PRAISE FO
KI

KISS OF DEATH

"Both paranormal and inspy romance readers will be captured by the new twists in this exciting novel and will be looking forward to the final title…"

—USAToday.com

"This compelling romantic adventure takes place across centuries and throughout Europe as humans and vampires work together believably, strengthening each other's faith as they struggle with questions of redemption and loyalty. The action is fast, furious and violent, interspersed with fascinating diary entries that are slowly revealed as the cousins translate pages, creating a rising excitement that doesn't stop when the book ends."

—*RT Book Reviews*

KISS OF NIGHT

"The premise is provocative: can a vampire be redeemed?…hordes of vampire fans who, after their introduction to the vampire Raphael, will clamor for book two and the movie adaptation that must star Johnny Depp."

—*Publishers Weekly*

KISS OF
Death

THE KISS TRILOGY BY DEBBIE VIGUIÉ

Kiss of Night

Kiss of Death

Kiss of Revenge

Kiss of Life (ebook short story)

Available from FaithWords wherever books are sold.

KISS OF
Death

A Novel

DEBBIE VIGUIÉ

NEW YORK • BOSTON • NASHVILLE

Copyright © 2012 by Debbie Viguié
Excerpt from *Kiss of Revenge* © 2013 by Debbie Viguié
All rights reserved. In accordance with the U.S. Copyright Act of 1976, the scanning, uploading, and electronic sharing of any part of this book without the permission of the publisher is unlawful piracy and theft of the author's intellectual property. If you would like to use material from the book (other than for review purposes), prior written permission must be obtained by contacting the publisher at permissions@hbgusa.com. Thank you for your support of the author's rights.

The author is represented by Alive Communications, Inc., 7680 Goddard Street, Suite 200, Colorado Springs, Colorado 80920, www.alivecommunications.com.

FaithWords
Hachette Book Group
237 Park Avenue
New York, NY 10017
www.HachetteBookGroup.com

FaithWords is a division of Hachette Book Group, Inc.
The FaithWords name and logo are trademarks of Hachette Book Group, Inc.

The Hachette Speakers Bureau provides a wide range of authors for speaking events. To find out more, go to www.hachettespeakersbureau.com or call (866) 376-6591.

The publisher is not responsible for websites (or their content) that are not owned by the publisher.

Printed in the United States of America

Originally published in trade paperback by Hachette Book Group
First mass market edition: September 2013

10 9 8 7 6 5 4 3 2 1
OPM

In memory of Sue Stark, who was like a second mother to me. Her courage and compassion were inspirational.

ACKNOWLEDGMENTS

I need to thank Kevin Roddy, Medieval Studies teacher at UC Davis for his passion and enthusiasm for his subject, which rubs off on his students. He helped bring that period of world history to life in a way that made me want to explore it more. As always, thank you to my agent, Andrea Heinecke. A big thank-you to my fantastic editor, Christina Boys, who makes the entire process fun. Thank you also to Chrissy Current whose unflagging support for this project helped inspire me, particularly when others told me that no one would ever want to read Christian vampire fiction.

Dear Reader,

You are about to read a vampire story.

Vampires in Christian fiction, can you do that?

That's just one of the questions I've been asked since the release of Kiss of Night, *the first book in my Kiss trilogy. Some people have been excited by the prospect while others remain skeptical. My answer is an emphatic, "Yes, I can, and I believe others should write them as well."*

First and foremost, the Kiss trilogy is a redemption story. As Christians we believe that even the most evil of people can still be reached and saved by the love of God and the sacrifice of Christ. I enjoy, as many Christians do, the fantasy genre. It helps make hard themes easier and less depressing to deal with than straight drama. It would have been simple to write a redemption story with a mass murderer as the lead character but it would not be a story I would want to read. By taking the mass murderer and instead calling him a vampire it helps you to hold the fiction at arm's length and tell yourself "it's just a story."

Using fantasy to tell a story is an old tool. C. S. Lewis wrote about talking animals, witches, and a fantasy land called Narnia as a way of making Christian themes accessible to children. His work has been read and loved by millions of Christians and non-Christians alike and has been used as a successful teaching tool. I'm writing these vampire books for Christians who enjoy fantasy in their fiction but I am purposefully using these books to also make Christian themes accessible to non-Christians.

This book series is a labor of love for me. In high school I read Dracula *and loved it. The struggle between good and evil is very real and very heartbreaking as seen through the eyes of several different people. In college I began to read more vampire fiction and I quickly became frustrated that there were no solid Christian characters represented in that fiction. Really, there's a lack of Christian characters in most horror novels and films. It puzzled me because I had read and loved everything Frank Peretti wrote, particularly* This Present Darkness *and* Piercing the Darkness *which dealt with angels and demons and had its fair share of horror. I loved his novel* Monster *and its portrayal of a real Bigfoot and genetically manipulated creatures. The Bible is filled with tales of miracles, angels, and demons and the supernatural in a real and present way. I wondered why when Christian characters were depicted in horror films or novels it was usually in a derogatory way such as people who had lost their faith. I decided I wanted to write a Christian vampire novel. It took years to make this series a reality, but it was worth it. It's for all those people who love a little fantasy with their morality play. And it is every bit as allegorical in its way as* The Lion, the Witch, and the Wardrobe *or* Pilgrim's Progress.

Every person, no matter their circumstances, past, or the evil they have done, can be redeemed by God through the blood of Christ. In the end, that blood is all that matters.

All the best,
Debbie Viguié

KISS OF
Death

PROLOGUE

The crumbling stones of the prison reeked of death. The stench of unwashed humanity and decay had long been in the nostrils of the warden of the lowest level of the ancient dungeon. Cut into the earth centuries before by nobles, the prison had once been a castle, proud and strong. It was still strong, but no longer proud. Generations of the vilest criminals that France had known had lived and died inside its walls. Murderers, rapists, thieves, and witches as well as religious and political dissidents had all met their end within the tiny, dank cells that the warden now walked past.

The warden stopped next to Marcelle, his protégé who would be taking his place. The young man nodded gravely as they went over, once more, his duties.

"Every day you feed the prisoners," the warden said,

as they paced slowly past each cell. "Someone doesn't eat for a couple of days, send men in to remove the body."

They walked a few moments in silence. Finally the young man asked, "Who is down here?"

The old man shook his head slowly. "I know all my prisoners, though I don't know who they were outside these walls nor what they did to be sent here. Men, women, gentlefolk and common, a few months in here and you can't tell them apart by conventional means anymore. But you learn to note differences."

He stopped before one cell. "This one won't eat anything that might be from a pig."

"Jewish?" the young man asked interestedly.

"Near as I can tell. And this one," he said, pointing to another cell, "sings after dinner."

"Good voice?"

"The finest I've ever heard."

"What about this one?" Marcelle asked as they stopped before the last cell. The massive door was ancient and battered, the wood bearing stains that might have been water or blood.

The old man paused for such a long time the younger one began to think he had not heard him. When the warden finally spoke it was slowly and in a hushed voice. "I do not know."

The young man felt as though a chill wind had just brushed against his spine. In the dim light he stared hard at the old man, waiting for him to continue, fearing that he would.

"There is—something—in there. I don't know what, but it's been there the whole time I've been warden, these last twenty years. The man who was warden before me said it had been here as long as he could remember."

"What is it?"

"I don't know," the old man repeated. "I only know that no food is ever slid beneath the door, but every so often a prisoner is put in there. I've seen dozens put in there, *and not a single one ever taken out alive.*"

He said the last in a whisper so quiet and fierce that it imparted a sense of danger and fear to the younger man. "Not ever?"

"Not ever," he said emphatically. "Never enter this cell, no matter the cause, if you value your life."

Marcelle stared hard at the door, trying to quiet the sudden sense of unease that had overtaken him. There should be nothing in this dungeon to cause him fear. He was, after all, about to be made the floor warden, in charge of the prisoners and guards for the entire level. It was a position of great responsibility and he had trained long for it.

Yet, suddenly he found himself wishing that he had never stepped foot inside the prison, even if he was a keeper and not a prisoner. Something about the giant door made him feel like running. He took a deep breath, though, and stood his ground. With a trembling hand he crossed himself, for he knew in his heart that he would be the one to discover what was on the other side.

Inside the cell *he* waited, listening to the murmurs from outside. He could smell the younger man's fear. The new warden was right to be afraid. He listened as the voices faded, the footsteps retreated until he was again alone with his thoughts and his thirst. He had spent far too long within the prison walls, but soon all that would change.

He dropped his head back against the stone wall, not feeling its cold. He didn't feel anything actually, anything but the hunger. It gnawed at him, a deep ache inside that he could not control. With the passing of each day it would grow until the pain was unbearable.

In the distance he heard a man begin to sing. Dinner was over, for all but him. Deep in his throat he growled.

CHAPTER ONE

See, I have set before thee this day life and good, and death and evil.

—Deuteronomy 30:15

*D*eath. *It's all about death*, Wendy thought in despair. She sat on a faded red velvet couch in a house somewhere on the outskirts of the city with her arms wrapped around her knees and stared at her cousin, Susan Lambert, willing her to wake up.

Susan lay on the floor, curled up, her chest gently rising and falling. *Proof that she's alive*, Wendy thought. A few feet away David Trent was also asleep. His face was bruised and even in sleep he kept wincing as though he was in pain. A soft whimper escaped every few breaths and it broke her heart.

And then there were the other three, the three who weren't breathing. The three who were dead.

Or not.

It took all her willpower not to feel like she was going completely crazy.

Vampires.

She shuddered. Wendy had hoped that when she went home to California she would be able to forget that vampires existed, write it off as some sort of bad nightmare.

Her eyes shifted again to David and lingered on his face. *Even if it meant I had to write him off, too.*

She and Susan had come to Prague the week before for their grandmother's funeral. Their grandmother had lived in Prague as a little girl and had chosen to be buried there. Wendy remembered hours spent sitting and listening to her grandmother talk about the city she loved, about its magic.

She'd said nothing about its vampires. But within a few hours of arriving in the city both she and Susan had drawn the attention of the monsters who walked at night. And when they were attacked David was the stranger who helped save them.

Maybe that's why she felt inexplicably drawn to him. He was a hero. He had saved both their lives. When the good vampires had asked him to stand and fight a coming war against evil with them he had agreed. So had Susan. It still seemed incomprehensible to her that there was such a thing as good vampires. She had wanted no part of it and had fled back home where it was safe.

And now I'm back.

She wasn't sure exactly why. All she knew was that one minute she'd been home, breathing easier, and the next she'd been on a plane back to Prague, compelled by something to return and help her cousin.

Looking around the room she realized her grandmother

was wrong. It wasn't a city of magic. It was a city of death. Last night, from what she had understood, David nearly became its next victim.

He had been unconscious when the vampires carried him in. He hadn't woken since then. Wendy thought they should have taken him to a hospital. But the vampires told her he'd be fine. So she watched over him, worried he might never wake.

He was handsome, and with actual color in his skin he looked so different from the vampires surrounding him. He was also kind and considerate and very funny.

Wendy took a deep breath.

She wanted to wake her cousin and David and run with them while they still could. They could all go to California and escape this madness. But she already knew they wouldn't go. They felt called to stay and fight.

Whereas she had just been called.

She rubbed her head. The voice inside it that had insisted that she had to return and help her cousin had been so overpowering, so strong, that she had been helpless to resist. She had felt like she was moving through some sort of dream state until she had actually made it back to Prague and been reunited with her cousin. It was the vampire Gabriel who had found her and brought her here to this house last night.

She glanced again from the clock to the heavy curtains covering the windows. Now, night was coming and with it evil would walk again. She stood and moved over to one of the windows. She wrapped her hand around the rich velvet drapes and was about to pull them to the side so she could at least see out.

Suddenly a hand clamped tightly around hers.

She screamed, spun around, and found herself confronted by a pair of smoldering eyes. Gabriel was staring at her.

Behind him she could see both David and Susan jump up, startled awake by her scream. Slowly Gabriel held up his other hand toward them, without looking away from her. They seemed to freeze.

What power does this man have to compel us all to do as he wills? she wondered. *Did he compel me to come back to Prague?*

He did have power, she could feel it. It was nearly tangible—thick and dark and far more menacing than anything she had ever felt before.

His jet-black hair was pushed back and he was dressed in dark clothes, though the cloak he had worn earlier was on the floor where he had been sleeping.

"The sun hasn't gone down yet," she heard herself squeak. It seemed a stupid thing to say, but weren't the vampires supposed to be asleep while the sun was up?

"The sun does not have as much power over me as some," he said. "They must sleep, but I may wake as I will."

He let go of her hand and she in turn let go of the curtain, arm dropping to her side. He didn't move away, though. Instead he just kept staring at her and she could feel her heart beginning to pound in her chest.

Something flickered a moment across his face, but she couldn't read the emotion behind it. Her chest tightened more with fear.

"You look like Carissa," he said.

Carissa. Who is Carissa? She looked at Susan and saw understanding in her cousin's eyes. She would have to ask her whom Gabriel was talking about. But later when the vampire wasn't around. Before she could say anything, he turned away. As if released from invisible chains, both Susan and David hurried forward.

David was blinking at her in disbelief, eyes wide. "What are you doing here?" he asked.

"I came back to help," she said.

He reached out and hugged her tight and she clung to him, trying not to cry in fear and relief. From the way he held on to her he must have thought he would never see her again either.

A sob escaped her. The world was so much more screwed up than she could ever have imagined.

She glanced at Gabriel, still troubled by his presence.

"What happened last night?" Susan asked, staring at Raphael who still lay unmoving on the floor.

He looked dead, but that was probably fitting. There hadn't been time for answers last night before the sun rose and the vampires were forced to sleep.

"If he was gone he'd be ashes," Gabriel said, answering the question Susan must also have been thinking and not the one she'd asked. It clearly did little to calm her fears.

Gabriel left the room and Wendy watched her cousin let out her breath. After a few moments, she moved to sit on the couch where she could stare at Raphael's face as he slept.

Susan reached up and closed her hand over the cross that hung around her neck. *The one Grandma gave her.*

Suddenly Raphael's eyes flew open and Susan jerked back. He stared, unmoving for seconds. Wendy had been told that vampires awoke at sundown but they did not all have instant control over their bodies. Wendy saw movement out of the corner of her eye and she turned to see the third vampire in their midst, the monk named Paul, rising to his feet.

She turned her eyes back to Raphael and Susan and a few moments later his entire body seemed to spasm and then he sat up.

Susan dropped to her knees next to him and threw her arms around him. "I thought you were dead," she whispered.

He returned her embrace. "I thought the same of you," he admitted.

It felt like a private moment, and Wendy wished she could give them some privacy, but with David and Paul also in the room, there wasn't much she could do about it. David still held his arm loosely around her, but she could tell that he was exhausted.

"What happened?" Susan asked.

"Captured. Then Richelieu set his pet scientist on me. He's running experiments in hell now," Raphael said.

Susan visibly shuddered. "And Richelieu?" she asked.

"I saw him when his minions captured me and brought me to him. I think I know where he is," Raphael said.

Then he wasn't dead as Wendy had hoped. *Not dead like he should be*, she thought, her stomach twisting in knots. Richelieu, the king of the evil vampires, like something out of a book. The absurdity of the thought suddenly hit her. He was actually in several books, fiction and nonfiction. The onetime cardinal of France had been reviled for centuries.

And no one even knows that he's a vampire or just how evil he really is.

"We're all listening," Gabriel said next to her.

She jumped, not realizing he'd been so close, but she forced herself to stand her ground.

"I think he's using one of the old palace complexes inside Prague Castle."

"It would appeal to his ego," Paul said.

"And his sense of purpose," Raphael said with a nod.

"Describe the place." Gabriel stared hard at Raphael.

Wendy glanced uneasily at David as Raphael described the room he had seen Richelieu in. David was still showing obvious signs of injury and favoring the ribs he had broken a few days before. It was too soon, not even twelve hours since they'd returned from the last battle. Maybe they could sit this one out.

"Not a chance, we need everyone we can get," Paul interrupted.

Wendy glanced over at him, startled. He gave her a grim smile. Susan had told her she suspected the monk could read minds.

"I know the palace you're describing," Gabriel said. "We will only have a small window of opportunity in which to strike if we are to maintain the element of surprise."

"He probably won't even hear about the attack on Michael and his lab for a few hours if we're lucky," Paul said.

Wendy knew that vampires could move swiftly but as she tried to follow the threads of the conversation she felt like they were also speaking abnormally quickly. She glanced at David, who seemed to be struggling more than she was to follow what they were saying. His hand was pressed to his side and he was breathing heavily.

What he needed were some of the painkillers the doctors in the hospital had given him. Wendy had searched his bag while he slept and couldn't find them.

He reached down and slipped his hand around Wendy's. She gave hers willingly, hoping it would give some measure of comfort.

Everyone had a sense of urgency about them and Wendy didn't want to interrupt to ask for clarification. David looked longingly toward the couch and she wondered if anyone would care or even notice if he lay down and went back to sleep.

He squeezed Wendy's hand and she squeezed it back. He turned and smiled at her. She offered a small smile in return. They both turned back to watch the drama. She noticed that Paul and Raphael were doing most of the talking but both of them kept deferring to Gabriel, though he rarely spoke.

They're afraid of him, she realized with a flash of insight. It was there in their body language, the way they stood, the distance that separated them, everything.

Susan was rubbing her cross necklace between her fingers obsessively. She was just afraid.

Wendy turned her attention to the conversation, focusing hard on what was being said.

"We know where he is and with any luck he'll have no idea yet that you rescued me and that Michael is dead. It's the perfect time to strike," Raphael said.

"Bearding the lion in his den is always dangerous, especially when we are so few and they are so many," Paul said. "It would be better to wait, figure out what he's planning to do, and confront him when he's exposed. Either that or find a way to lure him out. We could use Raphael's escape to our advantage there, too. Richelieu hates him and could be coaxed out of hiding if it gave him a chance to kill him."

Of the two arguments she liked Paul's best. It sounded safer to her, wiser.

"We don't know what he's planning. We haven't time to wait and find out because then it could be too late. We'll have no more warriors if we wait than we do now, and we'll have lost the element of surprise. I'm telling you the advantage is all on our side. It won't be for long because once he realizes we know where he is he'll vanish again," Raphael argued.

She wished David or Susan would speak up, give their opinions. After all, it was their fight, too. But both of them remained silent.

"We got lucky with the attack on the lab. We can't count on being that lucky again," Paul said quietly.

"What lab are they talking about?" Wendy whispered to David.

All three vampires turned to stare at her and she took a step back.

"A scientist, a vampire named Michael, who I had a run-in with during the Renaissance, was working with Richelieu. I was given to him to experiment on," Raphael said. "David, Paul, and Gabriel rescued me from there last night and we killed Michael."

"What kind of experiments?" she asked.

Part of her brain screamed at her to be quiet, to stop drawing the attention of the vampires, but she was there and she had a right to know what was happening.

"Experiments with blood. Poisoning it, draining it. He's spent his life trying to figure out the physiology of vampires and how they exist."

"Better he had focused on the spirituality," Paul murmured.

Gabriel held up a hand and the others turned to him.

"Paul, you've argued as a strategist. Raphael, you have argued as a warrior. I understand both your points of view. But, I am a hunter and I trust my instincts. An animal feels most secure in its lair, which means it is the best place to kill him. That only works, though, if the creature you're hunting has no reason to believe you're coming."

"Which brings us back to the fundamental question," Paul said.

"Which is?" Susan asked, breaking her silence.

"Did Richelieu hear about Raphael's escape before the sun rose this morning?" Gabriel answered.

They all stood and stared at each other. Finally David cleared his throat. "There's no way to know for sure, but odds are while we've been standing here talking about it he has."

Gabriel nodded. "He might be expecting us, but we can't afford to lose him again. We're going after him tonight."

"You know what they say, there's no time like the present," Paul said with a knowing look at Gabriel.

Raphael didn't trust Gabriel, even if they did agree. But then, how could he? His relationship with his sire had always been violent and tenuous at best. The fact that Paul was treating him more carefully than he once would have also gave him pause. Even as they scrambled to get the weapons they would need to lay siege to Richelieu's palace he wondered if he could trust the vampire who would be fighting beside him.

"He's one of the good guys," Paul murmured, at one point in the preparations, for his ears alone.

"But does he know I am?" Raphael whispered back.

Paul had simply clapped him on the back and gotten back to work.

It was bad timing. Half of them were injured. David was walking around with his mind seemingly more damaged than his body. Susan was worried for Wendy's safety almost to the exclusion of everything and *everyone* else.

And his body was not completely healed from the experiments Michael had performed on him. He needed to eat more and, truth be told, rest for another day before he'd be up for the battle ahead. Without both he couldn't fight, or even think, at the top of his game. But this might be their only chance to finish this war before it really ramped up.

Susan and Wendy began to rebandage David's ribs and patch up his other injuries. He wished they'd do it farther away where the smells and the sounds wouldn't be quite so distracting.

He smelled blood and he turned around with a hiss, struggling with the hunger that was threatening to overcome him. They had pulled off a bandage that was stuck on with dried blood and the wound started bleeding again. It was just a couple of drops but it was enough to set him off in this state.

And suddenly Gabriel was standing in front of him, fangs silently bared, eyes gleaming.

Raphael hunched his shoulders, panic flashing through him.

"It's good. He lost a lot of blood and hasn't had a chance to drink anything," Paul interjected quickly.

Gabriel continued to stare at him, as though daring him to move. Raphael caught the packet of blood that Paul threw at him and forced himself to meet Gabriel's eyes.

His sire didn't trust him, either.

He broke eye contact, ripped open the packet and downed it, belatedly wishing he had at least turned his back so Susan wouldn't see. When he was done drinking she was staring at him, eyes dilated wide.

He grimaced. He wasn't exactly putting on a good face for this little reunion for either of them. He closed his eyes. It had been centuries since he had seen Gabriel and those last few days had been anything but good.

CHAPTER TWO

*And he said, Behold now, I am old, I know not the day
of my death.*

—Genesis 27:2

Raphael woke up screaming. He was lying in bed and
the sheets were soaked with blood. He was sweating
it but even that didn't account for the staggering amount of
blood. He was starving and he felt his conscious mind begin to slip away. He fought it, but the smell of blood was
overwhelming. The stench filled his nostrils so completely
that he didn't sense the Lord of Avignon in the room until
he heard him breathing.

He turned and saw that Gabriel was sitting in a chair
across the room, fingers laced together, watching. Raphael
tensed. Gabriel only breathed when he was about ready to
attack. His chest was rising and falling with every powerful
breath. Otherwise he appeared as calm as always, his features giving nothing away. *He's even more dead than I am*,
Raphael thought as he launched a string of curses his way.

Gabriel just continued to stare at him.

"If you're going to attack me, what are you waiting for?"

"If I was going to attack you I would have already," Gabriel said, and his breathing stopped.

Hatred roiled inside Raphael. He continued to struggle to keep his mind clear. "What have you done to me?" Raphael asked, indicating the blood.

"You did it to yourself."

Raphael looked down and saw that there was blood under his fingernails. Faint scratch marks covered his entire chest and as he moved he could feel the skin on his face tingling slightly as it, too, healed. There was no pain. He didn't feel pain anymore, at least not in a normal way. Only fire hurt. When the pathetic knight they had encountered in their travels had pushed a cross into his face Raphael had burned and that pain had been very, very real and the first he had felt in months. The touch of the sun hurt almost as badly. Other than that he was invincible.

He thought daily of his old life. He remembered the battles he had fought, the power that had been his. *I thought I was a god, but now I am one and I will not be held captive forever.*

"Get dressed, we're going away for a few days," Gabriel commanded as he rose from his chair and glided to the door.

"One day I will destroy you," Raphael vowed.

"By the time you're strong enough to do that you'll be thanking me instead," Gabriel said.

He left and Raphael got up, and after washing as much of the blood off as he could in the washbasin, dressed. He paused at his door and listened to the servants as they scurried about the castle. If he focused he could pick out their individual scents. The hunger grew stronger and he closed his eyes and listened as one of the maids climbed the stairs. She passed by Gabriel's chambers and approached his.

He flattened himself against the wall and when she crossed the threshold she did not see him. He could hear her heartbeat, smell the soap she had washed with that morning, feel the warmth radiating from her skin.

He grabbed her and twisted her around to face him, clamping a hand over her mouth. Her eyes bulged in terror and he could feel her fear.

"Do you know what your master is?" he growled low, for her ears alone.

She shook her head. Some of Gabriel's servants knew exactly what he was. It was amazing to him that the rest did not.

"Do you know what I am?" he asked, dropping his voice to a whisper, letting it wash over her and soothe her like the touch of a lover. He smiled broadly so that she could see his fangs.

Slowly she nodded.

"And what am I?" he asked, replacing the hand over her mouth with his lips. He kissed her hard and deep, careful not to let his teeth pierce her skin. He could feel her moving in his arms but she was no longer struggling. He pulled her closer and she came willingly. He moved his mouth slightly and her own formed the answer to his question.

"Demon," she breathed.

"Shh," he urged, putting his hand back over her mouth. He looked into her eyes for a long moment and then twisted her head back and sunk his teeth into her throat.

She began to struggle again, but he only held her tighter as he drank her blood, feeling the heat and the strength of it coursing down his throat. Even as he drank he knew Gabriel would be furious. He had forbidden Raphael to touch any of the servants.

"But I'm a god, and I will be forbidden nothing," he whispered as he let the girl's lifeless body slip to the ground.

He licked his lips as he debated what to do with her. His first instinct was to leave her for the others to find. That would raise an alarm, though, and depending how quickly it could interfere with his other plans. He picked her up and walked over to his window. The castle stood on a rocky hill and his window overlooked a sheer drop to the valley below.

He threw the body out the window and watched as it tumbled downward. He thought briefly of jumping after for he was sure he could survive the fall. He might not find shelter in time, though, to survive the scorching sun. He turned away; soon he would leave the castle but it would have to wait. He had business to attend to first.

He paused at the doorway and listened for Gabriel's steps, but did not hear them. He left his room, glided down the hallway to the staircase and descended to the main hall. Once there he turned right and headed for the room where Gabriel held court.

There was no one inside the room. Writing tables lined two walls. Both were stocked with parchment, ink, and quills. Both held their share of books and papers. One belonged to Gabriel and the other to his chief servant, Andrew. A throne stood toward the back of the room on a raised platform. It was from there that Gabriel held court every Wednesday, listening to petitioners who came with grievances or requests.

It was one of the only rooms Raphael had not yet searched for the box entrusted to him by the king. Gabriel had taken it from him and hidden it somewhere. When he found it Raphael would attempt to escape. With the money he could get for the box alone he could go wherever he chose and live as a lord.

He moved to Gabriel's table and began searching it. Finished, he was about to search Andrew's table when he heard footsteps approaching the room. He spun around just in time to see Andrew enter.

"What are you doing?" the man demanded.

Fire exploded in Raphael's chest. "How dare you speak to me?" Raphael hissed before leaping at the man. He grabbed him, bit him in the neck and a moment later was knocked across the room.

As Raphael staggered to his feet Gabriel threw him a contemptuous glance before turning his attention to Andrew.

"Let me see," Gabriel commanded.

Andrew pulled his hand away to reveal two jagged wounds. Three seconds more and he would have been dead. "You'll be fine," Gabriel reassured him.

Andrew nodded and then left without a word. Gabriel watched him go before turning back to Raphael. A few drops of Andrew's blood were on Gabriel's hand and he carelessly licked them off. The moment he did his face twisted with rage again.

"I've spent years avoiding the taste of my servants' blood and in one moment you undo all of my effort," Gabriel said.

Raphael just continued to glare at him. Gabriel wanted to kill him. The vampire had been considering it for days, he could tell by the way he looked at him, the way he moved. But in the end something always stopped him.

Gabriel shook his head fiercely. "You won't find what you're looking for here," he growled. "Now, we're going."

Outside the castle walls they took their seats in a carriage. It was equipped with heavy black curtains that ensured no sunlight entered during the day. Now the curtains were drawn so that they could see the moon shining above.

"Where are we going?" Raphael asked at last.

"To the Château de Vincennes, the king has returned from the Crusades."

Raphael sneered. "With his tail between his legs like a dog no doubt."

Gabriel shook his head. "Kings never cower even if they wish to. It's the only thing that gives them their power, that makes them seem inhuman to the common man."

"You're going to give the box back to him, aren't you?" Raphael hissed.

"It was you he entrusted with the box and its contents, not me," Gabriel said darkly.

"If he sees me—"

The other vampire made a sound, almost like a laugh, that made him shudder inside. "And what makes you think I'm going to let you anywhere near the king? Or anyone else for that matter?"

Raphael bared his teeth at him. He hated him almost as much as he feared him.

"Why bother traveling this way? We could run and make it there five times faster than the swiftest horses."

"Yes, and then spend that extra time trying to explain away our unexpected arrival without a carriage. It is best to appear as human whenever you can."

The next two days were a torture of pent-up frustration interspersed with forced sleep. Raphael chafed under the restriction. Every time he turned his eyes to his master he could see him staring at him darkly.

He's going to kill me now, Raphael thought more than once. The wave of terror that would wash over him would keep him still for a few moments before he would again become consumed with his own frustration.

He busied himself with thinking about what it would be like when they arrived at the palace. He thought of the men parading around in their finery, bowing and scraping to the king. He thought of the pale-faced women looking for a real man. He smiled.

He would kill them all and drink down their blood. He could almost taste it now. And maybe it would be all the sweeter for having had to wait so long for it.

When they were near the palace he was ready to rip open the door and run the rest of the way on foot. The carriage veered suddenly, though, into the trees off the path.

"Where are we going?" Raphael asked.

"I told you before, I wouldn't trust you with people," Gabriel said, his voice filled with menace.

Raphael lunged forward, fingernails slashing toward Gabriel's eyes. But they never connected because his sire moved like lightning. Pain seared through Raphael and he looked down to see blood covering the front of his shirt. It was gushing from his throat. He clamped his hands over the wound just before Gabriel slammed his head into the side panel of the door.

"You are more trouble than you are worth."

Then kill me, Raphael thought, unable to talk, but suspecting that his sire could read his mind.

"I would, but that's not the point."

The carriage jounced along for a little ways and the wound in his neck healed. The carriage stopped and Raphael looked out. A small house was nestled among the trees.

"What is this place?" he asked.

"The home of a friend who owes me a favor," Gabriel said.

He stepped out of the carriage and grabbed Raphael by his shirt, hauling him out with ease. The door cracked open and an old woman stepped out onto the porch. Raphael could see the moonlight glinting off her fangs.

"She's going to watch you."

The next night when Gabriel returned Raphael practically jumped into the carriage, relieved to be away from the woman. She was old, ancient if her word was to be believed, and she had bled him half a dozen times for things Gabriel wouldn't even have raised an eyebrow over.

His sire barely glanced at him when he took his place in the carriage, which he noticed had been cleaned since he'd bled all over it the night before.

"The Marquis de Bryas was there with his new bride," Gabriel said, more to himself than to Raphael.

Raphael curled his lips. It was the marquis who had found the box, the box that had been entrusted to Raphael. The box that Gabriel had hidden somewhere within his castle.

"Did he or the king wonder what happened to their prize?"

Gabriel shook his head. "No. The king was busy making an announcement about it. He had a nice little box with a copy of the real thing inside."

"A fake?" Raphael asked, surprised.

"Yes."

"Why?"

"I've been trying to figure that out. The marquis looked as surprised as I was. He also knew the relic wasn't the real thing."

"What are they doing with it?" Raphael said, curiosity burning within him.

"Apparently it's going to be installed in a church in Paris. So you needn't worry, no one is coming to take the real one from you."

"Don't you mean from you?" Raphael growled.

Gabriel, though, had moved on to other thoughts. "The Bishop of Avignon was there as well," Gabriel said, his tone dark.

"Why should that bother you?" Raphael asked.

"He should have told me he was going. He and the king were speaking privately together and I don't like it."

Gabriel had had the king's ear for a very long time as far as Raphael could tell. Was it possible that the dark lord had fallen from favor? He curled his lips, wishing he could kill Gabriel and escape to freedom.

Freedom. He glanced out the window of the coach as the moonlit countryside swept by. What he would do with such freedom! The men he would kill. Others would worship him as he deserved to be worshipped. Even the king of France would have to bow before him.

But first, first I must find where he has hidden my prize from me.

When they returned to Avignon, Raphael renewed his efforts to find the box. Over the course of five nights he searched for it. Gabriel was preoccupied with other matters, something that had to do with his distrust of the bishop. Raphael did not care so long as it kept his master away from him.

Word of what he had done to the girl and tried to do to Andrew must have spread because the servants avoided him. It was just as well. With their frightened little hearts beating loudly and the veins in their throats and heads pulsing with blood they were a distraction he didn't need.

On the fifth night, just before dawn, he finally found it. The ornate bejeweled box was hidden underneath Gabriel's mattress. He had saved his sire's room to search last and when his hand seized around the box he felt a shiver of triumph.

The sun would be up shortly, though, and Raphael raced to his own room. He laid down and closed his eyes. He could hear the slight rustle of cloth when Gabriel came upstairs and checked on him before retreating to his own room.

Raphael waited a few seconds, he dared not wait longer as the pull of the sun was going to be upon him soon. He had to hide himself where his sire wouldn't find him before he could escape the next night. Now that he had the box and its precious contents he could flee.

He rose and ran as swiftly and silently as he could down the hall, down the stairs. He flashed past Andrew and the servant didn't even see him. He reeked of fear but Raphael didn't stop. He made it out of the house and all the way to the stables. There he had pried up some loose floorboards in the stall of his horse and dug out a burrow underneath.

The animal flattened his ears when Raphael entered the stall, but moved quickly away from the boards. Raphael pried them up, settled himself into the small, cramped space and pulled them back down over the top of the hole just as he could fight the pull of the sun no longer.

He managed to escape the next night, but it would be years before he discovered the reason why his sire had never pursued him.

CHAPTER THREE

Let that day be darkness; let not God regard it from above, neither let the light shine upon it. Let darkness and the shadow of death stain it; let a cloud dwell upon it; let the blackness of the day terrify it.

—Job 3:4–5

PRAGUE, PRESENT DAY

David took a deep breath. The moment of truth was upon them.

"I think we have everything we need," Paul said, dropping a final duffel bag at Raphael's feet.

Raphael looked from the monk to the others in the room, clearly avoiding Gabriel's gaze. "Wendy stays here," he said.

David was relieved when no one objected, not even Wendy.

"Raphael and I will go now so we can be in position when you arrive," Gabriel said.

Raphael turned and gave Susan a look of such passion that David felt like he should look away. "Be safe," he could hear the vampire mutter.

He heard the door open and close and Gabriel and Raphael were gone.

"It's time for us to go, too," Paul said.

David turned to Wendy. Tears were shimmering in her eyes and he wished that he could forget all about vampires and wars and take her far away from this place. If Richelieu succeeded in unleashing his evil on the world, though, there would be nowhere that they could ever go to be safe.

Wendy moved in close to him and he felt his blood quicken as she tilted her head back and kissed him. He could taste the salt from her tears on her lips and he kissed her back, knowing that it might well be the last kiss they would ever share. He didn't know what had brought her back to Prague but he prayed fervently that she would be safe no matter what happened. When at last they broke apart he felt as though a piece of himself were missing.

Wendy stepped back and Paul and Susan moved to the door. David felt like his heart was breaking as he turned to go with them.

Once in the car the exhaustion he had been battling seemed to take over. He didn't feel well, but he pulled himself together. He just had to focus long enough to get the job done. Then he could sleep as long as he wanted. *Just as long as that isn't forever*, he thought grimly.

They were driving over, a concession to Susan and him since they couldn't run like the wind. He glanced over at Susan and could see his own fear mirrored in her face. Paul was driving.

It all felt wrong. It seemed like they should have prepared, planned more. Paul and he had spent more time meticulously planning hits on houses that held two or three sleeping vampires. Now they were marching into the lion's den without enough weapons and without a solid plan. And worst of all it was the middle of the night so the lions would be awake and hungry.

His head was still buzzing, which just made things worse. He hadn't had a chance to eat let alone get painkillers and he knew he was in no shape to be fighting vampires. But that was war. You couldn't just fight when you were full and rested and healthy.

"Tell me again what we're doing," he said to Paul.

The vampire jerked slightly as though he, too, had been lost in thought.

"We're each going to take a section of the palace Richelieu is using. Other than the throne room we don't know what other rooms he has occupied. We will have to work our way through them before we get to the throne room so that once inside we aren't caught between two tides of his forces."

"That makes sense."

"You and Susan will be together in the area Gabriel has estimated is likely to have the least numbers of vampires."

"What about human servants?" David asked.

It was the question that was always foremost in his mind. He killed vampires, yes, but he couldn't kill a human who had been mesmerized into serving one. Taking care of them, and wherever possible freeing them from bondage, had been Paul's job.

The vampire shrugged apologetically. "I am sorry."

"What are you saying?" Susan asked suddenly.

"You will have to kill the servants yourself," Paul said.

"No!" Susan said, her voice laced with panic. "We can't kill people just because they've been mesmerized."

David winced. He knew it had hit a nerve with Susan

because her cousin had been mesmerized. Plus, like him, he was sure she wanted nothing to do with killing people.

Paul made a point of sighing, clearly for their benefit since vampires didn't need to breathe. "Then knock them out and I will deal with them later."

If there is a later, David thought to himself.

"Then what?" Susan asked.

"Head for the throne room."

"How will we find it?" she asked.

"Chances are you won't be able to miss it," Paul said, his voice grim. "We should be arriving there before you. Follow the sounds of fighting."

"Great," David said, tired beyond belief just thinking about it.

"And if that fails just check each room you come to but keep moving forward from where you start."

Paul parked a couple of blocks from their ultimate destination and David winced as he climbed out of the car. He slung a backpack filled with weapons over his shoulder, grunting as he did so.

"Let me carry that," Susan said.

He shook his head. "I've got it."

The truth was the pain was helping to keep him focused, alert.

They both armed themselves and then walked silently with Paul until they reached their objective.

Once inside, Paul left them and David took a steadying breath. He had half expected there to be guards of some kind outside, but apparently Richelieu felt pretty confident that he was hidden from the world.

Or maybe he's just got enough fighters inside that it doesn't matter.

After a few moments it was clear that there wasn't enough light coming in from outside to be of any value.

David pulled a penlight out of his pocket and turned it on. It wasn't much, but without it the two of them would be blind as bats. He grimaced at the metaphor even as he thought of it. *Vampires aren't bats*, he reminded himself, *no shape-shifting*. That was at least one thing they had going for them.

He shone the light all around the room. It was empty and he moved forward, Susan falling into step beside him.

As they approached the doorway he tensed, half expecting to see vampires rushing through it at any moment. The darkness was pressing in close around them. The beam of light cast by the flashlight narrowed, swallowed up by shadows that seemed to slither and move on their own.

It was almost like the shadows were whispering to each other. David shook his head, not sure what was real and what was his imagination.

When they finally reached the doorway he went through it in a rush, quickly playing his light across everything in the new space. It, too, was an empty room.

He should have asked Paul how big the palace was, how long before they all joined back up. How many rooms they were going to have to search.

A flash of motion in the corner of his eye caused him to spin around, stake raised. But there was nothing. Vampires could move at incredible speeds. It was possible one had run by, trying to get behind them. Getting in position to attack them perhaps.

Hopefully trying to escape instead.

He turned and looked at Susan. She shook her head. She hadn't seen anything. Not good.

They kept walking. They passed into the next room and instead of feeling relief when there was no one there he felt the pressure building. They were playing a dangerous game of Russian roulette and with every foot they progressed they were that much closer to being discovered, attacked.

He fought to control his breathing. The pain in his ribs was making it hard. That, combined with his fear, and he was one big target. If the vampires were smart, they'd attack him first. He was getting so tired and nauseated that he was having trouble just standing let alone moving forward.

I'm going to be useless in the fight, he realized in sudden terror. He began to sweat uncontrollably. All the vampires he had fought, all the things that had happened, and he had never felt as helpless as he did right then. He could feel panic rising in him.

He looked again at Susan, slender, fragile-looking in the dark with the light casting eerie shadows across her face.

God help us both, he prayed.

He glanced at his watch, the face luminescent. He hadn't worn a watch since he was a kid, relying instead on cell phones to tell the time. But he'd bought one the week before. When the exact minute of sunrise and sunset could mean the difference between life and death, time was important. And he had enough weapons to juggle without trying to deal with a phone, too.

Only four minutes had passed. He blinked, staring at it. That couldn't be right. It felt like they'd been walking for hours.

He had never been claustrophobic. He had spent a semester of his junior year of college sleeping in a glorified closet to save money and it had never bothered him. But now, in a giant room lined on one side with windows and three doors leading into and out of the space he felt completely trapped.

I should turn back.

The thought hit him hard enough to make him actually stop in his tracks. Susan stopped as well and looked at him, searching his face for answers and then looking at the room around them.

He wanted to tell her that he had a bad feeling about the whole thing. But that seemed ridiculous. Of course he had a bad feeling about it, how could he not?

He opened his mouth to tell her it was nothing, but then snapped it shut again. Vampires could hear a long distance off. What if he tried to whisper to her and that was the sound that gave them away, that rained hell down on them both?

He shook his head and made a grimace of apology. Then he pointed to his own head and made the crazy sign. She smiled slightly and nodded back.

He told his feet to start moving forward again but they refused. He stood planted to the spot, his fear and frustration and embarrassment growing with every moment.

He turned his head and surveyed the room, trying to buy time before she finally spoke to him to ask him what was happening. Because he had no answer for her. And he was sure the vampires would hear. *They can hear footsteps as well*, he thought. But they wouldn't know whom they belonged to.

He took a deep breath and reminded himself that the

vampires could be closing in on them from any side, even from behind at this point. It made no sense to go back because the fight was going to happen with or without them and with them their side had a much greater chance of winning.

But at the moment he was less concerned with winning and more concerned with surviving. The pain and exhaustion had worn him down, that was all.

And then he thought of Wendy and the way she had looked at him when she'd kissed him back at the house. He'd seen himself reflected in her eyes, a hero, going off to battle, a knight off to slay the dragon and save the village and win the heart of the princess in the process.

And he had to be that for her. Because if he wasn't, if Richelieu wasn't stopped, then Wendy would always be in danger, and that was intolerable. No matter how tired or hurt or distracted he felt, he had to persist.

He took a step forward and then another and then a third. He was able to resume his regular rhythm of walking. Susan didn't say anything and he didn't risk a glance at her. Better she not know about the war he was fighting inside. She needed to focus all her energies on the greatest war, the one they had to win. And so did he.

He shoved all the pain and fear and confusion to the tiniest corner of his mind he could. He could still feel it but it no longer controlled his thoughts, nor drove his actions.

They moved into the next room and the shadows pressed in more closely. There was even less light here. They continued their slow, steady march toward the throne room. Soon the shadows would be made of flesh and bone and he would be able to fight them.

Soon, but not just yet.

* * *

The silence weighed upon Susan. It was thick and heavy and felt oppressive. So many buildings felt wrong when they were empty, but this was unlike anything she had ever experienced before. She had the insane urge to scream just to break the silence.

She glanced over at David and saw the tension on his face. Was the silence getting to him, too? They continued walking and they stepped so softly that even though she struggled to listen she couldn't even hear their footsteps.

This must be what it's like to become deaf, she thought. *Trapped in your own head in a silent world that feels so wrong. And all you want to do is shatter the silence like you'd shatter a mirror.*

This whole thing is insanity. We shouldn't have rushed here to fight him. We're walking blind into what is probably a trap.

She couldn't help but wonder if anyone else felt as she did. There was something wrong with David, she could tell. She couldn't tell if it was his injuries that were causing him trouble or if something else was wrong.

Maybe he thinks this is a trap, too.

They continued creeping forward and she could feel the sweat rolling down the middle of her back. She clutched a stake in her right hand and a cross in her left and both were becoming too slick to hold.

What am I even doing here? she wondered. David, Raphael, Gabriel, they were the warriors, not her. She tried to remember what she'd been told about killing vampires, but she wasn't even sure she'd remember how to angle the stake to put it through a heart.

You managed to kill a vampire while ill and lying in

bed, a voice whispered in her head, reminding her. She shook her head as she wondered if that was the still small voice she had come to associate with God or if it was Gabriel who she had heard whisper in her mind before.

It was disturbing and it made her question what was real in a way that frightened her. How long had he been watching her and why? He had mentioned back at the house how much Wendy looked like Carissa. Susan knew that Carissa was one of their distant ancestors. She had seen a portrait of her in the decaying castle in Bryas, France, wearing the very same cross necklace that Susan's grandmother had left her.

She'd had no idea the heirloom necklace had been a part of her family's history for so long.

She reached up a hand to grab it, to steady herself. Touching the necklace to a vampire could make him burn.

She thought of Raphael, hoping, praying that he was safe in whatever part of the palace he was in.

So far they had found nothing. She couldn't even tell if she had been in this section when she had explored the castle on her own as a tourist in what seemed a lifetime before.

How she wished she had paid more attention and memorized the layout then. It would help ease her fears now. She wished she at least had had a moment to look at a map tonight, see where the exits and entrances were. She wasn't even sure where the palace was situated in relation to the rest of the castle.

She thought about the day she had visited. Was it possible she had been within steps of Richelieu and hadn't even known it? She remembered the section of the castle that she'd wandered into that had felt so evil to her. She remembered how fast she'd moved to get out of there.

At the time she'd thought it was part of the castle's dark history. Now she wondered if she had been sensing the presence of the vampires. The thought made her sick, made her stomach twist in knots. Could she have been that close to pure evil and not known it?

Of course there were entire sections of Prague Castle that were off limits to the public. Surely that was true of this section. Richelieu would have wanted to take over a section that would be undisturbed by the normal flow of tourists and staff. And presumably he had many working for him that were all calling the place home.

So why hadn't they seen anyone yet?

She glanced over at David. He didn't look good. He was sweating even more than she was and his eyes were glassy. His cheeks looked drawn and the rise and fall of his chest was uneven, labored. He had been acting strangely for a while. Did he see things she didn't? Was the pain of his injuries getting to him?

We shouldn't have come, she thought to herself. *This was a bad idea.* But they were here now and there was nothing to do but press on. If they were lucky this night would put an end to all the fear and running and uncertainty. If they were lucky they would win the war. If they were very lucky they'd even live to tell about it.

And what then? she wondered. What would happen to her, to Raphael? Without a common enemy to fight, there'd be no need to work together, to see each other. The thought of never seeing him again was unthinkable. She wanted to scream in frustration at the thought.

Or maybe she just really, really needed to break the hold the silence seemed to be gaining on her. She could feel the tension in every muscle in her body. Her arms and legs felt stiff, and she reminded herself to loosen her aching hands from around the weapons she clutched. She looked again at David. He still looked terrible but he was starting to walk a little more briskly. He probably wanted this to be over even more than she did. But his face looked paler than before.

She was about to ask him if he was okay when her foot slid out from underneath her and she fell onto the floor with a thud, the stake in her hand striking the stone, sounding like a gunshot in the silence. David jumped and then grabbed at his side with a gasp.

The sound of her fall and his gasp were caught by the walls and bounced around, echoing back to them until she cringed. She had managed to hold on to both the stake and the cross somehow. She gripped both tightly, waiting for the enemy to swoop down on them.

She could hear David's breathing now, ragged and labored. He sounded like he was in terrible pain. At least he was still alive. They both were. But for how much longer?

She didn't know how long they stayed like that, waiting for an attack that didn't come. Finally she sighed and let herself relax slightly. David tilted his penlight down at her. She looked at the floor and saw that she had slipped on a glossy brochure someone had dropped.

She transferred her stake to her left hand, grasping it and the cross together, so she could reach over and pick up the brochure. A stupid piece of paper nearly had them discovered and killed. It was so ridiculous that she wanted to laugh, but knew that she didn't dare risk it.

The echo alone would be too loud. She blinked at the thought and remembered the sound of the echoes from earlier. Only empty places echoed. Even though it was night and all the workers and tourists had left for the day it shouldn't be empty. Vampires and human minions should be around. She had always been able to sense evil, feel its presence before she saw or heard anything. Tonight, she'd felt nothing...until now. Susan slowly twisted around to see a dark figure framed in the doorway behind them.

CHAPTER FOUR

*He made a way to his anger; he spared not their soul
from death, but gave their life over to the pestilence.*

—Psalm 78:50

Raphael crept through the palace grounds. He'd insisted on taking the most obvious route in. Richelieu might be expecting him but if they could hide the presence of the others, particularly Gabriel, it would be a great advantage. He twisted his head left and right, senses straining as he tried to pinpoint his enemies before they could discover him.

It was dark, without a star shining in the night sky. The air was still and it carried far-off sounds of cars and people. To the left of the door he was heading for, obscured by shadows, there was a figure. Raphael paused, debating which approach to take. The way the vampire's body was angled it would be nearly impossible to get behind him unseen. That left the direct approach.

Raphael walked up to the door. That was often the secret. Act as though you belonged and most people would never question you.

He got within a half-dozen steps before the guard

stepped out, posture menacing, full of swagger. "Identify yourself."

It was hardly original, but at least the other vampire hadn't asked Who goes there?

Raphael smiled and locked eyes with the other vampire. "Your master's sire," he said.

The other vampire never ticked his gaze downward and so never saw the stake coming. Raphael rammed it home in his heart and then stepped back as the sentry turned to ash.

A branch snapped behind him and he spun and dropped to the ground just as another guard thrust a stake through the air above him. He kicked the man's legs out from under him. When he fell with a grunt, Raphael leaped on top of him and straddled him. He tore the stake from his hand and twisted it around, angling it downward for the guard's heart.

At the last moment he heard that heart beating and he stopped himself from completing the swing. The man was human and from the looks of him, mesmerized. He hit him hard enough to knock him out for a long time.

Raphael jumped to his feet and yanked open the door before storming inside the palace. Once inside he melted into the shadows and slipped from room to room.

Tonight I'm going to kill Richelieu and there'll be an end to this, he promised himself. No matter what else happened the twisted vampire had to be stopped. After that his followers would vanish back into the shadows and others could spend a lifetime hunting them down. Cut off the head of the beast and the body was useless.

He worried about Susan but they had positioned her and David as far from the main entrances and the throne room itself as possible. With any luck the battle would be over by the time the two of them made it that far.

And then she could go home to California and forget all about wars and vampires and bloodshed. *And me.*

The thought was so distracting that he nearly ran into the next guard. As it was the vampire's phone rang shrilly in the silence and brought him up short. Raphael flattened himself against the wall and listened as the guard answered.

"Yes? Yes, it is taken care of."

He strained, but couldn't hear the other end of the conversation.

"We've got guards at the entrances. We'll know if anyone's coming. Yes. No. Nothing will disturb the master and his guests."

The man ended the call as Raphael ended him with a well-placed stake.

Who could Richelieu's guests be?

If all went well he'd find out soon enough.

He kept moving, trying to stay focused. Everyone was probably either in the throne room with Richelieu or scouring the city for him.

No need to have your underlings search for me, I'm coming to you, he thought grimly.

Still, he couldn't rush and get sloppy. He'd gotten this far without an alarm being raised but the farther he got the better for all of them. Since he hadn't heard anything else he assumed that the others were doing as well as he was. He hoped that was the case.

Richelieu had already gone. Gabriel had yet to find a single follower, and that was the only explanation. Maybe there was something he had left behind that would help them find him. Gabriel could follow a trail better than most as long as he had something, anything, to go on.

But so far there was nothing.

A whisper of sound and the smell of a vampire alerted him to another presence at last. He coiled his muscles, sinking deeper into the shadows of the corridor he was in, and waited.

Moments later a lone figure came into view, headed in the same general direction that he was. He stepped out of the shadows when he recognized Paul.

"Anything?" he asked his sire in hushed tones.

Paul shook his head.

Gabriel didn't like anything about the empty palace. Something was wrong. He lifted his head, straining as he tried to hear or smell or see something that seemed just out of the range of his senses.

"What do we do?"

"Keep going, for now," Gabriel said.

Together they moved forward, covering ground faster. They were nearly at the throne room.

And it still felt so wrong. Just as it felt wrong to be working with Raphael.

"When was the last time you saw Raphael?" Paul asked. "I mean before last night?"

"Better to ask when the last time he saw me was."

"Always the hunter," Paul said, lips twisting into a wry smile.

"Some things never really change, no matter how long you walk the earth."

Paul put a hand on his shoulder and he could feel the older vampire's sympathy in the touch.

"I have watched him on and off for a while. But the last time we interacted, the last time he was aware of my presence, was the night they came for me."

FRANCE, AD 1149

Gabriel lay down on his bed but before he could shut his eyes he realized that something was wrong. He couldn't feel the box beneath the mattress. He growled low in his throat. It had been a hiding game he'd been playing with Raphael and it was getting old.

The sun rose, pulling at his mind. As he succumbed he promised himself that he would kill Raphael when he woke up. And then he'd ask Paul how he'd managed to stand being around him during his first few years as a vampire.

When Gabriel awoke with a start, he could tell it was still morning. He had not been asleep more than a few minutes. Something was wrong. He sat up in his bed and strained his senses. Someone was on the staircase. He knew it couldn't be Raphael. Young vampires were nearly impossible to wake during the day. So were many older ones. Gabriel had spent decades training himself to be able to come awake quickly if he heard or smelled something that was out of place. Still, it was rare that something woke him. Most of his servants kept the same hours as he did and should have been asleep.

And yet at least one was not. He smelled Andrew on the staircase outside his door even before he heard the rustle of cloth. He threw back the covers. Andrew knew better than to wake him.

As his bare feet hit the floor he was suddenly over-whelmed by the scent of at least a dozen other men and the sound of running footsteps. A moment later he smelled burning wood. As the first men flooded into his chambers he lunged forward, breathing heavily.

Before he could touch them, others appeared waving torches and crosses. The crosses he tore from their own-ers' hands but the torches he shied away from, the fire singeing him when he passed close.

One priest dove after the cross Gabriel sent flying and he pushed him away. The man hit the floor with a crack, and was still. As he turned to take out another someone threw a rope of garlic cloves around his head and shoulders.

His knees gave way and he hit the ground, vomiting as the smell filled his nostrils. Rotting blood mixed with bile beneath him but all he could smell was the garlic.

Pain seared through his legs and he realized that some-one had set them on fire. He tried to roar and roll over to extinguish the flames. All that came out was a cough and more blood. He collapsed onto his back and found himself staring up into the eyes of the bishop.

"So, you're going to kill me," he hissed. He had known something was amiss when he'd caught the man talking with the king days before.

"Not exactly," the bishop said with a faint smile.

Gabriel hooked a finger around the garlic rope and tossed it as far away as he could.

"Look out!" someone shouted as he lunged to his feet, flames still licking at his ankles.

Gabriel turned just in time to see Andrew throw open the heavy drapes and let sunlight fill the room.

"You," he promised the traitor, "I will find."

A moment later the sun touched him. There was an instant of blinding pain. He heard a voice from far away say, "The other one's gone," and then nothing.

PRAGUE, PRESENT DAY

When Gabriel and Paul reached the throne room, it was empty. Gabriel advanced slightly. "I can smell vampires, they were here an hour ago."

"We're too late," Paul said, defeat in his voice.

Gabriel crouched down, inspecting some scraps of cloth and drops of blood in front of the throne. Richelieu had been busy in his last few minutes here in the room. He could smell humans, their scent was stronger. They had left more recently.

There was something else, too: a faint hissing sound. It was too consistent to be made by an animal.

He heard a step and looked up. Raphael appeared on the far end of the room, gave his head a brief shake, and disappeared out the doors again.

Gabriel growled low in his throat.

Raphael stepped back into the room, his face worried. "Have you seen Susan or David?" he asked.

Gabriel was about to tell him that he hadn't when his eyes fell on some canisters sitting behind the throne. And suddenly Gabriel realized what was wrong about the empty palace. "Trap!" he roared at Paul as he turned and sprinted toward the exit.

A figure appeared in the doorway, a match in hand. Gabriel spun in midstride and shoved Paul ahead of him toward the door Raphael had entered through.

Behind him he heard a popping sound as the match was lit and then a moment of absolute silence before the world exploded around them in light and sound and fire.

The blast wave slammed into Raphael and lifted him off his feet, hurling him through the air like a rag doll. He crashed through the wall into the next room and debris showered on top of him. His clothes were on fire and he twisted, trying to roll to extinguish them. Behind him he could hear several more explosions and the earth beneath him shook. His eardrums burst and blood flowed from ears and nose.

He pushed himself to his feet, dizzy, disoriented. He couldn't hear anything. Another blast picked him up and hurled him through the air again.

He had to get out of the building before it collapsed completely. *Susan, where was Susan?*

She'd never made it to the throne room. Maybe she and David had already left the building. Maybe they had already been killed. He struggled back to his feet, as fire rushed around him. He twisted and turned, trying to remember how to get out.

His shirt was still on fire and he ripped it off his body as he ran back the way he'd come into the building. There had to be a closer exit. He shot into a large room where the tapestries hanging on the walls were on fire. The air was so hot it burned his eyes. And to his right he saw six feet up on the wall a stained-glass window.

He crashed through the window face-first and landed on the ground outside in a shower of glass. Even as his skin tried to heal more glass showered down on top of him, slicing him open again and again. Several pieces were embedded in his face, legs, and abdomen and the pain seared through him as his body tried to reject them but couldn't.

The ground shook again. Another explosion? He scrambled away from the building on all fours. His ears began to heal and the pain was excruciating. He collapsed onto the ground and moments later heard his own screams.

He reached down and yanked a piece of glass out of his chest and tossed it as far away as he could. The sensation of relief was instantaneous, but there were more pieces that were burrowing in, trapped.

Trapped.

He turned and looked at the building even as part of the roof caved in. If the others were alive and inside there was nothing he could do for them. Fire was deadly to vampires and he wouldn't make it very far before he was ashes.

If the others hadn't made it out by now they were likely already dead. He squeezed his eyes shut. Richelieu had won. He had blown up half a historic landmark to do so.

We should have never gone inside. I should never have permitted Susan to come, he thought, despair filling him.

Emergency personnel would be arriving shortly and when they did he needed to be gone. But how could he go without knowing for sure the fate of the others? Gabriel and Paul had been much closer to the heart of the explosion than he was. Had they burned to death? And what of Susan and David?

Despair gave way to rage. It was his monster, his creation that had caused all this death and destruction. And he wasn't even here to witness it. Why? Where was Richelieu? How many minutes had they missed him by?

Raphael thought of the guards. There had been so few.

And Gabriel had shouted that it was a trap. *Just enough guards so I wouldn't suspect until it was too late*, he realized bitterly. *He should have stayed around and made sure the job was finished. That will be his undoing.*

But he didn't have another century to track him down. He needed to kill Richelieu now, before he could put his plans into motion.

Then he remembered the guard he had knocked out. It was possible the man was still alive. He ran back closer to the building, heading around to where he had first entered, picking his way through the rubble and dodging the debris that was still falling. And there, just a few feet from the entrance, he saw the man, his body trapped beneath some fallen stone.

Raphael was relieved to hear the man cry weakly for help and he dropped down beside him. Blood was trickling out of the man's mouth and it looked as though the stone had crushed most of his organs. He didn't have long to live. *That's what you get for serving the devil,* he thought bitterly.

"Tell me where Richelieu is!" he demanded.

The man just looked up at him with pain-filled eyes.

"Tell me where your master has gone."

"Far away," the man slurred.

Hope flared in Raphael. Maybe he actually knew. "Tell me," he insisted, dropping his voice low.

"Don't know."

"But you know he's gone far. How do you know? How far?"

"Blood, it's all about the blood."

Something in the way he said it gave Raphael a sick feeling. "What blood?"

"Not what," the man wheezed. "Whose."

"Whose then?" Raphael demanded, fighting the urge to shake it out of the man.

"Wouldn't...you...like to know?" His eyes closed.

Raphael took a deep breath, struggling to control the rage he was feeling. The man was dying, losing his sense of place and self. There were only a few moments left to get the information he needed out of him.

Raphael didn't have time to undo the mesmerism Richelieu had put upon the man, even if he could. But he could use it to his advantage. He changed his voice slightly, raised it to sound more like Richelieu and put as much persuasion as he could into his words.

"You have done well and I will reward you generously."

"Master?" the man asked, senses failing him, almost gone.

"Just tell me you remember the plan."

"Yes."

"Where am I going?"

"To get the artifacts," the man said, coughing violently at the end of it.

"Which ones?"

"Blood," the man said, struggling to get the word out.

"Very good. Whose blood is it?"

"You know."

"I'm testing you, your memory."

The man began to cough and his eyes started to roll back in his head. Foam and blood mixed on his lips.

"The name!" Raphael barked sharply.

"Mess—"

And then he was gone.

Raphael shook him, but there was nothing more the

man could tell anyone. Richelieu had left Prague in search of something. Something to do with blood.

He staggered to his feet and moved away from the dead man. He circled around as much of the palace as he could at a limping run, looking for the others.

He found only more destruction.

Another section of roof collapsed with a crack. He could hear trucks, people. They were coming to put out the fire. They would save the rest of the castle.

If they knew what was coming, they wouldn't have bothered.

CHAPTER FIVE

Then thou scarest me with dreams, and terrifiest me
through visions: So that my soul chooseth strangling,
and death rather than my life.

—Job 7:14–15

Susan ran, heart pounding in terror, legs and lungs on fire. She had to find someplace to hide because she couldn't outrun the monster chasing her. But where could she hide that it wouldn't smell her fear or hear her breathing?

She shook her head. She had to find the others. She shuddered to think what might have happened to David. *Dear God help him, please save him*, she prayed. *And please save me.*

The vampire who'd entered the room had looked familiar, both in face and in manner of dress, and it had taken her a moment to realize that he was the second of the four Raiders Richelieu had sent to hunt her down. The Raider had called her by name. That's when David had thrust the flashlight into her hand and shouted at her to run. So she had.

She hoped to find the others but she had gone the wrong way, exiting the palace and making it into another part of the Prague Castle. It was possible David had killed the vampire or that the others had arrived to help, but she couldn't take that chance. Raphael had told her that the other Raiders would never stop hunting her when he had killed the first one.

For all she knew, all three were stalking her even now.

She needed to turn off the flashlight but if she did she wouldn't be able to see where she was going. And the vampire could see her even without the light so maybe it didn't matter if she left it on or not. Unless she found someplace to hide.

She heard what sounded like explosions in the distance and it only increased her terror. No one had said anything about explosives so that couldn't be her side that was setting them off.

She snaked through a series of corridors and then found herself in a chapel. She rolled underneath a pew halfway down on the left-hand side and turned off her flashlight.

She struggled to bring her breathing and heart rate under control. She was shaking from the exertion and the adrenaline and her teeth were actually chattering together.

I see you, Susan.

She heard the voice in her mind and she jerked, slamming her head into the pew. She gritted her teeth against the pain and her vision swam for a moment.

Laughter followed, deep and cruel, it pulsed in time with the throbbing of her head. She wanted to scream but she kept her mouth clamped shut. If he was inside her head like that then he might not know where she was. Otherwise he would have just pulled her out from underneath the pew and killed her.

Terror surged through her. If she could hear him then

he could probably read her mind. She squeezed her eyes shut, refusing to give away her hiding place.

Think of something else, anything else, she commanded herself. *The color blue.*

She fixated on the color blue. The blue of the sky at sunrise, the blue of the sky on a summer day, the blue of the ocean back home, the blue in her favorite pair of earrings.

You can run, but you can't hide, the voice taunted.

Blue, blue eyes. Raphael's blue eyes, glowing with light as she had seen him that first day in the church.

Church, mustn't think of churches. She thought about Raphael more. He would find her. She thought about the kisses they'd shared.

Her head hurt even more and she felt dizzy.

You know what I'm going to do to you when I find you?

She cringed, trying not to think of the answer.

You'll be praying for death by the time I'm finished with you.

Raphael had said that the Raiders were vampires who had ridden with Quantrill during the American Civil War. They had committed atrocities most people had never heard of. Her mind went to terrible, dark places and fear whipped through her harder, accelerating her pulse again.

She began to breathe in short, rapid bursts.

I'm hyperventilating, she realized. The sound was like thunder in her ears. She felt like she couldn't get any air.

He wants me terrified so he can hear me breathing.

She had to calm down.

Dear God, please save me, rescue me. Let Raphael find me, she prayed. *And let David be okay.*

* * *

David opened his eyes with difficulty. The ground beneath him was moving. Earthquake?

He smelled smoke. His eyes focused slowly. He was lying on the floor in the palace.

He remembered telling Susan to run and then he had turned to face the vampire in the darkness. In the brief beam of the light as he'd thrust the flashlight at Susan, the man had looked like something out of a nightmare. David had hefted his stake in his hand, wishing he'd had a chance to drop the backpack first.

"You won't touch her."

The vampire had laughed. "Of course I will, but I'll kill you first." There had been a sound of movement, and David had jumped to the side, and then he felt a sharp pain in his skull and after that, nothing.

He moved his hand to his head and pulled it back sticky with blood. The vampire must have hit him as he ran by after Susan. Jumping to the side at the last moment had probably saved his life, causing the vampire's blow to glance off his skull instead of crush it.

But all that was moot if he didn't manage to make himself move because David realized the palace was on fire. He shoved himself to his feet and then fell down. His head was spinning and he began to cough.

Smoke.

Closer to the ground was safer anyway. He shrugged out of his backpack and crawled across the floor. How many rooms had they crossed on their way in? How far did he have to go and did he have the time to make it out?

He pushed the terror from his mind and focused on his goal. All he had to do was keep going. He prayed for the strength to do just that. As he went the smell of smoke grew stronger and the flames seemed to chase him from room to room.

He was getting close, he had to be. Suddenly a roaring sound filled his ears. He turned and saw a wall of flame approaching behind him. There was no way he could get to his feet and outrun it.

His hand came down on something sharp. He looked down. It was a shard of glass. He swiveled his head. On the other side of the room there were a set of windows, their glass blown out.

He headed for them, using the wall to stand when he reached it. He sucked in smoke and began to cough. He moved to the window. It was chest high and he gathered his strength to try and jump. He grabbed the casing, trying to throw his body over the windowsill. It didn't work and he began to fall back just as the flames reached him.

He screamed and a hand reached through the window, grabbed his shirt and yanked him out. He landed hard on his back on the ground outside with an anguished cry.

Raphael moved into his line of sight and the vampire's face was blotchy with blood.

"Where's Susan?"

"A vampire went after her. She ran. I don't know where," he managed to say around the knifing pain in his ribs.

Raphael picked him up and carried him several yards from the building before depositing him back on the ground underneath a tree.

"Stay here!" the vampire commanded before turning and running back to the building.

As David stared at him, struggling to keep breathing

against the pain in his ribs, he wondered just where Raphael thought he could go.

Raphael was frantic. Was Susan still alive? Or had the vampire or the explosions killed her? He ran the perimeter of the great structure, not daring to go inside among the flames.

He had to trust that she was still safe, that he could still reach her in time. He tried to think but his thoughts seemed to scatter like ash in the wind.

If she had run away from the throne room there was a chance she'd made it into one of the other sections of the castle. And that was exactly where he needed to go.

He ran through the night, straining, listening for anything that would tell him which way to go. If Susan was running, she would try to hide. Where would she hide?

Someplace she felt safe.

A chapel. The thought came to him suddenly and it spurred him onward. Maybe she had sought refuge in one of the chapels. His mind raced trying to remember which chapel she would have happened upon first if she was running away from the palace.

Susan screamed as a hand wrapped around her ankle. She lashed out at it, kicking and thrashing. It tightened around her leg and began to pull her out from underneath the pew.

She cried as loud as she could for help.

And then the hand was gone.

She blinked rapidly. She realized she was still underneath the pew. Her head was spinning.

Just a matter of time until I get my hands on you.

It hadn't been real. She bit down on her fist to keep

from sobbing and screaming all at once. He had the ability to speak inside her mind, read her thoughts, and apparently manipulate them.

She felt like she was going to throw up.

He doesn't know where I am, she told herself.

No, but one more good scream and I will.

Which meant she couldn't scream, no matter what happened, no matter what she saw.

There was more laughter in her head and she closed her eyes praying she could shut it out. *God, keep me calm, give me strength.*

Your friends are dead.

Her heart stuttered.

I killed the man with one blow.

David.

And the others? The explosion took care of them. Richelieu's little trap. But see, you're special. You are going to get the…personal…treatment.

And then he showed her an image of exactly what he meant. She kicked and fought, slammed her fist into the underside of the pew, which helped to remind her that what she was seeing, feeling, couldn't be real.

Some people call me a monster. But I'm an artist. And you will be my greatest masterpiece.

Raphael ran toward the first chapel and as he got closer the acrid stench of smoke was replaced by the smell of fear. No, not just fear, terror. He shot through the back doors and slowed down. He could hear the sounds of a struggle and he ran toward it, fearing the worst.

And then he saw her.

Susan was curled up on the floor half underneath one of

the pews and she was kicking and lashing out at an invisible attacker. He dropped to his knees and grabbed her.

A scream ripped from her body unlike any he'd ever heard before. He pulled her out from underneath the pew and grabbed her head. She tried to hit him but she was flailing wildly, as though in the throes of a nightmare.

And as he looked into her eyes, pupils dilated, he realized she was living a nightmare. The vampire had been playing tricks with her mind, causing her to see things that weren't there.

"Susan, it's Raphael, you're safe," he said.

Her head lolled to the side and he couldn't tell if she had even heard him. She screamed again and the sound sent chills down his spine.

"It's going to be okay."

"Women know when you're lying to them about that kind of thing."

Before Raphael could move something punched into his back. He gasped and dropped Susan onto a pew as a stake emerged from his chest.

"You missed," he spat as he spun around, coming face-to-face with the vampire. He recognized him instantly as one of the Raiders who was after Susan. "And now I'm going to kill you just like I killed your brother."

Susan lay on the pew and watched as the two vampires fought. Was it real or was it another illusion? She gripped the edge of the pew so tightly her knuckles ached. Was that pain real?

She wanted to believe that Raphael had come to rescue her, wanted to believe it with all her soul, but she didn't know if she could trust it.

The Raider had said he was dead. Maybe it was just another one of his lies, another one of his tricks. She felt herself starting to lose consciousness but she forced herself to stay with it. She had to know.

The struggle escalated, raging all around the room. Raphael felt the other's desperation growing and a moment later he heard him speaking inside of his head.

He roared. Only Gabriel did that to him. He had never been able to kill Gabriel, but he could kill the Raider.

He yanked the stake from his own chest and plunged it into the Raider's heart. As the vampire turned to ash there was a sob of relief from Susan.

He rushed to her side. Her eyes were clear now, though she still seemed dazed. She reached out a shaking hand to touch his cheek.

"Are you real?"

He cursed the vampire he'd just sent to hell for what he'd done to her.

"Yes, Susan," he said, struggling to keep his voice calm. "I'm here. I'm real. You're safe."

She nodded and he helped her to stand. Her legs started to buckle and he caught her. He carried her out of the chapel and made it as swiftly as he could back to the tree where he'd left David.

Closer to the burning palace, emergency personnel had gathered and fire hoses were hard at work quenching the rage of the fire. They had to get out of there before someone noticed them and started to ask questions. He was in no state of mind to properly mesmerize someone and the last thing he wanted to do was kill an innocent person who was trying to help.

"We should go," he told David.

The man nodded, but he was unable to stand. Raphael would have to carry both of them if they had any hopes of getting out of there.

He knew where Paul had said he was going to leave the car. He took Susan first since he was already holding her. She faded in and out of consciousness as he ran and he was grateful for that.

After he had her safely in the car he sprinted back. The fire crews had done well, and he couldn't see any more flames. When he reached David, he found the man had managed to prop himself up against the tree. He was staring at the buildings.

Raphael followed his gaze.

A hulking figure loomed through the roiling smoke. Gabriel—burned, charred, dragging one leg behind him and still more frightening than anything he had ever seen.

He was carrying something. Raphael moved forward until he could see that it was the limp, charred body of a man. He looked up at Gabriel's face for confirmation and read everything he needed to in the other's eyes.

Paul.

CHAPTER SIX

The fathers shall not be put to death for the children, neither shall the children be put to death for the fathers: every man shall be put to death for his own sin.

—Deuteronomy 24:16

Susan couldn't remember how she got there but she found herself standing in the living room of the house where she'd been earlier. Wendy had quickly hugged her before following Raphael upstairs where he was putting David in one of the bedrooms. Gabriel had already taken Paul upstairs.

Susan stared at the staircase, wondering what she should do next. She wanted to collapse into a ball on the floor. But that wouldn't help anyone. She forced herself to move and she headed for the kitchen. Once there she looked around.

I had to have a reason that the kitchen seemed like a good idea.

Her eyes landed on the coffeepot and she moved to it. Coffee. Someone would need coffee. She didn't think it was her, but someone would.

She rinsed the pot, filled the machine with water, then carefully measured the grounds. She focused on the sensation in her fingertips. This was real, this was concrete. She could touch it, see it, and smell it. If she wanted to, in a few minutes, she could even taste it. As she turned the machine on she could hear it begin to percolate. Touch, taste, smell, see, hear. She could observe it with all five senses. That had to make it real.

Didn't it?

A few minutes later Raphael came back downstairs, face grim. He had a pair of tweezers and a towel with him. He set them both on the kitchen table. He took off his shirt before sitting down on one of the chairs.

Susan stared at him. There were a dozen red cuts and splotches across his chest. She saw something glistening in one of them and realized as he picked up the pair of tweezers that it was glass. She watched as he pulled several pieces from his skin and dropped them on the towel. As each one hit the towel the wound it had left sealed up.

She should offer to help, but she felt awkward and shy. She realized it was the first time they had been alone together in days, since he'd disappeared while they were in Bryas. It felt like she should say something.

"You didn't come back," she blurted out.

And even though she was still struggling to keep her grasp on what was real and what wasn't she knew that in anyone's reality that was the wrong thing to say.

He looked up at her slowly, eyes angry. The final piece of glass clinked onto the table. "It's not because I didn't want to," he said.

She shook her head. "I know that."

She didn't know what else to say. Clearly, neither did he. They remained silent for a couple of minutes while the coffee brewed. As she listened to it percolating and the aroma filled the kitchen she realized how ridiculous it was.

Vampires only drank blood. David was unconscious. Wendy hated it and so did she. There was no one to drink the stupid coffee.

And for some crazy reason that's what made her finally start crying. In a moment Raphael was there, his arms wrapping around her and pulling her close. She sobbed against his chest and he stroked her hair.

"I don't know who I made the coffee for," she said at last. "Why does Gabriel even have a coffeemaker?"

"You made it for your grandmother."

She went still, tears checked in midstream. And then she pulled away from him and sat down at the table. She put her head in her hands. He was right. Her grandmother drank coffee and she had always made it when something had upset her.

It was still so hard to believe that she was gone. It was even harder to believe that her grandmother never told Susan about the vampires; that she'd let her find out on her own.

She looked up at Raphael. "How do you know my grandmother drank coffee?" she asked.

He shrugged. "Lucky guess. Lots of Americans do and she helped raise you."

It sounded completely logical but he didn't meet her eyes. Suspicion cut through Susan.

"My grandmother left me a letter. I found it in Bryas after you were kidnapped. It was down in the dungeon."

She saw him flinch. He had admitted to having been in the dungeon at some time in the past but he had not wanted to talk about it while they were staring at the door leading to it there and he clearly still didn't want to talk about it now.

"The letter told me that vampires were real, that there was a war coming."

That got his attention and he looked up at her, listening.

"My grandmother said that I should find you because you would be at the heart of it."

He jerked slightly and Susan felt some reward for her efforts. "She said you probably wouldn't remember her, but that she had met you once as a young woman."

A strange smile twisted Raphael's lips. "Of course I remember her. She was not an easy woman for anyone to forget."

A sick feeling wrenched Susan's stomach. All the times that Raphael had talked so knowledgably about her family, particularly the women of Bryas, came back to her. "Were you in love with my grandmother?"

The question hung in the air between them and Susan held her breath, waiting for the answer, terrified to hear it.

Slowly Raphael shook his head. "I was not the vampire who was in love with your grandmother."

Susan sagged in momentary relief until she realized the full impact of what he'd said. "So another vampire was?"

"Yes."

Before she could ask who, he turned and left the room.

Raphael didn't want to have that conversation with Susan. There was so much she didn't know. So much she shouldn't. It was safer that way.

The sun would be up shortly. He hesitated for only a moment before climbing the stairs to the room where Paul was. Gabriel was already stretched out on the floor between the bed and the door and Raphael winced as he had to step over him to get to the other side. He lay down on the floor on the other side of the bed.

It probably wasn't a smart move. *Shouldn't put all your eggs in one basket or all your vampires in one room with a window*, he thought.

There were still bits of glass embedded in his legs, he could feel them. He should have asked for Susan's help to get them all out before the sun rose. That would mean having her touch him, though, and he didn't trust himself enough.

Even hugging her briefly had been difficult. The memory of her blood was still fresh in his mind. And being around her made him feel things that it was dangerous to feel.

For just a moment he thought he heard a low chuckle from the other side of the room.

Raphael barely managed to growl and bare his teeth before sleep claimed him.

Wendy watched David as he slept. She had been so relieved to see everyone return. It had been torture sitting, waiting, wondering for hours. She had imagined all kinds of horrors.

David looked terrible but Raphael had assured her that he would be fine. Just as he had yesterday. She wanted to remind him David was human, that he didn't heal like a vampire. But not only was that obvious, she didn't have the courage. He was sleeping, which was best for him.

Wendy brushed back a strand of hair from David's forehead.

Susan came into the room after some time had passed. She handed her a mug.

"What is this?" Wendy asked.

"Coffee."

She wrinkled her nose. "You know I don't drink coffee." She noticed that Susan also had a mug. "And when did you start drinking coffee?"

"About ten minutes ago. It seemed like a good idea."

Wendy rolled her eyes.

"He seems to be sleeping okay."

"Yes."

"Then you should get some rest," Susan said.

Wendy shook her head. "I'm going to be sitting right here when he wakes up."

"In that case drink the coffee, you're going to need the caffeine."

Wendy took a sip, trying not to taste the bitter liquid as it slid over her taste buds. It was warm though and it made her feel a little better.

"Next time I'll try it with some sugar."

Susan patted her on the shoulder. "I'll be downstairs on the couch if you need me."

"Thanks," Wendy said, sparing a smile for her cousin. Susan had dark circles under her eyes and looked pale. "You enjoy the sleep," she urged her.

Susan nodded and left.

Wendy turned back to David's still form and touched her hand to his cheek. "Alone again," she whispered.

Susan awoke later that afternoon feeling worse than when she went to sleep. The couch was not the most comfortable and she'd been plagued with nightmares. Wendy had

come down once to wake her, telling her she was screaming in her sleep.

Susan didn't doubt it. As the nightmares retreated to the
corners of her mind she prayed they would never return.

She had discovered that the cupboards were stocked
and the refrigerator had regular food as well as the packets
of blood she had seen the vampires drinking from the
night before. She made a quick meal of hamburger and
rice and took some upstairs for Wendy.

Her cousin smiled wanly at her but still refused to get
some sleep. Susan sat with her a few minutes until she
heard a voice coming from the room next door.

The vampires were awake.

Raphael awoke and mentally cursed when he saw Gabriel
standing over him. His sire was the only vampire he knew
who'd found a way to circumvent the initial paralysis of
waking and could awaken at will even when the sun was
up. He didn't know how he managed it but he would pay
dearly to be able to do the same.

"I remember feeling as helpless as you are now,"
Gabriel said.

Is he taunting me? Raphael wondered, hating him even
more in that moment.

"You know, I've often wondered where you went, the
night you escaped."

That was one secret Raphael intended to keep no matter what. There was no practical reason, but it was the
only advantage he had against his sire. He knew and the
other didn't. It was a small victory, but he clung to it
all the same. He could have asked him the same, for
Gabriel, too, had disappeared that night. But he had since

heard stories, rumors, and he wasn't sure he wanted to know the truth.

His entire body spasmed as the sleep paralysis passed and he sat up with a gasp. "Better we should be asking where Richelieu has gone," Raphael said.

Gabriel cocked his head to the side. "You know?"

"No, I questioned a human minion as he was dying, but wasn't able to get the final piece from him."

"What did he say?"

"That Richelieu had left the city in search of relics, in search of blood."

"Whose blood?" Gabriel asked sharply.

"He died before he could say. All he got out was 'Mess,' nothing more."

Gabriel narrowed his eyes and Raphael saw the surprise burning in them.

"Mess? Are you sure?" his sire demanded.

Raphael nodded. "I don't know what that—"

"Messiah," Gabriel whispered.

Silence hung heavy between them as Raphael struggled to grasp what it was Gabriel had said.

"Surely not, *Him*."

Gabriel nodded. "He's going after artifacts that have touched the blood of Christ."

"But...do they even exist? I mean the probability—"

"Would you have thought that the treasure the king entrusted you with in the Holy Land was real until you beheld it with your own eyes, felt its power?"

Raphael looked away. Until that day he had not even believed in the possible existence of God or the supernatural. And yet within hours of receiving the relic, he had been cursed by Gabriel to a life of darkness.

"What are we talking about?" he asked.

Gabriel cursed quietly. "Paul would be of great use to us in this. He takes interest in such things."

"I wonder why," Raphael said sarcastically.

Gabriel threw him a look of such menace that Raphael winced as though he'd actually been struck.

He glanced down at the badly burned body of the monk and shuddered. He couldn't understand how the vampire was still alive.

"So, are we seriously talking about the holy grail?" Raphael asked hastily.

Gabriel shook his head. "As far as I am aware if that exists no one knows where."

"So, what are we talking about?"

"Crown of thorns, nails, the spear that pierced His side."

Raphael blinked at him. "Do we know that those things exist?"

Gabriel shrugged. "There are places, churches, that think they have things. We won't know until we see them if they're real. The good news is, Richelieu will have to get near them to tell if they have power, too. And if he believes enough to go after them, then we know how to find him."

Raphael thought of the little jeweled box, of what it held inside. He had never believed, not really. But he had feared.

Richelieu had always believed. And that belief made him strong.

And now he was seeking to make himself even stronger before the end. Raphael couldn't let him do that. He would have to find those artifacts first. And in finding them, he just might find Richelieu as well.

"There are many relics that he might be going after," Gabriel mused.

"We should split up, we can cover more ground," Raphael said.

Gabriel shook his head sharply. "We do not know how many allies Richelieu will have with him and if he acquires a viable relic before we find him, we will need to band together."

Raphael hissed sharply.

"Don't worry. I won't enjoy it any more than you will," Gabriel assured him.

"What of the others?"

"They'll stay here for now. If Richelieu has truly left the city they should be safe enough. I went to a lot of effort in choosing this place." He looked down at Paul who lay still, unmoving. He placed a hand briefly on the monk's shoulder. "It will give them all a chance to heal."

Susan had finished washing the dishes when Raphael and Gabriel came downstairs. She met them in the living room. Their faces were grim and for a moment she thought that Paul might have died.

"Good evening," she said, when they didn't speak.

"We need to go," Raphael said, refusing to look at her.

"Okay, when will you be back?" she asked.

"I don't know."

She looked from one to the other. "What's going on?"

"Richelieu moved his headquarters before we got there yesterday. I don't know if he's even still in this country, let alone this city."

"And we need to find him quickly," she said.

"Yes, that much hasn't changed."

"But something else has," she said, feeling her pulse accelerate.

Raphael ran his hand through his hair, a gesture so human it almost made her smile.

"I might not know where he is, but I have a pretty good idea where he will be. Last night I discovered that Richelieu is going after some artifacts, objects of power. Gabriel knows where some of them are, where he's likely to go looking for them."

"And?"

"And I need to find them before he does. Ideally, I'll find him in the process and be able to kill him and end this whole thing."

"But how do you know he'll go himself and not just send some of his men to find these objects?" she asked.

"Trust me, he'll go in person. He wouldn't risk having these objects in the possession of others, even for a minute."

"Okay, well this gives us a chance at least. That's better than nothing. When do we leave?"

"Tonight, in about an hour."

"I'll go grab my stuff," she said, heading for the living room.

He caught her arm as she walked by and spun her to face him.

"I can't take you with me."

"Of course you can. You'll need someone to help you, someone who can walk in the sunlight."

"Not this time."

She pulled her arm free, anger racing through her. "What's suddenly different? You needed my help to stop Richelieu before, why not now?"

"It's too dangerous."

"How is it any more dangerous now? You said I was special, that you needed me."

"I don't now. Not for this," he hissed.

"Why not?" she demanded.

"You'll just slow me down and get in the way."

She felt as if he had slapped her. She blinked up at him in shock.

He crossed his arms over his chest. "You, David, and Wendy will be safe here. You don't need to do anything for Paul. We'll be back when we can."

"We?" She looked over his shoulder. "Gabriel's going with you?"

"Yes."

"I see."

"So all of you should just sit tight here."

And wait.

As horrific as the night before had been, as terrified as she was at the thought of coming up against more vampires, the idea of just waiting was the worst torture she could imagine.

She cleared her throat. "At least tell me where you're going, what you're looking for. Maybe there's something I could do here."

Raphael hesitated.

"Tell her," Gabriel said.

"We're looking for relics that hold the blood of Jesus, like the crown of thorns, the nails…" He drifted off.

"That's what Richelieu is looking for?" she asked.

"Yes," Raphael said.

"I don't understand," Susan said. "Why would he want those things?"

She could see the uncertainty in Raphael's eyes. There was something he didn't want to tell her. He hunched his shoulders and bared his teeth, though she didn't think it was on purpose so much as a reflex.

Still it made her back away slowly. Gabriel stepped forward, which just made her want to get farther away.

"Do you know why the Bible says you're not supposed to eat or drink the blood of any creature?"

Because it's wrong? she wanted to say. But clearly he was looking for something more than that. "No."

"Because the life of the creature resides in the blood. By taking the blood of the creature into yourself, you make its life, its spirit, a part of you. That's why there are so many prohibitions against drinking blood in the Old Testament. Paul could quote them all to you. It was an ingrained law, one that the Jews understood very clearly. That was why at the Last Supper, when Jesus said that the drink was His blood and commanded His disciples to drink it, it would have run contrary to everything they were raised to believe. What He was commanding them was to symbolically take His life, His spirit, into themselves and make Him part of who they were."

"Wow," Susan said, blinking and suddenly feeling a new appreciation for the communion ceremony she had taken for granted since childhood.

"The spirit, the life of every one of our victims, becomes a part of us," Gabriel said.

She thought about the inn, about giving Raphael her blood to save his life. "Am I a part of you?" she asked Raphael wonderingly.

"In so many ways," he whispered.

She felt a thrill run through her. What did he mean by

that? She wanted to ask him, but her eyes turned back to Gabriel. She wasn't comfortable talking about such things in front of him.

"Blood is life, its strength and power and spirit," Gabriel said.

She nodded slowly. "And the blood of Jesus, the son of God, was enough to atone for the sins of all mankind."

"It's the most powerful blood that ever has been," Gabriel affirmed.

"And Richelieu thinks it will make him powerful. How?"

Raphael turned away but Gabriel stood his ground. "How do any of us vampires gain power from blood?"

She felt her legs beginning to give away and she sat swiftly. Her ears roared and she caught her breath.

"What would that make him?" she asked, her voice shaking.

Only silence greeted her. She looked up and Gabriel was gone and Raphael was all the way across the room. "We don't know. But we don't want to find out," he whispered.

And then he, too, vanished.

Her heart stuttered for a moment and then she realized she hadn't heard the door close. That probably meant they had just gone back upstairs. They weren't gone yet then.

Wendy came downstairs and walked past her heading for the kitchen. "More coffee," her cousin said with a yawn. "I'm going to add more cream this time. I think I'm getting closer to figuring this out."

At least that makes one of us.

"Good luck," Susan said weakly. She stood in the living

room and realized she had no idea what to do with herself. It felt like déjà vu.

The waiting had already begun.

She climbed the stairs. She could at least check in on David. When she walked into the room she was surprised to see his eyes fluttering open. Finally he turned his head slightly to look at her.

"Hey, how's my defender?" Susan asked, plastering a fake smile on her face.

"A little the worse for wear," he said with a weak smile in return. "Raphael told me what happened. Sounds like we all got lucky."

She nodded, trying not to think about Paul in the next bedroom.

"I want to thank you for coming to my rescue. Again."

"I'm trying not to make a habit of it."

"Is there anything I can do for you?"

He grimaced. "Call in sick for me. I'm supposed to start work in the morning."

She sunk down in the chair next to his bed. "I completely forgot; I am so sorry."

"Hey, it's not your job to remember my job," he said. "My bosses are going to think they sent me on a three-month assignment and I just vanished."

"Well, I'm sure we can get you a letter from a doctor or something when this is all over." She grimaced. "I can certainly make the call for you if you tell me where."

"No, it's my responsibility. If you could get my phone for me, though, I'd appreciate it."

"Sure, where is it?"

"Back at my apartment."

"Sure thing."

She heard pounding steps on the stairs and she hastily stood up. "I think Wendy heard that you're awake," she said, moving toward the doorway.

Wendy ran in and threw her arms around David with a squeal. Susan heard him grunt in pain, but she couldn't help but smile.

"I leave the room to get a cup of coffee and you wake up," she heard Wendy say, her words muffled against David's chest.

"That'll teach you to leave my side," he said, sounding better than he had before Wendy arrived.

Susan stepped into the hall and jumped when she realized Raphael was standing right there.

"I'll get his phone for him. It will just take me a few minutes," he said.

"Thanks."

It was lame, but she didn't know what else to say after his proclamation that he was going to be leaving to try to hunt down some artifacts before Richelieu could. When they hadn't managed to stop the other vampire she had anticipated that she and Raphael would still be together, spending time together, and now she couldn't help the strange aching she felt.

She was afraid she was never going to see him again. She was afraid that he would be killed. She was even more afraid that he would find and kill Richelieu and never return to tell her. Then she'd spend her life wondering what had happened to him and fearing that Richelieu and his minions were lurking in every dark corner.

She swallowed hard. She had no right to keep him there. And he had made it clear that he could move faster without her by his side. It shouldn't have hurt, but it did.

Yet as she stared up at him all she could think about were the stolen moments they'd shared, the taste of his lips, the feel of his arms around her. She felt herself flush. He bent down as though he was going to kiss her.

Sudden nightmarish images filled her head, memories of the things that the Raider had tortured her with in the chapel. With a sob she took a step back.

Raphael turned and disappeared down the stairs so fast she almost didn't see him. She reached out and grabbed the banister, feeling herself go a little weak.

Of all of them she had been the least injured, but the most frightened. Everyone else had physical wounds to attend to, proof of what they had been through. For her the wounds were only mental and she was terrified that the scars they would leave would be deep and disfiguring in their own way.

She needed someone to talk to, someone to help her dress her own wounds. *And clearly it's not going to be Raphael.*

She turned and stared at the bedroom down the hall where Paul was fighting for his life.

She walked to the doorway and then hesitated for a moment, gathering her courage. The heavy curtains were drawn over all the windows even though it was night and there was no sun to guard against. A small lamp was on in the corner and it cast strange shadows around the room. Her eyes moved to the bed where Paul was lying so still even though he shouldn't have been asleep. He was loosely covered by a sheet from the waist down. The skin on his chest, arms, and head was black in the few places it was left. The rest was a mass of open wounds. She saw muscles and bones laid open. Even his face was completely unrecognizable.

"How come he hasn't died?" Susan asked, unable to keep the quaver out of her voice.

Gabriel was standing half in shadow, face a mask as he stared at his sire. He shrugged. "I guess God's not finished with him yet."

She wanted to smile at that but she just couldn't. "Will he live then?"

Gabriel looked at her and something like a shadow passed across his face for just a moment. "I do not know. I have never heard of a vampire burned like this who did not die instantly."

"Then there's hope," she said.

He shook his head. "His body isn't healing."

She blinked. "I thought your bodies always healed from wounds that weren't fatal."

"So did I. It is like he is suspended between this world and the next. And until something changes he is part of neither. Either way, it is best to prepare for his death."

She choked back a sob. She barely knew Paul. David had spent much more time with him than she had. Still, there was something about him that touched her. And she couldn't stand to see any creature suffer. She breathed a quick prayer for him then she forced herself to look away.

"Have you tried feeding him some of the blood that's in the refrigerator?"

"No, I've been afraid to touch him too much. I'm not convinced in his state it would help anyway."

She turned and started to leave the room.

"I have been watching you with Raphael," Gabriel said.

She froze. Gabriel still terrified her, though she couldn't say why. He'd done nothing, said nothing. It was a primal fear, an instinct. She tried to ignore it, but the sudden thought of him watching her made her a little sick with fear and dread.

"Yes?" she asked, forcing herself to raise her chin high, praying she looked braver than she felt.

"You care for him."

"I—no—well, I guess—" She cut herself off as she realized he had been making a statement and not asking her a question.

He turned and looked full at her, his dark eyes piercing flesh and bone and heart and soul. She trembled, like the rabbit trapped by the serpent.

"The path we walk is not an easy one. It is fraught with peril not just for ourselves but also for those for whom we care."

She didn't know what to say so she just stared back at him, wishing she could read him even as he was reading her.

"He needs you. More than even he realizes."

"The war—"

"This has nothing to do with the war and everything to do with him."

She felt her heart begin to beat faster and by the way his eyes narrowed slightly she could tell he heard it.

The question is, do you need him?

She started, realizing he had spoken the last in her mind. She wondered why he could do that and Raphael couldn't. Her heart began thundering harder as she watched him. She realized that this time he expected her to answer.

She opened her mouth but no words would come out and the fear she had been feeling was nothing compared to the overwhelming rush of terror she felt now. What was he asking her? And even if she knew the answer could she admit it to him or to herself?

Raphael was a monster. But he was more than just that. And he was struggling so very hard to be good. His quest to stop Richelieu was noble and worthy of what little help she could offer.

But that wasn't what Gabriel was asking. He was asking about the aftermath of the war. If they managed to stop Richelieu would she return home to California, allowing Raphael to fade back into the shadows from which he had stepped?

The thought of not seeing him made her feel like she was falling inside. *What is wrong with me?* she wondered in desperation.

She thought about the way Raphael had kissed her, the fire he had ignited within her. How could she turn her back on those feelings? It was dangerous, and wrong, to want to be with him, to want to kiss him. There was no life they could share. She had everything to lose by just being near him: heart, future, life.

Gabriel reached out swiftly and before she could move he had put his hand on top of her forehead. A peace she had never known swept through her, driving all the pain and fear out before it. She should care, she should fight, but she just wanted the peace.

Your choice is not yet made, nor does it have to be, he said inside her mind again. *You do not have to be in such turmoil now.*

"You did something to me," she said.

"I merely calmed your mind," he said out loud. "You are not mesmerized as your cousin is."

"Can you help Wendy?" she asked, feeling like she was slurring her words.

"I could, but it's best if I don't. Raphael will release her when it is time, I will see to it."

And there it was again, the chilling sound of menace in his voice. But it was aimed at Raphael, not at her. And she didn't want to care.

She closed her eyes and sighed, focusing instead on the peaceful feelings he had gifted her with. Who knew how long they would last? She wanted to take comfort from them while she could.

"I have something for you," he said and she forced herself to open her eyes.

He was holding a small, ancient-looking book.

"What is it?"

He smiled. He had the most beautiful smile she had ever seen and yet it made him more menacing and terrible than ever before.

No wonder the others fear him so when the expression that is meant to put people at ease only sets their teeth on edge.

"It is the diary of my lady, Carissa."

She almost asked about his relationship with Carissa, but something in his eyes stopped her.

"It looks old," she said instead.

"Eight hundred years. Treat it with care."

She was afraid to accept it, but even more afraid to refuse. Gingerly she took it from his hand, careful not to touch his fingers as she did so.

"What does it say?" she asked.

He shook his head. "I do not know. I have never read it."

"Why?" she asked, stunned.

"Because it was not meant for my eyes."

"Why give it to me?"

"It may help you in your time of need. It belongs to the ladies of Bryas, and it is time it was in their possession once more."

"Thank—"

She blinked. He was gone.

Gingerly she opened the book and her eyes fell on the first page.

"Of course," she said with a bone-weary sigh. It was in French.

CHAPTER SEVEN

*And he said unto them, Verily I say unto you, That there
be some of them that stand here, which shall not taste
of death, till they have seen the kingdom of God come
with power.*

—Mark 9:1

Where are we going first?" Raphael asked as he and
Gabriel left the house behind.

"I've been debating that. For sheer number of artifacts
Notre Dame in Paris is a likely destination. The relics
housed there include a crucifixion nail, a piece of the
cross, and the crown of thorns, or at least, the band minus
the thorns."

"Don't you mean *alleged* relics?" Raphael said.

Gabriel shook his head sharply. "We won't know for
sure until we get close to them."

"But then again, neither will Richelieu. And the number of artifacts there would seem to make it a good bet."

"Yes, but what he's after is the blood. The question is,
will any real amount of blood be on those items?"

"What are you thinking?"

"I'm thinking that since every relic is a gamble until one
gets close to it and can tell whether it's authentic that he
would go first for something proven to have blood on it."

"I thought we already ruled out the grail, what could have a greater chance of blood than that?"

Gabriel smiled slowly and the sight chilled Raphael. He began to run through the night, heading for the airport and Raphael followed. After a moment he drew next to him. "Where are we going?"

"Italy. The city of Turin."

An hour later they were seated on board a plane for Frankfurt where they would then change planes for one bound for Turin. Travel time was going to be three-and-a-half hours. Raphael reflected that he had once spent three-and-a-half weeks sitting motionless in complete silence in one of the rooms in the monastery where Paul lived and yet that seemed like only a second compared to what it was going to be like trapped with his sire on a plane for a few hours.

"I hate planes," Raphael growled once they were seated.

"If you meditate on something you can learn to ignore the smell of the people, the sound of their pulses," Gabriel said.

Advice. Where had the other vampire been when Raphael was younger and could have used some? Even though he'd chosen to leave, the resentment was still there. Modern kids with absentee fathers had nothing on him.

"It's not that. I hate the contraptions," Raphael said as they began to taxi.

Gabriel looked at him, a single eyebrow raised. "Surely you're joking."

"If God meant us to fly He would have given us wings," Raphael said.

A vampire who is afraid to fly, funny.

The words echoed around in his head and set his teeth on edge. He hated when Gabriel did that. It felt like the ultimate intrusion on his privacy.

What could you be afraid of?

"I don't know, falling, burning to death, being decapitated, having something wooden shoved into my heart," he hissed.

"Only three of those would kill you," Gabriel murmured.

"Isn't that enough?" Raphael snapped.

"You know what happens to our kind when they fail to embrace progress?"

"They move to the country and live as hermits. That's what they would have done in the old days."

"The old days, maybe, but in modern days it could get you killed."

The plane took off and Raphael dug his fingers into his armrests, hearing the groaning of the plastic as it gave way.

"Calm down," Gabriel said.

And even though Raphael was a vampire he still felt the words wash over him, pull at him.

"Don't mesmerize me," he ground out.

"Don't tear your seat apart," Gabriel countered.

It had been easier on his flight to Paris with Susan. He had been able to focus completely on her. The seriousness of their mission, the sound of her voice, the smell of her skin—

"Do you love her?" Gabriel asked.

Raphael cringed. "No," he said quickly, silently cursing the other vampire for bringing up the subject. It was a conversation he didn't want to have with himself, let alone his sire.

"She has feelings for you," Gabriel continued, conveniently not responding to the malevolent thoughts Raphael was leveling at him.

He shrugged and turned to stare out the window, seeing the lights as pinpricks in the darkness. But if he focused, he could still see the cities they were flying over, make out their buildings. "How could she care for a monster?"

Gabriel laughed and the sound caught Raphael by surprise. He had never heard him laugh and the sound was rich and full.

"What?"

"Raphael, it's one of the oldest stories mankind has."

"What's that?"

"Beauty and the Beast," Gabriel said with a grin that exposed his fangs.

At the sight of them Raphael flinched involuntarily.

Gabriel cocked his head to the side.

"Your fangs are longer than I remember," he admitted.

"As are yours," Gabriel answered.

It was true. A vampire's fangs continued to grow after he was cursed so that they could tell each other's approximate age by the length. Paul had the longest fangs Raphael had ever seen on a vampire.

"Answer the question," Gabriel said.

And even though he didn't want to think about it, didn't want Gabriel to see his private thoughts, his memories, Raphael couldn't help but remember the inn where Susan had given her blood to save his life. And when he had realized that if she died he would kill all those who had been involved.

"Even yourself?" Gabriel asked softly.

Raphael stared out the window and refused to answer. He told himself it was because he didn't know the answer, but deep down he knew it was because he was afraid of it.

Susan and Wendy sat together on the couch, feet drawn up underneath them. It was ridiculous in its own way. It felt like they were kids again and they were waiting for their grandmother to read to them before bedtime.

Though Wendy would be doing the reading, in a twisted way it was like having an older relative tell them a story. After all, this was Carissa's diary, and according to Raphael, Wendy and Susan were direct descendants of Carissa's cousin Fleur. Which would make Carissa their great-aunt centuries removed.

Raphael and Gabriel had left an hour before, to where neither said. Once she'd been able to talk to David for a few minutes Wendy had let him go back to sleep but she had been too overcaffeinated to take advantage of the downtime to sleep herself.

Susan was thrilled because it had given her a chance to start hearing about what was in the diary.

"Ready?" Wendy asked, her voice trembling slightly.

Susan looked down at her clasped hands in her lap and realized she, too, was shaking. What could a woman who lived so many centuries before she was born possibly have to say that would affect her? Why had Gabriel entrusted her with the book? Why did Gabriel have it?

She bit her lip and forced herself to nod.

"Okay," Wendy said. She looked at the page and began to translate it slowly.

" 'My life is not my own. The death of my father is still

fresh upon me and I find myself weeping bitterly for him with every day that passes.'"

Susan felt her stomach clench even as tears stung the back of her eyes. Gabriel had claimed not to know the diary's contents and yet could it be coincidence that Carissa's story began with the death of her father?

Isn't that the beginning of my story as well? The death of my grandmother? What before that? Childhood, growing up, the pains and stresses and joys of doing so. Had it not been the loss of her grandmother that had changed her story, rewritten it? Without it she would not have come to Prague and met Raphael, would not have known vampires existed.

Wendy, too, must have felt the irony because when she continued her voice was shaking.

"'My cousin, Fleur, has shown me great kindness and has been selfless though she is mourning her uncle nearly as much as I am. But this world does not care for the tears of women and they, like our lives, are not our own.

"'Today the king's messenger came bringing the news that I dreaded. We are to travel to the palace where in a fortnight I am to be wed at the king's command. All I know of the man is his name.'"

FRANCE, AD 1198

Carissa rode upon her favorite mare, Dancer, in the middle of the small cavalcade. She turned for one last glance back at the castle that was her home. The rising sun colored the sky above the stone towers in shades of fire. "I'll be back soon," she promised the glistening walls, the servants within, and the farmers without. She twisted back around and urged Dancer to a trot. The mare whinnied delicately before picking up her speed.

She rode up beside the carriage and Fleur leaned out. "Are you sure you don't want to ride in here?" the younger girl asked.

"There'll be time enough for that later," Carissa answered. "I want to ride Dancer for a little while first."

Fleur shook her head before settling back into the carriage. Carissa smiled. Fleur had been bitten by a horse when they were children and had never been on one since.

She touched her heels to Dancer's flanks and they passed the carriage. More than anything, she needed to feel free, not confined to the gilded cage in which her cousin sat. She was grateful for Fleur's presence, though. Just knowing that she was close by comforted Carissa.

She glanced around at the king's guard who were escorting them to the palace. She'd heard it said that the number of the guard sent to escort a noble was in direct proportion to that person's importance. By her count, it would seem that she was a very important person indeed. In reality, it was her deceased father's title and lands that were important, not her. Instead of feeling like the king's honored guest, she felt like a prisoner. Within the fortnight she would be married, to a stranger, and all her father's possessions and land would belong to him.

She began to feel nauseated, fear nibbling at the corners of her mind. She kicked Dancer into a canter, and they left the cavalcade behind with the exception of one guard who kept pace with her.

She felt the wind blowing in her face and slowly she began to relax. Dancer's gait was so gentle it was like being rocked in a mother's arms. After the chaos that had surrounded their departure from the castle it provided welcome relief.

Her life was changing so fast, she didn't know how to handle it. She wasn't sure she was ready to be anyone's wife, let alone a stranger's. Still, it was not her place to make that decision and when the king called she must obey. She squeezed her eyes shut for a moment and whispered a prayer for strength.

Reluctantly she pulled the mare back to a walk. She glanced at the guard riding beside her, and he gave her an encouraging smile. It made her feel better. He was a stranger to her and yet he offered her a bit of kindness. Perhaps things were not so bleak as she imagined.

Impulsively she asked him, "Are you married, good sir?"

The man looked at her with startled eyes. He clearly was not used to being addressed regarding anything more than an order or a pertinent travel question. "Yes, milady, ten years now."

"Is she a good woman?"

"The finest," he responded, a smile lighting up the whole of his face.

"Did you know each other well when you married?" she asked, surprised by her own impropriety.

He shook his head. "We were strangers to each other. I did not see her face until we stood before the priest."

"Then God smiled upon you," she told him, feeling her own burden lessen slightly.

"That He did," the man replied, his eyes alight with joy.

"Thank you."

"Milady?"

She could only offer him a small smile as way of explanation before turning her eyes back to the road ahead. If God could grant the man beside her such happiness, surely He could grant her the same. *I have done everything I could to live a blameless life. I have attended church, done penance whenever I committed the slightest sin, and kept my mind and body pure. I have also been gentle, self-controlled, and dutiful, always dutiful.*

Duty, it was a word she knew well. Duty had kept her by her father's side, caring for his castle and lands after her mother died and he was sick with grief. Duty had kept her from ever riding as much as she wished or joining her father when he hunted so that her skin could remain pale and soft, the hallmarks of a lady. Duty now compelled her on toward the king's palace, to fulfill her destiny—to be a stepping stone for a young man of ambition seeking a way to fulfill his.

Surely God can forgive me what trespasses I have committed and grant me a good husband and happy marriage. That is all a woman can hope to have.

The sun was overhead when she finally consented to ride in the carriage. Fleur was eager for her company by then and prattled on about seeing the palace. Every once in a while the carriage would bump over a stone in the path, and Carissa would long for the smoothness of Dancer's gait once again. Her skin tingled lightly where the sun had warmed it and she could see the soft flush of pink upon the backs of her hands. It gave her a small surge of pleasure, which was soon replaced with thoughts of the creams she would have to put on later.

The hours slipped slowly past and at long last they stopped at an inn where they would rest for the night.

Carissa peered out anxiously as Jacques, the guard she had spoken with earlier, disappeared inside the building. To the side of the structure she saw several carts of strange design with shaggy ponies hitched to them. There were symbols upon the carts, but in the gathering dark she could not make out what they were.

After a minute, Jacques returned. "There is room for us to stay tonight," she heard him inform his captain. "There are some gypsies here, but they are friends of the innkeeper who are visiting briefly and will not be stopping overnight."

"Gypsies!" Fleur exclaimed next to her. "How exciting."

Carissa smiled at her enthusiasm. She had heard of gypsies, much of it unflattering. She felt secure, though, in the men that were with them. No harm would befall them while they were with the king's guard. Safe in that knowledge she found herself craning her neck to take a closer look at the gypsies' caravan.

A guard opened the carriage door and extended his hand to help her out. She accepted gratefully and stepped down, careful to lift her skirts to keep them from dragging in the muddy earth at her feet. Fleur stepped out of the carriage and stood at her side as they gazed at the door of the inn.

"I've never stayed in an inn before," Fleur whispered.

Neither had Carissa. She had spent the whole of her life in and around the castle where she had been born. She felt a moment's hesitation, but quickly brushed it aside. The captain of the guard would have chosen the safest route for them, and they would not have stopped unless he felt it necessary and appropriate.

She took a deep breath, and gripping Fleur's hand, strode toward the door. Inside, they were greeted by the innkeeper and his wife, a jolly couple who made much over them. They were seated at a long table, in a corner opposite from where another group, presumably the gypsies, sat.

The men with Carissa and Fleur sat at several tables around them. For a moment she thought of inviting the captain, or Jacques, to eat with them but dismissed it, knowing that it would be inappropriate. She thought of what her father used to say. *Our rules and social mores must be upheld at any costs. They are all that keep you and other women safe. They are all that separate us from animals.* He had lectured her time and again about how to act with common men, so as not to invite trouble. He had managed to instill in her a healthy fear of men, in general, even though he had always praised the virtue of godly noblemen.

He had also warned against gypsies. Her curiosity was too much, though. Carissa risked a glance at the gypsies on the far side of the room. Not wanting to seem rude or be caught staring, she only looked once and then away. There were about fifteen of them. Several of them were women and there were two children. They all wore colorful clothes and the women let their hair hang down, free and unfettered. The children had cherubic faces and black, curly hair. The men wore heavy beards with beads braided into them. She had never seen the like.

Dinner was a humble affair of roast meat and thick slices of bread. The meat was spiced in a peculiar way that made her wrinkle her nose. It didn't taste much better than it smelled, but the bread was at least hot and fresh and there was ample butter. Across from her Fleur picked at her food, obviously too excited to even notice how it tasted. Her cousin kept staring unabashedly at the gypsies.

As she finished her own meal Carissa watched in interest as the gypsies rose to leave, with many fond salutations to the owner.

One, a woman Carissa guessed to be a few years older than herself, smiled at her.

Carissa blushed at being caught staring, but smiled back as Fleur giggled.

"Would miladies like their fortunes told?" the gypsy asked. "No charge to friends of our host."

"Can we please?" Fleur asked, somewhat breathless.

Carissa hesitated, looking to the captain of the guard.

He nodded slowly. "It should be all right."

Carissa called, "Yes, please, milady."

The woman came forward and drew up a chair. She had long, curly black hair and deep green eyes that seemed to pierce through Carissa. Silver rings glittered on the woman's thumbs. On a belt around her waist hung many objects, which swung back and forth when she walked. One of them, a wooden bowl, she untied and placed upon the table.

"Who first?" she asked.

"Me, please," Fleur answered breathlessly.

The woman laughed at Fleur's eagerness. "All right, child, give me your palm."

Fleur held out her hand and the gypsy took it, carefully studying the lines. "This one"—her fingernail tapped a line—"means that you will have a long life. Your love line is strong, showing a bond between you and your husband with three children born to you."

Fleur practically squealed with excitement. Carissa smiled, pleased at her cousin's happiness. She didn't know if she believed the gypsy's proclamation. One of her servants back home was superstitious and swore that gypsies could tell the future. Carissa had never known what to think of such claims. She hoped, for Fleur's sake, though, that what the gypsy had said was true. Even if it weren't, the woman's kind eyes and cheerful proclamation caused Carissa to relax. Maybe there was nothing to fear from gypsies after all.

The gypsy woman then produced a pin. "I need three drops of your blood."

Fleur nodded and the woman pricked the tip of her finger over the bowl. Fleur bit her lip and her already pale cheeks seemed to grow whiter still. From her belt the gypsy pulled a small vial of powder and sprinkled some over the blood.

"Within the month you will know sorrow, but it will be brief and your joy magnified after. Your days will be spent with the sun shining upon your face and love surrounding you."

Fleur sighed contentedly. "Thank you so much."

"You are welcome," the gypsy said, smiling.

"Are you sure you won't take something, just a coin or two?"

The woman closed Fleur's hand into a fist and placed it down on the table.

"No, this is a gift."

"Thank you," Fleur said again. "Can you read my cousin?"

"Of course," the gypsy said, turning to Carissa.

Something icy touched Carissa's spine and she wanted to

decline. There was no way in which she could think to do it gracefully, though, so she reluctantly extended her hand.

The gypsy's smile quickly faded as she traced the lines on Carissa's hand.

"What do you see?" Carissa asked, fear beginning to course through her.

"I need three drops of your blood, and a lock of your hair," the other woman answered.

She produced another bowl, larger than the first. With a small knife she cut the smallest end off one of Carissa's locks and dropped it in. She added a foul-smelling clear liquid to it. Next she took the pin and pricked Carissa's finger. She winced at the pain and then watched in fascination as three crimson drops splashed into the clear liquid. The mixture suddenly turned black as night.

The gypsy looked up, her face ashen. "You shall wander long in darkness before you find love. There is much pain ahead of you. Blood shall be your downfall, and also your redemption."

The woman dropped Carissa's hand and stood hastily. "I must go," she said. She paused for a moment and then looked into Carissa's eyes. "I am sorry," she whispered in a fierce voice. Then she turned and fled out the door leaving her bowl behind.

Carissa sagged slightly, and stared into the bowl of inky liquid that the gypsy had left behind in her haste, wondering fearfully what the woman had seen. The blackness mocked her, though, keeping its secrets.

"I am sorry if she upset you, milady," the captain hurriedly said. "Pay the gypsy witch no mind. You know they cause mischief where they can." He waved his hand and a guard stepped forward to take the bowl away.

"I have forgotten it already," Carissa lied, though she knew the trembling of her voice betrayed her.

"We should retire for the evening," Fleur urged, her voice contrite. "We have a long journey in the morning."

A long journey, indeed. Her misgivings of the morning returned full force as she remembered the gypsy's words. "To wander long in darkness," Carissa whispered, "would be a long journey indeed."

Upstairs the girls changed quickly and in silence. Carissa lay awake long after Fleur had fallen asleep. She listened to the gentle rhythm of her cousin's breathing, but found no peace in it. She could not banish the events of the evening from her mind.

She closed her eyes and tried again to pray, but her thoughts kept straying too much. When at last she did fall asleep, her dreams were filled with images of a shadowy creature made up of darkness.

Though Carissa was weary of traveling, as they neared the palace she found she would have given anything for another day on the road. From the way she clapped her hands, Fleur clearly did not feel the same.

The palace stood, white walls sparkling under the noonday sun. Its very size took her breath away and made her life and her fears seem small by comparison. Surrounding the palace were gardens as far as the eye could see. Her eyes were drawn to the lush greenery, which offered comfort to the weary.

As humbling as the sight of the palace was, though, Carissa could not help but feel like a queen as the carriage rolled to a stop before a score of liveried servants waiting to receive them and escort them inside.

As one of them helped her and Fleur down from the carriage, another stepped forward and bowed deeply. "His Majesty, the king of France, has been expecting you."

"As have I," a strong voice said.

Carissa turned to see a man approaching. He was a little taller than she was with light-colored hair. The smile on his lips did little to lighten the severity of his piercing blue eyes, but his manner seemed pleasant enough.

He stopped before her and gave her a deep bow. "You will excuse me for this informal introduction. I saw the carriage approaching and could wait no longer. I am your fiancé."

Carissa curtsied hastily. "Monsieur, you take me by surprise. I had hoped to rest and gather myself after the long journey."

"Apologies, milady, it was thoughtless of me."

"No, I spoke in haste, it is you who must forgive me. I, too, shared your eagerness to meet."

"Then upon us both the sin of impatience," he said, a smile still upon his lips.

"Let us forgive each other and pledge to meet again at a more appropriate hour," Carissa answered.

"Milady is as wise as she is beautiful," he answered with a deep bow. "Until later today, mademoiselle."

He turned, leaving Carissa feeling flustered. Fleur touched her arm and she jumped, having forgotten her cousin was there.

"Handsome," Fleur murmured.

"Oh. Nothing. I— We should go inside." Carissa mused, watching him leave. There was something about him that she found disquieting, but she was at a loss to discover what it was.

"What's wrong?" Fleur asked, sounding alarmed.

"Hmm?" Carissa asked, turning to her cousin.

"You were making the sign of the cross."

Carissa glanced down and saw her hand hovering in midair. She paled. "Yes, I suppose I was."

Carissa tried to put the incident behind her as she and Fleur were escorted to their chambers in the palace. Maids were waiting there to help them.

Buckets of hot water were brought from the kitchens and poured into two large tubs. The two girls were soon stripped and soaking in the baths while fresh clothes were laid out.

Carissa scrubbed and scrubbed until she felt like she'd taken off a layer of skin. When she exited the bath her skin was pink and glistening. After drying off she was dressed in one of her finest gowns made of pale gold cloth. Her hair was wound on top of her head and covered with a filmy veil. Last she donned the cross necklace that her father had given her. It was silver, of Byzantine design. He had been given the cross by her mother and wore it while he was away in the Crusades.

He had always told her there was a secret about it, but he had died before ever telling her what that was. She touched it and closed her eyes. She could almost hear his voice and she missed him so. Why had he never told her before it was too late?

PRAGUE, PRESENT DAY

"What?" Wendy asked when Susan gasped, looking up from the diary.

Susan grasped the cross necklace around her own neck. "In Bryas, when I was in the hall of the castle I saw portraits of some of our ancestors. There was a young woman whom Raphael identified as Carissa. She was wearing this cross in the portrait."

Wendy carefully put down the ancient book. "What on earth are you talking about?"

And then Susan remembered she hadn't told Wendy, or anyone else in the family, about the deed to the French castle that the attorney, Pierre, had given her. She took a deep breath.

"After Grandmother's funeral, I was contacted by a lawyer here in Prague. His name was Pierre. His family's firm had helped Grandmother find this cross. Apparently it was a family heirloom hundreds of years old that was lost during the Renaissance."

"Wait, if that cross was lost during the Renaissance, how did Grandma even know about it?" Wendy asked, looking bewildered.

"I'm coming to that. It turns out that she left some things for me with Pierre. One was a key and the other was the deed to a dilapidated castle in France, in Bryas to be exact."

Wendy's eyes bulged. "A castle? In France? Are you kidding me?"

Susan threw her hands up in the air. "I know, it all seemed completely crazy."

"Is that why you went to France?" Wendy asked, leaning forward.

"Yes. I felt I just had to go and see it. See what it was that she was keeping secret."

"And the key? What did it open?"

"A safe locked inside a stuffed animal in the dungeon. Inside were a bunch of papers. One of them was a letter to me from Grandma, saying she knew I'd find it and that it was time I learned the secret of this cross necklace."

Wendy reached out and touched the necklace. "What is the secret?"

"I don't know. The other papers were a letter from a French knight named Jean to his daughter, Carissa, explaining what the secret was. Grandma said she thought it best I read the letter instead of just hearing about it from her. It was in French, though. So I brought it back with me to Prague, but my bag was stolen at the airport."

Wendy fell back among the couch cushions with a strangled sound. "I shouldn't have left. If I hadn't left you I could have translated it and we'd know."

Susan grabbed Wendy's hand. "You did what you had to. I never wanted you to get caught up in any of this nightmare."

"And yet, I'm here, back, right in the middle of it," Wendy said, her voice thoughtful. "I'm still not sure how that happened."

Susan looked away, not sure that she wanted to explain to her cousin that she had been mesmerized by Raphael and that he still hadn't lifted it from her. She was compelled to do as he said. No, she couldn't tell her, not just yet. With any luck she could get Raphael to release her from the mesmerism and she'd never have to know about any of that.

"God works in mysterious ways," Susan said instead, hating herself for it.

"So we have no way of knowing what secret she was talking about," Wendy mused, staring at the cross.

"Grandmother did say in her letter that the key ring she gave me for my sixteenth birthday would help reveal the secret. I had your mom mail it to me."

"Where?"

Susan bit her lip. "I didn't know where I'd be, so I gave her the mailing address for Pierre, the attorney."

Wendy leaned forward again to touch the cross. "I hope it gets here soon. My curiosity is killing me. I knew it was old, I just had no idea how old. So this is Carissa's cross?"

"Yes, it looks exactly like the one in the portrait."

"What does...did...she look like?" Wendy asked.

"Exactly like you, but with my dark hair instead of your blond hair."

Wendy smiled. "Then she was one gorgeous lady."

Susan laughed and smacked her with a pillow. Her mind was still reeling, though, from everything they had just learned. To find out how much she had in common with Carissa was a shock. Both had been given the cross by the person who should have also told them its secret, but both of them had been kept in darkness by the death of their relatives.

I'm tired of dwelling in the darkness, with the shadow of death upon me, she thought.

Sometimes death is all you have, a still, small voice seemed to whisper in her mind.

And just like that the tears came.

"Hey, what's wrong?" Wendy asked.

Everything. But how could she tell her that? Fear washed over her as she remembered the voice inside her head in the chapel, the things it had made her think.

"I can't believe they left us alone," she whispered.

"We have David."

"Who is too injured to even stand at the moment," Susan said. It was true. David was going to be bedridden for a few more days at the least. She hadn't listened when he'd called in to his work, but she hoped it was going to be okay. But *okay* had become such a relative term, not meaning what it once had to her. Now it just meant that at the end of all this they'd be alive.

"I don't know what to say," Wendy said in a small voice.

Susan turned to look at her cousin and then gave her a quick hug. "Say that it will be okay," she whispered.

"It will be okay."

Susan closed her eyes and prayed that was true.

"I'm going to go check on David," Wendy said, getting up after a minute.

She yawned and Susan looked at her closely. "Then you should get some sleep."

"Only if you promise to get some yourself," Wendy said.

It was a good idea. As much as Susan wanted to know more about the contents of the book, sitting up and waiting while Wendy slept would do neither of them any good.

She got up. "I'll look in on Paul."

Upstairs Paul lay, still unmoving. He had not regained consciousness once since he was injured. And it still looked like he wasn't healing at all.

God, what's happening to him? she asked.

She shook her head and started to leave the room. She stopped, though, and turned back. She wasn't ready to be alone with her own thoughts yet or memories of recent events. She pulled up a chair and tried not to stare at the ruined face of the monk.

"Hi, Paul, it's Susan," she said quietly. "I just wanted to say hi, spend a few minutes with you." She swallowed hard against a sudden lump in her throat. "Everything— everything's going to be okay."

Looking at him, she knew it was a lie. Everything wasn't going to be okay.

"Everyone's doing well. David is getting plenty of bed rest. I'm fine." She swallowed. *Another lie.*

"Gabriel and Raphael are off hunting down Richelieu who apparently is after some kind of relics or artifacts." She sighed in frustration. "They wouldn't tell me exactly what it is that they're looking for or where."

No movement still, not even a twitch to show that Paul was even in there or could hear her. Still she felt compelled to press on. "So, now all we need is for you to heal up so we can go kick some more vampire butt."

It sounded laughable, especially coming from her. In the end there were no words of comfort she could offer him or herself.

"Before I go, I guess, I'll just pray here for a little bit. I'll pray for both of us," she whispered.

She slipped onto her knees and rested her head on the edge of the bed. Tears streamed down her face and she began to shake uncontrollably. It was all too much. She still had nightmarish flashes from when the Raider had been playing with her mind. The worst part was, it wasn't going to get better any time soon. They hadn't won the war. They hadn't even won this particular battle.

She prayed there in the room like she'd never prayed before in her entire life.

CHAPTER EIGHT

He that hath an ear, let him hear what the Spirit saith unto the churches; He that overcometh shall not be hurt of the second death.

—Revelation 2:11

Gabriel was tense. He didn't like going into any situation blind. He liked it even less when he couldn't trust those who were supposed to be on his side. He glanced at Raphael. Paul was right. The younger vampire had grown much, matured in the years since they had last seen each other. He shouldn't have been surprised. It was, after all, the way of things, the grand design.

Vampirism was a curse bestowed only upon the most evil so that they could live long enough to understand the horror of their crimes and repent and find the forgiveness and mercy of God.

That was how it had always been, the true and proper order of things.

And it still shocked him every time it worked.

Even so, he could feel the conflict that burned inside the other vampire. Every moment was a struggle not to forget himself, not to slip into the old ways. He cared deeply for Susan; Gabriel could feel his emotion. But at the same time Raphael lusted after her blood, a lust that was made all the worse by the fact that he had actually tasted it.

Hunter and prey, lover and beloved. Sometimes the distinction was far too subtle.

They slipped through the darkness, the few people who were actually out never saw them. It was best that way. He had grown used to moving among the shadows, seen only by those he wished to be seen by. Raphael had always been more of a warrior than a hunter and stealth wasn't second nature to him. He did well, though, and they made their way to Turin Cathedral unseen.

At last the cathedral loomed in the darkness. Out of habit Gabriel stopped, turning slowly in all directions, sniffing the air for anything that seemed out of place.

Raphael stood beside him, saying nothing, but Gabriel could feel his impatience. Impatience could get you killed. Gabriel had learned that lesson when he was still human and nothing that had happened since had shown him anything different. At last he began to move again and he could feel Raphael's agitation growing with each step.

The Sindone Chapel was where the shroud was housed. The chapel had been designed and built just for the relic. They circled around until they found a door that was unlikely to be noticed because it was in shadows.

It was an easy thing to break the lock and force the door open. Once inside they kept moving until they were walking down a long, dark corridor. When it ended they were inside the chapel. Rows of pews stood silent, pillars and arches soaring above them on either side, drawing the eyes toward the front where underneath a dome the relic was housed.

They walked forward, their footsteps making no sound

that could echo around the building and give away their presence. He could feel Raphael's hesitation. The younger vampire was still terrified of crosses and the churches that housed them. Still, he maintained pace with him as they marched toward the front.

Gabriel kept his head constantly swiveling as he tried to catch even the slightest movement or the hint of a whisper. There was nothing, though. Given the experience at Prague Castle, that did little to ease his mind.

When at last they were standing under the dome he resisted the urge to look up. It was dark and there was not enough light in the night sky to illuminate the figures above.

In front of them was a replica of the shroud, slightly smaller. There was also a large replica of the negative image of the face on the shroud. He felt his eyes drawn to it and he stopped for a moment as he couldn't help but wonder if he was looking at the face of Christ.

There were many marvels, many mysteries in the world. Could the shroud be one of them?

A vault kept the actual shroud safe. But even though distance and metal separated them from it, he should have been able to feel something from it if it was real.

He closed his eyes, reaching out with his senses. He was looking for power, real power, like he had felt a few times before in the presence of objects touched by the hand of God.

After a minute he opened his eyes and shook his head.

"There is nothing here," he said.

"It's fake?" Raphael whispered.

"I do not know if it has already been stolen by Richelieu or if it isn't what so many have believed. For all we know it could even be absent, off somewhere being subjected to more religious and scientific analysis. Regardless of whether or not the actual shroud is real, there is nothing here for us."

Raphael turned to go, but Gabriel stopped him with a hand on his shoulder. "That does not mean there is nothing we can learn."

He inhaled deeply. So many scents flooded his nostrils. Most pronounced was the smell of incense. But there were other, subtler scents as well.

He had once met a vampire who worked in the perfume industry. He was one of the most renowned "noses" of his age. He could smell anything and not only tell you what its component parts were but re-create it perfectly. His enhanced vampiric senses had made him exceptionally skilled, much to the delight of his patrons and the puzzled despair of his rivals.

He would have been able to tell Gabriel exactly what he wanted to know. He closed his eyes. *Patience. Concentration.*

He inhaled again.

There it was! The scent he had been trying to detect. The smell of death and decay. It was the scent of a vampire.

He straightened. Richelieu had already been there. They were one step behind him but at least they were on the right path.

He turned and raced from the building, Raphael on his heels. Once outside he explained to him.

"He's been here, but we have no way of telling if he found anything."

"Then what do we do?"

"I suggest we try the next most likely place in case he, too, came up empty-handed."

"To Paris?" Raphael said, his voice laced with hesitation.

Gabriel couldn't blame him. His last trip to the country had not turned out well.

"To Paris," he affirmed.

"We won't be able to find any flights that land before dawn."

Gabriel growled, knowing he was right. "We'll have to seek shelter for the day."

He stopped and turned to look back the way they'd come. And with the wind now blowing toward him he smelled what he should have before.

He barely had time to shout a warning before three vampires were upon them.

The first one rushed him and Gabriel dropped into a crouch and threw the creature over his head, snatching the stake from its hand as he did so. The vampire hit the ground hard and Gabriel swung the stake down into his chest. He yanked the stake out just as the creature disintegrated.

He turned just in time to see Raphael rip out the throat of the second vampire with a roar. From the size of the attacker's fangs he couldn't be even a century old. He was no match for the seasoned warrior of the Crusades.

The third vampire was slightly older and more cautious. He approached, holding a stake in his hand, eyes darting between the two of them.

"Tell us what we want to know and we'll let you live," Gabriel said.

"If I tell you what you want to know I will not live long," the other said, sneering.

"Join us," Raphael said. "You do not have to follow Richelieu. We can show you a different way, a better way."

"I don't think so." The vampire rushed at Gabriel. When he got close Gabriel twisted, letting his enemy slam his stake into his chest. His eyes opened in horror as he realized that he had missed. Gabriel grabbed him and staked him through the back.

As the vampire started to turn to ash Gabriel plucked a piece of paper from his jacket pocket a split second before it, too, was dust.

"What is it?" Raphael asked, wiping the blood from his mouth with the back of his hand.

"Plane reservation for tomorrow night. Looks like he was about to join back up with his master."

"Paris?"

Gabriel shook his head. "It appears I was wrong. Richelieu is headed for Vienna."

"What's in Vienna?"

"I don't know, but we need to find out."

Raphael pulled out his phone and called Susan.

"Hi, it's me. I need you to do some research. See if you can find out what relics that could have touched the blood of Christ might be in Vienna. We're going to ground soon so just leave a message when you find something."

He hung up and Gabriel felt the sun beginning to rise.

"Let's move," he said.

They ended up finding another church, much smaller. They broke in and made their way down to the basement. If Richelieu had left any human minions to hunt them they'd be unlikely to search a church.

They found a utility room that was thick with dust.

Raphael collapsed on the threshold and Gabriel dragged him inside and closed the door.

He had time only to find a darkened corner before crashing to the ground, unconscious. His last thoughts were of the diary he had given to Susan. He hoped he had done the right thing. And, rare for him, as he slept he dreamed.

FRANCE, AD 1198

Locked in the prison cell the thirst gnawed at him, making him half crazed and he hallucinated from time to time. For a while he imagined that the last four centuries had been nothing but fever dreams and that he would awake to find his mother standing beside his bed placing a wet cloth upon his brow as she had done when he was a child. Just when he felt himself slipping away, into oblivion, he would hear the heavy clank of an iron door and smell fresh meat. He would wait, still for a moment, unable to believe his good fortune, until the meat, moaning in anguish, would venture too close to his corner. Then he would strike and he would drink, the blood trickling down his throat, quenching his thirst, and the bones snapping in his jaws.

As his hunger subsided his reason would return and he would find himself crouched over the body of yet another dead human. The souls of his victims found an escape in death that he would never know. He was death and yet he still lived.

As he stared down at the corpse of an old man cradled in his arms he knew that the cycle had to stop. He didn't know how exactly, but he couldn't go on like this. His captors were using him. He was kept alive as their unwitting accomplice, the monster in the dungeon that killed the prisoners they did not want to dirty their hands with.

He stared at the face of the old man and wondered what crime he could have committed to merit such treatment. A political dissident perhaps? A would-be religious reformationist? He let the gray head slip from his cold fingers to the ground, where it landed with a dull thud. He put his hands to his face, smelling the blood upon them, and was unable to stop himself from licking his fingers.

Slowly he stood, feeling the power surging back through his limbs. He took five short steps and was at the end of his tether. Then, as he had so many times before, he began to systematically test the strength of each link in the chains that held him captive.

Was it his imagination or did one of them seem weaker this time? He pulled with all the strength he had. It did seem a little weaker, but still too strong for him to break. He flexed his long fingers and listened closely to the sound of the muscles and sinews as they moved beneath his skin.

Outside he could hear the other prisoners breathing, in cells far away from his. He heard the rats rustling around. Years ago their ancestors had grown wise enough to avoid his cell. He paced his small corner of hell, his eyes able to see things in the dark that a human could not.

He forced himself to lie down, though energy was still flooding through his body. He forced everything to slow, and he put himself into a kind of trance.

A few days later a prisoner in a nearby cell died. He had heard the death rattle in a dying man's breath often enough to recognize it instantly. The sound had awoken him from his sleep. He listened with a touch of envy as men came to take away the body. He wondered if they would ever come for him or if he would be trapped in the cell until the walls fell down around him.

As the warden's footsteps retreated into the distance, his thoughts returned to a more pressing matter. The thirst had grown unbearable.

CHAPTER NINE

He discovereth deep things out of darkness, and bringeth out to light the shadow of death.

—Job 12:22

When Susan woke she saw that she had missed a call from Raphael. Fear and regret mingled together as she checked her voicemail. She sagged in relief when she realized he was okay. She played it a second time just to listen to his voice.

Get a grip, Susan, she told herself.

There was a computer set up in the living room and she hurried down to it. After about an hour of searching she was pretty sure she knew what Richelieu was looking for in Vienna.

She dialed Raphael's phone, knowing he wouldn't answer because the sun was up.

"Hi, it's Susan. My best guess is he's going after a relic in the Hofburg Treasure House. What you'd be looking for is a lance or a spear-type thing. Although, from what

I can tell it isn't the spear that pierced the side of Jesus. It's thought to be the lance of Constantine the Great. It was said that Constantine's lance had one of the crucifixion nails inside it. Anyway, I hope that helps. Let me know if you need anything more. Please."

She hung up. The thrill of finding the information passed now that she had shared it. Still for those few minutes she hadn't felt helpless. She'd felt like she was actually doing something.

She got up from the computer and made herself some breakfast. It would be hours before she even had a chance of hearing back from Raphael. Hours with nothing to do but sit and wait. She wished she could read the diary for herself and silently cursed the fact that she had taken Spanish in high school and not French. Instead she had to wait patiently for Wendy. They hadn't made it very far in the diary and she was eager to see what came next.

She went upstairs to check on the two patients. Paul was no different. She lingered in the doorway for a moment, wondering how he would feel if he knew the others were hunting for relics without him.

She moved into David's room next and saw that he was awake.

"Are you hungry? I can fix you something to eat," she said, seizing upon the opportunity to busy herself with something.

"Just some soup would be great," he said with a weak smile.

She ran back downstairs and while the soup was heating made some breakfast for Wendy, as well. She told herself she would wake her when she went back upstairs.

When the soup was done she carried it up on a tray

and discovered that Wendy was already awake and talking with David. The two were holding hands when she entered the room and Susan felt a pang of jealousy. They could hold hands if they wanted to. They were two normal humans and it wouldn't send one of them into a fit of bloodlust.

She forced herself to smile as she dropped off the tray and then she scurried back downstairs. It wasn't Raphael's fault that he had a hard time being close to her, but it made things difficult.

Not that things should be easy. He is, after all, still a monster, she reminded herself. But when she thought of him she thought of the way he looked at her, the way he had kissed her, and it was hard to remember that part.

Susan stroked the cross necklace as she thought about the portrait she had seen of Carissa. Carissa as a young woman, before the darkness took her, before blood was her downfall, if indeed it was.

But was it also her salvation as the gypsy woman predicted?

She thought about all the secrets that had been hidden and forgotten in her family. What was it they said? Those who forgot the past were doomed to repeat it.

That's why I have to know about her, about what happened to her. So that I can escape whatever fate befell her.

Wendy came downstairs, looking tired. There were circles under her eyes. She ate her breakfast in the kitchen while Susan took her place on the couch and tried to imagine everything that Carissa must have thought and felt. Had she known that vampires walked the earth?

Did she fall in love with one of them?

She thought of what Raphael had said about her own

grandmother. He had implied that a vampire had been in love with her. Had her grandmother been in love with the vampire? And if so, who was it?

It wasn't Raphael, which relieved her to no end. She thought about Gabriel and shuddered. She prayed it wasn't him.

By the time Wendy finished eating and came into the room Susan felt like she was going to scream in frustration. Wendy settled herself down on the couch with a yawn.

"Ready?"

Susan nodded, not trusting herself to speak, and handed her the book opened to the page where they'd left off.

Wendy took it and began to read. "'Dinner at the king's table is something everyone should strive toward. I only wish I had been there under happier circumstances.'"

FRANCE, AD 1198

The food was exotic and elaborately prepared in stark contrast to the food Carissa had eaten during her journey. She tasted none of it, though. Instead her time was spent stealing glances at her betrothed and wondering what type of man he was.

As the meal drew to a close, the king rose. A hush fell upon everyone at the table as they waited for him to speak. He lifted his glass in the air and looked purposefully at Carissa. She blushed as she guessed what was coming next.

"A toast to the good health of our bridegroom, one of the finest and youngest magistrates in all of France, and a good and righteous man, and to his bride-to-be."

Carissa nodded acknowledgment, her mouth dry. She

raised her glass to her lips but did not taste any of the liquid that flowed across her tongue. Magistrate. The young man who was looking at her, who would soon be her husband, was one of those involved with the Inquisition, protecting France from witches and heretics.

The king sat back down, and her intended rose to his feet. "I am honored and humbled that the king would choose me to be the husband to this young woman. It is a tremendous responsibility that he has laid at my feet. Not only must I learn to be a husband, I must also learn to care for a vast estate. I only hope that I am equal to the challenge that has been set before me."

He sat and everyone drank again, everyone but Carissa. Which did he value more, her hand or her lands? She shook her head to rid it of such thoughts.

When at last she and Fleur returned to their chambers, she sat upon the bed wearily. Fleur, on the other hand, was spinning around the room, her cheeks flushed with excitement. Carissa couldn't stop herself from laughing out loud at her cousin.

"Does your exuberance have anything to do with the young man who was sitting next to you at dinner?" she said, hazarding a guess.

Fleur sat down next to her with a guilty laugh. "It does. He was simply wonderful. I think he liked me as well."

"I'm happy for you."

Fleur's smile quickly faded. "What about you? Are you happy for yourself?"

"I don't know what to feel," Carissa admitted, shaking her head. "My mind just feels so muddled."

Fleur patted her shoulder sympathetically. "Maybe things will be clearer in the morning."

"I hope so. Speaking of the morning, though, we should get some rest. We want to look our best for mass."

As she slowly began to undress, though, Carissa couldn't help but worry that the morning wouldn't bring any change. Even when she got into bed and closed her eyes she couldn't settle her mind. She prayed for what seemed an eternity and tried to coax sleep but it seemed no use.

She heard a footstep and she jerked, startled. There was the whisper of cloth and she twisted her head slightly so she could look at Fleur's bed.

It was empty.

She turned her head again and saw her cousin very quietly dressing, her movements hurried.

Carissa thought about calling out to her, questioning her, but something held her tongue. What was her cousin doing?

A few moments later Fleur tiptoed from the room. As soon as she had left Carissa leaped to her feet and threw on a dress with a heavy cloak over it, praying no one looked at her too closely.

She glided out the door and hurried down the hall to the staircase, anticipating that Fleur would be headed downstairs. Many in the palace were still awake and the sounds of revelry echoed through the halls.

She hesitated for a moment, wondering if Fleur had decided to rejoin those in the great hall. Then she caught sight of the hem of Fleur's dress as it disappeared out a door leading into the gardens.

Carissa followed. As she stepped foot outside her heart began to pound in her chest. Where could her cousin be headed at this time of night, alone?

Torches scattered around the grounds cast eerie shadows on everything and she could see her cousin a ways ahead. Fleur slowed when she reached a stone bench and Carissa moved off the path behind a row of hedges that lined the walkway.

The girl seemed excited, shifting her weight from foot to foot and clasping her hands together.

Something dark crept into Carissa's mind. What had the gypsy said about sorrow touching Fleur?

She looked around. There didn't seem to be anyone else about. It was just them and the shadows, which seemed to crowd in, thick and dark. The air was still and all noise from birds and insects had ceased, as though the night creatures had sensed the intrusion into their domain.

Either that or there's a predator nearby.

Something didn't feel right about any of this. Fleur had always been a bit fanciful, but she wasn't the type of girl to come out here by herself and—

One of the shadows suddenly moved, detaching itself from the others. Carissa jumped and clamped a hand over her own mouth. She relaxed only slightly when she recognized Étienne, the young man Fleur had been flirting with during dinner.

And suddenly her cousin's mysterious actions didn't seem quite so mysterious. Carissa ducked down so she could see them clearly, but they would not be able to see her. She should make her presence known, insist on acting like a chaperone, but one look at the smile that lit up Fleur's face and she prepared to wait it out.

Someone deserved to be happy. Even if it wasn't her.

"I didn't mean to frighten you," Étienne said as he took Fleur's hand and kissed it.

She smiled coyly. "It was a good kind of frightened."

"I thank God that He brought you to this place."

"You should thank the king and my cousin as well," Fleur said lightly.

"I will not hesitate to do so."

"And what will you say to my cousin?"

"That she is a blessed woman to have family such as you."

From her hiding place Carissa couldn't help but smile. She was indeed blessed to have Fleur as her family.

"In a couple of weeks she'll have a new family," Fleur mused. "What do you know of her fiancé?"

Carissa held her breath, not wanting to miss a word Étienne was about to say.

"Not much," Étienne admitted. "I have had very little interaction with him, a fact that I am grateful for."

"You don't approve of the Inquisition?" Fleur asked intently.

"A wise man would not admit to that."

"What *would* a wise man admit to?" Fleur asked.

"Loving you."

"Oh," Fleur said, sounding as startled as Carissa felt.

"Do you believe in love at first sight?" Étienne asked.

"I must confess I am a recent convert to the idea," she said, and even in the dim torch light Carissa could see that Fleur was blushing.

"I am in love with you," he said, taking her hand in his.

Fleur pulled her hand away. "You are too bold, sir. I'm not to be pawed at."

"I do not transgress lightly. You know my intentions," he protested.

"Nay. I know your emotion but naught of your intentions," Fleur countered.

"I am yours, your own knight. Command me in all things," he said, dropping to his knees before her.

From her hiding place Carissa could see his eyes burned with a passion so intense that she could nearly feel the heat of his gaze. Her breath caught in her throat. What would it be like to be her cousin and to be the recipient of such passion?

"Today you are mine, but what of tomorrow, and the next?" Fleur pressed.

"Always yours."

"When I am no longer young, and my hair is gray and my body crippled?"

"Always yours," he repeated.

"And how then shall you prove this devotion?" Fleur demanded with a boldness Carissa could only dream of.

"In every way."

Something rustled in the bushes nearby. Fleur jumped and Étienne leaped to his feet and placed himself between her and the sound. Carissa swiveled her head from side to side but could see nothing.

"Who's there?" he commanded.

Carissa froze, her fear of whatever might be lurking nearby vying with her fear of being discovered. She waited to hear what response would come to Étienne's question.

Silence greeted him. "Perhaps it is nothing," he said at last.

Fleur's hands were trembling and she shook her head. "There is something, I am sure of it. There's something...evil."

"Then let us leave this place. You should get your sleep. I will escort you back inside," he said.

The surprise was clear on Fleur's face. "You believe me?"

He nodded and offered his arm.

She took it and gazed at him in wonder. When they were children, Fleur had told her about sensing things— good, evil. Carissa had believed her when they were young, but hadn't given much thought to it in years. Neither had she heard Fleur speak of having such a feeling in a long time. She couldn't help but wonder if the feeling of something watching her was the same as whatever her cousin was sensing.

Evil.

It was a harsh word and Fleur would not have used it lightly. Suddenly Carissa wanted nothing more than to be back inside the palace, asleep in her room, and only dreaming of dark things.

"If it would ease your mind I could ask my uncle about your cousin's fiancé. My uncle is also a magistrate and would be in a more knowledgeable position," Étienne said as he and Fleur began to walk back toward the palace.

"It would be good of you."

"No, it would be selfish of me. It would give me an excuse to see you again."

When they were down the path a ways Carissa stepped out cautiously from behind the row of shrubs. Somewhere in the darkness behind her there was a cracking sound, as if someone stepped on a twig. She picked up her skirts and ran after her cousin and Étienne. At the last moment she realized she couldn't just follow Fleur back to their room or her cousin would know she had been spying on her.

There was another door farther down the wall and she rushed for it, praying that no one saw her in her disheveled state. God smiled upon her and she reached it in time to beat her cousin to the stairs without anyone seeing her.

Once in their room Carissa threw off her cloak but did not have time to remove her dress. She laid down on her bed, tucked the covers under her chin, and closed her eyes, pretending to be asleep. Moments later her cousin slipped into the room.

When she could tell from Fleur's breathing that she was finally asleep, Carissa slipped out of bed and removed her dress. Then she laid back down again as her mind feverishly worked on trying to figure out who or what had been watching them in the darkness.

PRAGUE, PRESENT DAY

Susan sat and waited breathlessly as Wendy turned the next page. She couldn't help but think about the night she had met Raphael, when Wendy had gone off with a stranger who turned out to be a vampire. She thought of Carissa chasing after Fleur and realized that they were even more alike than she had at first thought.

But Fleur's man was a man and not a monster.

At least, she hoped so. She hoped that Étienne had been everything he seemed to be. That would make for a nice story. And Fleur was the one she and Wendy were actually descended from. If she was their great-grandmother many times over was Étienne their great-grandfather?

" 'They say that if you keep your eyes open you can see signs and omens all around you,' " Wendy continued to read. " 'Today something else happened, but I don't know what it means. I just know that I am afraid. Maybe the gypsy woman's words have set fear in my heart where I should feel none.' "

Susan shuddered. There was something horrific coming, she could feel it. Had Carissa been about to encounter a vampire? Had it been a vampire watching her and Fleur and Étienne in the gardens? And what about her fiancé?

FRANCE, AD 1198

Carissa felt the heat rise in her cheeks as the priest spoke of love. She risked a glance over to the next pew where the man she was to marry sat. Next Sunday they would be sitting in church together, as husband and wife. As though he felt her eyes upon him, he glanced in her direction and smiled.

She smiled back before hastily dropping her eyes. She was not at all sure that God would approve of her flirting during mass.

The last week had been strange. She had seen more of him and heard many people speak highly of him. Her fears had not been allayed, but she was doing her best to try and get to know him and to become his friend. So far she had learned that he was a righteous man, with an important job, who worked hard for king and church. All those traits were admirable. Maybe he was a little too serious, but he was probably just nervous around her as she was around him.

"And Christ loved the church as His bride, sacrificing everything, even His life, for her," the priest continued.

Tonight I shall be his bride. Does he love me like that?

Would he sacrifice his life for me? She didn't risk glancing at him again, though she burned to. *Do I love him?*

She didn't know; she was not even sure she knew what love felt like. She admired him, respected him, surely that was part of it. *And if I do not love him, I will grow to love him as husband and confidant. It is part of my duty, part of the mystery of becoming one in marriage.*

Or, at least, she hoped. Carissa's mother had gone to her grave years before she had been able to ask such questions.

At last the mass was over and Carissa rose to her feet, feeling the need for fresh air. She hurried outside, Fleur trailing behind her.

"Are you frightened?" the other girl asked.

"No," Carissa lied.

Fleur wrinkled up her nose. "You know what is supposed to happen tonight, when you're alone together?"

Carissa nodded.

"I know I shall be terrified when it is my turn," Fleur said with a shudder.

"Maybe it will be wonderful," Carissa countered.

"Not very likely."

Although she would never have said so, Carissa enjoyed Fleur's blunt manner of speaking. It was a refreshing change from courtiers who said one thing while meaning quite the opposite. Indeed, Carissa had spent as little time as possible with the others of the court, preferring instead to take long walks upon the palace grounds and dream of going home.

"Come, we need to get you ready," Fleur urged, picking up speed.

"I wish to walk first."

"You walk every day," Fleur protested. "Surely you have seen all there is to see by now."

"Yes, but tomorrow it shall all be different. *I* shall be different."

Fleur gave her a hard look before giving in with a sigh. "Very well, but be to our rooms quickly. There is much to do."

"I shall," Carissa promised.

She watched Fleur hurry off and knew in her heart that she should be going with her. She needed a few more moments to herself, though. She wandered into the rose garden, breathing deeply of the perfumed air.

The small stone bench she had seen when Fleur met with Étienne a few nights before called to her, and she took a seat. She closed her eyes and let the warmth of the place wash over her, nourish her. She sat still for several minutes, letting the sunshine soak into her bones. She felt her cares begin to slip away.

"You look very beautiful this morning," a soft, masculine voice said.

She jumped, startled, and opened her eyes. There before her stood her fiancé, a smile on his face, but a slightly disapproving look in his eyes.

"Thank you, monsieur," she replied lightly, though her heart was still racing in startlement.

"King Solomon strayed from God's will because of his beautiful wives," he mused, almost as if to himself. "I wonder if you shall lead me astray?"

"I have no intentions of doing so," Carissa protested with a blush.

"What a woman intends and what she does are often two different things," he answered sharply.

He thrust his hand toward her suddenly and she recoiled. "Come," he said, a tight smile brushing across his lips. "You need to prepare for the wedding."

She stood slowly, knees trembling, and took his arm. They walked in silence back to the palace and once inside she pulled away.

"Thank you for the escort," she muttered. She walked off quickly, her chest feeling constricted, and made her way to the rooms she shared with Fleur.

Her cousin was waiting for her, impatiently pacing the floor. "Where have you been?" Fleur scolded. "We barely have time to get you ready."

"I was in the garden, talking with *him*."

"And?"

"He frightened me," Carissa whispered.

"What did he do?"

"It wasn't anything he did, really, but something he said."

Fleur stepped forward and embraced her. Carissa rested her chin on the other girl's shoulder. Fleur rubbed her back and made cooing sounds.

"You're probably both just nervous."

Carissa nodded. "Probably," she answered, not sure she believed it.

She spent the next two hours being dressed in a gown of pale blue silk and having her face painted. At some point during the whole proceeding she felt herself go numb.

She shivered and turned, but nothing was there.

"What's wrong?" Fleur asked.

Before Carissa could answer her, a large black bird flew through the open window at the far end of the room. The bird landed at her feet, and she jumped backward. Fleur screamed as the bird wildly flapped its wings.

"Death!" Fleur shrieked. "A bird flying into the house is death to someone within it."

Carissa knew that to be true. A bird had flown into the house on the day Carissa's father had died. She felt herself grow faint even as the creature hopped forward and pecked at her slippers.

"Get it away from me," she choked.

A maid who had been laying out Fleur's clothes darted forward and caught the bird up in the dress she had been holding. She ran to the window and threw both dress and bird outside.

The three women then collapsed onto the floor.

"'Tis a bad omen," the maid breathed, crossing herself.

From where she sat on the floor with Fleur and the maid, Carissa looked at her satin slippers. Little drops of blood appeared on the material where the bird had pecked her toes. "I'm bleeding," she said, dazed.

The maid leaped to her feet and scurried over to look. She bent low over Carissa, carefully studying her slippers, and then straightened with a look of fear on her face.

"What is it?" Carissa demanded.

"Nothing, milady, beg your pardon," the maid answered before fleeing the room.

Fleur crawled across the short space separating them. She touched the blood on Carissa's shoe and then looked up at her with tears shining in her eyes. "It will be all right. We will get you some other slippers."

Carissa felt a chill hand on her spine, but this time she did not turn around. "No, these will be fine."

Fleur clasped her hard in her arms, and Carissa felt herself needing the other girl's strength. Fleur had done well at the palace, really coming into her own. She was more confident, stronger, than Carissa had ever seen her, and she envied her that.

A different maid suddenly appeared in the doorway, interrupting the moment. She kept her eyes down, not looking at either of them. "Miladies, do you need anything?"

"My cousin seems to have—lost—her dress. She will need another," Carissa said.

Between Carissa and the maid Fleur was dressed in short order. At last they were both ready. She prepared to leave the room, but Fleur put a restraining hand on her arm.

"Leave us," Fleur commanded the maid who curtsied before exiting.

"What is it?" Carissa asked.

"It's not too late to join a convent," Fleur blurted out.

Carissa stared at her, speechless.

"I know things seem hopeless. Maybe it will all work out and you will be happy. However, if you want to leave here, right now, Étienne will help us."

Carissa hugged Fleur and fought back the tears. She had thought about running away to a convent herself. The thought of never seeing her home again, though, broke her heart. "I just want to go home," she said, praying that Fleur understood. "If I marry him I can do that. Besides, I'm not the first woman to be married off to a stranger. If they can survive so can I."

"All right then. We've still got a few minutes before they send for us. What do you want to do?"

"I'd like to spend them by myself, if you don't mind."

Fleur looked hesitant but finally left. Carissa retrieved the little book from her things that she liked to write in.

She had just enough time to write down a few thoughts before hiding the book from her new husband.

PRAGUE, PRESENT DAY

"What's wrong?" Susan asked Wendy as the other girl stopped reading abruptly.

"The handwriting is different on the next page," Wendy said, sounding puzzled.

Susan could feel her stomach twist in knots. "What does it say?"

"It says, 'God help me, something has happened to my cousin, Carissa.'"

CHAPTER TEN

For the wages of sin is death; but the gift of God is eternal life through Jesus Christ our Lord.

—Romans 6:23

Susan moved over so she could see the words. Even as she looked at them a chill touched her. "Fleur, that has to be Fleur's handwriting," she said. Fleur, the woman who was their many times great-grandmother. She touched the ink and it almost felt alive to her, warm and electric.

"How is that possible?" she whispered.

"She must have found it in Carissa's room," Wendy said, not understanding what Susan was talking about. How could she? She didn't feel what Susan was feeling, the intensity of connection, the immediacy. If she held her breath she could almost imagine that Fleur was in the room with them, alive and real and not dead hundreds of years before they were born.

"Are you okay?" Wendy asked.

"Yes, I'm fine."

Wendy stared at her cousin. Susan had gotten really pale and her eyes had taken on a faraway look. She'd seen that look before, mostly from their grandmother. She'd seen it on Susan's face once, the night of her parents' death.

Something was happening to Susan. Something that she couldn't be a part of. She'd always envied her, that ability to sense things. Their grandmother had it, but Wendy had never had it.

As much as she envied Susan, sometimes she was also sure that it would scare her too much. Life was hard enough without getting strange feelings. She remembered staying with her grandmother when she was little when the older woman had felt a sudden urge to drive three hours in the car to pray over the bed of a pastor she had never met. Wendy had had to go with her and the whole experience had been overwhelming.

She took a deep breath. But it had also been exciting.

She wondered how Susan felt. Did she realize the gift she'd been given?

"What?" Susan asked suddenly.

"Nothing," Wendy said, biting her lip. "I'm just worried about Carissa."

"It's weird, right?" Susan said.

"How you can care for someone you don't even know? Yeah, totally weird," Wendy said. *Just like Grandma.*

She cleared her throat and picked up the diary. She turned the page and discovered some parchment folded up neatly and inserted between the pages. She showed it to Susan and then, very carefully, unfolded it. She scanned the first few lines.

"It's Carissa," she said, feeling an absurd sense of relief.

"What does it say?" Susan asked leaning forward, voice eager.

Wendy began to read. "'So many terrible things have happened. I'm terrified to write them down. But I must make sense of it all somehow. The things that have happened are so monstrous, so unspeakable. There is no one I could tell. No one who would believe me. I wouldn't want to burden anyone with these secrets. I shall destroy these papers after I'm done with them. If I don't die first.'"

France, AD 1198

Carissa felt as though a shadow was behind her, just out of her sight. She sat next to her husband of an hour at their wedding banquet and felt a chill growing within her. She lifted her goblet and let the sweet mead trickle down her throat. *'Tis just wedding night jitters*, she told herself.

"How are you?" he asked, turning to her.

"Well," she said, forcing herself to smile.

"Forgive my lack of attentiveness, I am rarely in the company of such a lady as you," he said, kissing the back of her hand.

This time her smile was genuine. "You flatter me."

"Hardly," he answered airily. "I spend my days trying heretics and evildoers."

It was the first time he had spoken to her directly about his work. "That must be very difficult," she murmured.

"It is hard work, but someone must root out the types of evil that infect a people. Some have such dangerous ideas, so contrary to all we believe, that they cannot be allowed to walk free and spread their poison. Chaos would result."

His eyes grew bright with passion as he spoke, and Carissa began to tremble inwardly.

"This world is full of heretics and witches and the worst sort of demons," he continued. His voice dropped down to a fierce whisper, "I've seen things you cannot even imagine."

She hurriedly picked up her glass of mead and swallowed some of the liquid, trying to warm herself. The brighter his eyes burned, the colder she felt, though, and the mead did nothing to help.

Her fear was beginning to mount as well, for as the hours passed, she drew closer to the time when she would be alone with her new husband. She looked for Fleur, but her cousin was hemmed in by young men, all seeking her attention, although it was clear to her that Fleur only had eyes for one of them.

Meanwhile, beside her, her husband was still speaking about the heretics and witches whom he had tried, and, often, ordered to be executed. A servant came and filled her glass, and she was beginning to wonder just how much she had drunk.

"Is there no way that one of these wretches may redeem himself?" she asked at last, mostly just to have something to say.

He wrinkled his nose. "There is no redemption for such ones as I see. They have gone too far, violated the laws of God and men in ways too horrible to mention."

She thought about that for a moment. She had always believed that anyone could be redeemed and so what he said made no sense to her. She shook her head lightly. He was a righteous man and a magistrate, surely he knew more of such matters than she did.

Before she could ask him another question, she heard someone shout, "To the bed!"

The shout was taken up by others in the room and several women rushed forward and laid hands upon her. Terror filled her as they bore her with them out of the room and toward the chambers she would share with her groom.

As they bustled down the hallway, several young men trailed behind, snatching at Carissa's legs, trying to rip off her garters. She shrieked as their hands scratched at her. At last one garter came loose, its new owner whooping loudly and waving it over his head. It was said that to snatch a bride's garters was good luck and guaranteed a man's wife would be faithful.

The rest of the young men redoubled their efforts, and she heard a sickening ripping sound. The other garter came free, and the men beat a hasty retreat, congratulating the two lucky ones among them.

In the room, the married women stripped Carissa of her gown and put her naked into the bed. She clutched the bedclothes around her, shivering the entire time. Tears streamed down her cheeks, and there was nothing she could do to stop them.

Then the women left, except for one, an elderly matriarch. She stood for a moment beside Carissa and touched her cheek. The look she gave her was one of pity. "It will be okay, dear. I know you're frightened, we all have been there. I fainted. But tomorrow, the sun will still rise, and you will be fine. Just relax if you can, it will make it easier."

The older woman gave her a smile before turning to go. At the doorway she turned back. "I know you won't believe this now, but someday, you might actually enjoy it."

And then she was gone. For a minute all was quiet before Carissa heard the sounds of another procession as the men brought her husband down the hall.

In a daze she watched him enter the chamber. She averted her eyes as he undressed. Her heart was pounding as he slid into bed beside her. He didn't say a word, but he put his hand on the inside of her leg and slowly moved it upward.

She closed her eyes and tried not to sob. She prayed the pain would go away. Suddenly he made a strangled sound deep in his throat. She opened her eyes and saw his face contorted with rage.

"Witch!"

"What?" she stuttered.

"You do not bleed. You have already been with another."

"No!" she cried, fear ripping through her. "I have been with none, I am untouched."

"Your own body betrays you. Were you pure I would touch you and you would bleed."

"I swear to you, I am pure," she said, struggling to a sitting position.

He hit her with the back of his hand, and she fell back among the pillows, pain exploding across her cheekbone and her vision briefly going black.

"Fornicator, you will pay for your sins," he hissed.

An icy knot formed in her stomach and swiftly spread its cold throughout her body. She began to shake uncontrollably, and she prayed that it was all a nightmare from which she would soon wake. "I have done nothing," she whispered.

"We'll just see about that."

A minute passed in which she slipped further inside herself, relegating the rest of the world to a small corner of her consciousness. When she felt his hand on her arm, roughly dragging her out of bed, she looked up, surprised that he was still in the room.

She was further surprised to see that he was dressed. He threw her chemise at her. Numbly she slipped into it, eager to hide her body from his accusing eyes. She snatched up her cross necklace, which she had been wearing earlier, and hurriedly put it on.

He pulled her through the hallways at a rapid pace, and she stumbled along behind him. As they were about to exit the palace a manservant hurried up to them. Her husband barked a few words to him, and he scurried off.

Outside the palace a carriage was waiting for them. A horse and rider thundered by and the darkness swallowed them up. Soon even the hoofbeats were lost to her ears.

He shoved her roughly inside the carriage and climbed in behind her. His face was hard, unyielding. She shrank into a corner and wrapped her arms around herself. They drove for what seemed an eternity and then, finally, the carriage came to a stop.

He stared coldly at her. She shifted uncomfortably and his eyes moved to her cross. He reached forward and tore it from around her throat.

"Sinner," he spat. "How dare you wear this?"

PRAGUE, PRESENT DAY

Susan gasped and gripped the cross around her own throat. Wendy was pale and looked like she was going to be sick.

"The cross, it wasn't lost until the Renaissance," Susan muttered. "That's what the lawyer said, the one whose firm found it for Grandma."

"Maybe she got it back somehow. Maybe it was all a mistake and he gives it back to her," Wendy said, her voice a little shaky.

Blood was her downfall. Or rather, the lack of it. Why does it always come back to blood?

Susan gripped the cross tight and it was as though she could feel Carissa's fear, humiliation, pain. Her mind flashed back to the terrible things the Raider had made her see and feel while she was hiding in the chapel.

"You're crying," Wendy said.

"We both are," Susan realized, reaching out to embrace her cousin.

"I don't want to know what happens next," Wendy whimpered.

"Neither do I, but I think we need to."

Wendy dashed away her tears with the back of her hand.

"'My neck burned where the chain cut into me as he ripped it from my neck. How could he? The one thing I had of my father's, the one sign of my faith. I fought him, but he was too strong.'"

FRANCE, AD 1198

Carissa cried out and lunged for it, but he struck her and she reeled backward. With great ceremony he put it in his pocket and then exited the carriage.

"Out," he commanded her and she obeyed, shaking with cold and fear. He grabbed her arm and pulled her into a shadowy building before she even had a chance to look at it.

He led her down a long hall, which ended in a large

room with chairs ringing three walls. Shadows flickered and danced along the walls and lent a sinister air to the room and the two men already in it.

They sat, their eyes hooded in shadow, and did not move. Her husband, her accuser, pulled her to the center of the room and then stepped back from her. As she faced the two men she began to vomit in terror.

When the nausea at last stopped, she straightened slowly.

"Why have you brought this woman here?" one of the men asked.

"She is my wife of a few hours. When I came to the bedchamber I caught her engaged in secret rituals, pagan fertility rites. She was offering prayers to the dark prince. She is a witch."

Horror filled her at the lies he was speaking. She had to tell them, it was all lies. "I am in—"

"Silence the witch that she may not speak her blasphemies here," the man who should have loved her ordered.

A guard appeared from out of the shadows, and before she knew what was happening, he had stuffed a dirty rag into her mouth and bound her hands behind her. She began to gag on the stench of bile from the rag.

"Have you any proof against her?" the second man inquired.

"The proof of my own eyes and ears. Plus when I touched her, she did not bleed."

"Impure," the first man muttered.

Carissa shook her head fiercely.

"We would not expect a magistrate of this Inquisition to be married to such a carnal creature," the second said.

Carissa stamped her feet, trying to gain their attention as the two men began to whisper together. Surely they must let her say something in her defense! No move was made to remove her gag, though, and after a moment the first man rose to his feet.

"We find this woman guilty of adultery and witchcraft. As we cannot release you from your bond of marriage to her we hereby order her to be burned."

"For mercy's sake, I ask for a more private death. She is, after all, my wife," the vile serpent answered.

Carissa stared at him wide-eyed, unable to believe what was happening.

"Very well, throw her into the Cell," the second man answered.

The guard who had gagged her stepped forward and grabbed her. His filthy hair was pulled back from his face and he leered at her with dark eyes. She struggled against him in terror, but he was too strong. He dragged her back along the hall that she had been down a few minutes before. The stones cut her feet, and she bit her tongue. Her mouth filled up with blood but with the rag still in her mouth she had no choice but to swallow it.

Outside he threw her into the carriage and after a sharp word to the driver stepped in behind her. She moved as far away from the guard as she could and stared at him.

The carriage careened along at a wild pace, and she was slammed hard against the wall. She struggled to sit back up, dizzy and more frightened than ever.

Something flashed by the carriage and she realized that there was someone on horseback traveling beside them. She stared outside, hoping desperately that it was someone who could help her. The rider had passed out of her sight, though, and after a minute she turned back toward the guard in the carriage with her.

She recoiled when she saw him leering at her. He slid closer to her.

"So you're a witch?"

She shook her head violently from side to side.

"I didn't think you were. You are an adulteress, though," he said, his voice husky.

She shook her head again, her heart beginning to pound wildly in her chest. No one had ever looked at her the way that he was and her terror reached new heights.

"Sure you are," he said, putting his hand on her leg. "You didn't bleed for the good magistrate."

She tried to jerk her leg away, but he dug his fingers in, his dirty fingernails slicing through her thin chemise and scratching the skin above her knee.

She tried to scream around her gag, but only a squeak came out. She shoved herself back even farther into the wall of the carriage, praying that she could break through it and fall outside, away from his reaching hands.

"You know, every bride needs to be bedded on her wedding night. If your husband wasn't up to the job, I guess I'll help myself."

She kicked out at him as hard as she could, her bloody feet hitting him in the chest. He started to laugh at her futile effort, but the carriage lurched to the side and it threw him off balance. She kicked out again, and her right foot connected with his chin. His head snapped back and hit the door.

He slumped down onto the floor, unconscious, and she sobbed in relief. *God protect me*, she prayed.

The carriage continued to bounce along, and she kept

an eye on her guard, watching for any sign of his waking and hoping that he wouldn't.

They stopped once to change horses. Carissa stared in frustration at the closed door. Even with her hands tied behind her she might have been able to open it had her companion not been slumped against it. They quickly started moving again, and she gave up on thoughts of escape while she was trapped inside.

The man groaned and started to move. She jumped and then quickly kicked him in the head again. He stopped moving and she fell back upon her seat whimpering to herself.

The sun rose and hours later began to set. The guard woke, and though he glared at her he did not accost her again. Finally the carriage rolled to a stop and Carissa stared numbly out the window. Before her was a giant castle of dark stone. The structure was ominous and oppressive and she shivered. The door to the carriage was yanked open by her husband.

They dragged Carissa kicking and screaming through the sour gag into the old castle that now served as a dungeon. The warden looked as if he had been roused from sleep and he stared at her in surprise.

She flushed, aware that in her thin chemise she was all but naked. She was freezing cold too. She could swear she saw pity mingled with the curiosity in the warden's eyes as he stared from her to her husband.

"I am Marcelle, the warden. What can I do for you, Magistrate?" he asked.

"Warden, I have a prisoner for you."

"I figured as much," he grunted in reply.

"She is to be placed straight away in the Cell."

Marcelle looked at the magistrate sharply. "The Cell?" he asked slowly, as if not sure he had heard correctly.

"Yes. And be careful. She brutally attacked and wounded a guard during transport," the magistrate added. Having concluded his business he turned on his heel and left, the guard slinking behind him like a cur.

She sagged in relief when they were gone. The warden hastily untied the gag, and though the air was dank, it tasted fresh to her as she inhaled.

"You have the most innocent face I've ever seen," Marcelle said suddenly.

She began to cry. "I'm not supposed to be here. I don't know what's happening. He lied about me."

Marcelle looked like he was in almost as much distress as she was.

"Don't cry, milady," he said.

"I am innocent," she whispered.

"I know," he answered, simply.

"Then help me," she begged.

"I can't. You're a prisoner and I have to do my duty, no matter how terrible it is."

This couldn't be happening to her. She was a noblewoman, the king's ward until a few hours before. She was a good and faithful daughter of the church.

"Come with me," he said, heading toward a door, a key ring in his hand.

She stood, rooted to the spot, terrified of what was behind that door.

"Please, milady, don't make me call one of the guards."

She moved forward like one walking through a nightmare. They spiraled down a seemingly endless stairway and then finally came out onto a floor of cells. The stench was unbearable and she thought she was going to be sick again.

She shook like a leaf as she followed him past cell after cell. Finally, at the very end, they stopped before a massive door. Marcelle turned and looked at her. "I'm so sorry," he whispered.

He opened the door and she stepped inside. The clank of the door as Marcelle closed it behind her was a death knell.

CHAPTER ELEVEN

*I call heaven and earth to record this day against you,
[that] I have set before you life and death, blessing and
cursing: therefore choose life, that both thou and thy
seed may live.*

—Deuteronomy 30:19

TURIN, PRESENT DAY

A sound woke Gabriel from his slumber. A priest had
entered the storage area looking for something. He
struggled to bring himself fully awake, but he had been
dreaming and part of him did not want to wake.

Raphael was safely unseen, hidden behind some boxes
where Gabriel had dragged him. Gabriel rolled deeper into
the shadows and the priest found whatever he was looking for and retreated back to the church above. There were
still hours of daylight left, he could feel it as sleep seized
him again.

FRANCE, AD 1198

Gabriel heard the warden nightly as he made his rounds,
but he did not move. What could only have been a few

more days passed and the door opened again. He listened as someone stepped inside and the door slammed shut.

He opened his eyes and saw a young woman, strikingly beautiful and equally terrified. She was leaning against a wall, sobbing. He could smell dried blood and his stomach spasmed with pain. The thirst raged at him. He ignored them both. He continued to lie still, watching her even as she surveyed her surroundings.

"Of what crime are you accused, Lady?" he croaked, the first words he had spoken in years.

She screamed and jumped. "Who's there?" she asked in a panicked whisper.

"Another prisoner, like yourself," he purred, making his voice as gentle sounding as possible.

There was silence for a minute and he closed his eyes and listened to her frightened breathing.

"Don't come near me," she said, breaking the silence.

"I assure you, milady, I cannot. I am chained to the wall."

There was another silence and he opened his eyes again. She was standing with her hand pressed to her breast. Her eyes were wild and her body tense. She looked like a deer that had just heard the distant baying of a hound.

He remained quiet, letting her adjust to her surroundings, waiting for her to relax. After a moment the fight left her body, her shoulders slumped, and she slid slowly down the wall to a sitting position.

She took a few rapid, shallow breaths and for a moment he thought she might faint. Finally her breathing began to slow, and a minute later she looked back in his direction.

He smiled, knowing that she could not see him in the darkness of the cell.

"What are you doing here?" she asked.

He flicked his tongue briefly over his eyeteeth, feeling their sharpness. "Let's just say that my visage offends those who put me here."

"I'm afraid I do not understand."

"That's all right," he assured her. "Some days neither do I."

"Are you deformed?" she asked.

He could tell from the sound of her voice that he had piqued her curiosity. "Some would say so, yes."

"I am very sorry," she answered.

Her answer amused him. Something terrible had just happened to her, she had been locked into a prison cell from which she would never return, and yet she could feel sympathy for a cellmate whom she imagined to be hideous. Few in her position would have cared for the plight of another.

"And what, fair lady, is your crime?"

"My husband believes that I am impure," she whispered.

"Impure? He believes that you have been with another?"

She nodded but said nothing.

"How long have you been married?"

Tears began streaking down her cheeks. "We were wed last night."

That she should be here so swiftly surprised him. He studied her for a moment more before pushing. "Was he right?"

"No!" she declared, her voice and head lifting. Even in the dark he could see the fire blazing in her eyes and knew that she spoke the truth.

"Then your husband is a fool."

She crumpled slightly. "He touched me, with his hand, and said there was no blood."

At the mention of blood, his stomach renewed its protests and he had to take a moment to refocus his errant thoughts. He breathed in slowly and deeply and tried to meditate on something else.

Prague, Present Day

" 'The stranger told me that he was deformed in some manner and he believed me that I had not been with another,' " Wendy read. She looked up. "I believe her, too."

Susan nodded. "There are dozens of reasons she may not have bled that have nothing to do with chastity."

"I wonder if they knew that then."

"It seems whoever she was talking to must have." Wendy turned back to the papers in her hand.

"Despite that, why do I have a feeling there's someone bad in that cell with her?" Susan whispered.

"Well, it is a prison," Wendy pointed out.

"Yes, but do you think it was a vampire?"

Wendy licked her lips and glanced back down at Carissa's diary. "I don't know, but I think we're about to find out."

France, AD 1198

Carissa sat, stunned by the stranger's words. Could her husband have known it was possible she had not been with another? She thought of her father's wealth and lands that now belonged to him. Had that been all he really wanted? Had he taken the opportunity to dispose of her?

She had always thought him such a righteous man, could all of that have been but a façade? She shivered and looked around at her cell. Could a righteous man have falsely accused his wife of witchcraft and sentenced her to live out her life here?

"They wanted to kill me," she blurted out. Her fear returned tenfold with the sudden realization.

For a minute she didn't think her mysterious cellmate was going to answer and then he said very quietly, "I don't doubt it."

"They said they were going to put me in a particular cell, wanted my death to be a private one." She hated the tremor in her voice.

"Many have been sent here to die."

"How?"

This time her cellmate didn't answer. Slowly she moved farther away from the shadows that concealed him.

"Do you kill them?" she asked, holding her breath to hear the answer.

Again there was only silence.

"Who are you?"

"I'm a prisoner, like you," he answered. "Well, not *entirely* like you."

There was something in the way he spoke that terrified her more than all the events of the last day. She took her eyes off the shadows for a moment to glance at the door. If she pounded upon it loudly enough would the warden hear her? Would he rescue her? Would he even care?

Probably not, but she couldn't sit here and wait for the

man in the shadows to kill her. For all she knew he wasn't even chained to the wall. She carefully measured the distance to the door. The only light in the cell came from beneath its heavy wood and she fixated on that.

Quietly, she moved her hands to brace them beside her on the ground so she could push herself up. She winced as a sharp stone sliced across her palm.

"Are you all right? I smell blood." The voice spoke from out of the darkness.

"What do you mean? I just cut myself, how could you possibly smell it?"

"Years in here can sharpen one's senses. There isn't much to see, and unfortunately, there is a lot to smell, so that sense has become heightened."

It sounded plausible. There had been a child born to one of her father's servants who was blind from birth. It hadn't stopped him from doing everything the other little boys did, though. He had ears as keen as a fox and could tell who entered a room by the sound of their footsteps.

"Are you all right?" he asked again.

"Yes, it's little more than a scrape," she lied, wrapping the hem of her chemise tightly around her hand to stop the bleeding.

"Ah," he answered.

Was it her imagination, or did he sound vaguely disappointed? She hastily banished the thought and got shakily to her feet. She began to move, catlike to the door, hoping he didn't see her and praying he didn't hear her. "You said you've been here for years. How long?"

"I've lost track. What year is it?"

"The year of our Lord 1198."

"Then I have been here about fifty years."

"Fifty!" she gasped. "And you're still alive? You must have been a child when you were imprisoned."

"Something like that," he said.

A great surge of pity swept through her. "Pray tell, what was your crime?"

"None that they could prove. I was imprisoned, for lack of a better explanation, because of my countenance."

"You said before that you were malformed. Is that truly why you are here?"

"Yes, some found it to be disturbing."

She was at the door. She stood carefully to the side so that he would not see her legs in the tiny shaft of light below the door. She reached out her hand to touch it, but before she could he spoke.

"They won't listen to you."

"Who won't?" she asked, her fingers hovering an inch from the worn wood.

"The guards. They are trained to ignore threats, begging, and screaming. You can scream all you want, they won't come to help you. You have been abandoned, that is why you are here."

"So that you can kill me?"

"That is their intention, yes," he answered.

She felt like she was going to be sick to hear him actually say it. "And is it *your* intention?"

"It is not my intention, but it may happen whether I wish it or not."

"I do not understand. How can you do something you do not wish to do?"

"Did you wish to get married?" he asked, sounding bemused.

"No."

"And yet you did, anyway."

"It was my duty to do so," she protested. "The king commanded."

"Your own heart should make such decisions, not a man who knows you little and cares less."

Stung, she retorted, "And your own heart should dictate whether or not you kill someone, nothing else."

"Ah," he answered, "but it is my heart that I am fighting."

"What do you mean?" she demanded.

He fell silent.

She stood, her fingers absently stroking the wood of the door as she wondered what he meant and whether she would survive the night.

There was a muffled cry from her cellmate a few minutes later and she turned sharply, trying again in vain to pierce the darkness and see him.

"Are you all right?" she asked, taking a tentative step forward.

"No, I'm not," he said, his voice husky.

"Can I do anything to help you?" she asked.

"There is something you can do for me, though I do not think you will wish to."

She backed away hastily, repulsion flooding through her. Surely he couldn't mean—

"All I need," he said quickly, "are a few drops of your blood."

It was a strange request and not at all what she had been expecting. Instead of frightening her it intrigued her.

"My blood?" she asked.

"Yes."

"A few weeks ago a gypsy woman read my fortune. She took a lock of my hair and three drops of my blood. Do you wish my blood for something similar?"

"Not to tell your fortune, no," he answered. "What did the gypsy woman tell you?"

Her eyes flew open wide and she began to tremble. "Oh my—"

"What did she tell you?"

"That I would wander in darkness before finding love."

"It doesn't get much darker than this," he answered with a short laugh.

"She also said that blood would be both my downfall and my salvation."

"Well, I do know that your blood could be *my* salvation," he answered quietly.

It only took her a moment to think about it. "Have you a bowl?" she asked.

A rusty, deformed bowl slid across the floor out of the darkness. She grasped it and pulled it to herself. Then she unwrapped her injured hand above the bowl and very carefully squeezed it. She felt drops of blood roll down her palm and drip off her fingers into the bowl. She gritted her teeth against the pain.

"How much do you need?" she asked.

"As much as you can spare," the words were spoken softly, but for the first time she could hear him breathing. They were great deep breaths, heavy and regular.

As a child her father had had a wolf-dog that breathed like that, slow and deep. It had always seemed menacing to her and she had learned to associate that kind of forceful breathing with predators.

She squeezed her hand tighter and the blood began

to flow faster, now in a steady stream. It was hot and sticky and slowly coated the bottom of the pan. At last she stopped with a gasp.

She carefully felt in the dark for the sharp stone and used it to tear off a clean strip of fabric from the bottom of her chemise. She quickly wound it around her hand, tying it off tight.

"What do you want me to do with it?" she asked.

"Slide it over here," he said. His voice sounded deeper, more like a growl.

"It might spill, I'll just carry it," she said, starting to pick it up.

"No! I don't want you getting that close."

She set the bowl back down. She wondered if he was ashamed to have her see him, his deformity. Another thought occurred to her. Maybe it had something to do with what he had said about possibly killing her even if he did not wish to.

Carefully, she slid the vessel across the floor. It stopped, an inch from the deepest part of the shadows. She watched in fascination as a hand moved like lightning and snatched the bowl. She blinked, stunned at how quickly he had moved.

"Is that enough?" she asked.

There was a pause and then, "It will do."

She didn't know what else to say. She turned and retreated to the corner of the cell farthest from him where she sat down and drew her knees up to her chest.

Carissa had only sat for a minute before she realized how exhausted she was. She glanced furtively toward the darkness. What would happen if she fell asleep? She yawned and felt her eyes grow heavy. Perhaps if death was going to come it was better if it came quickly. Despair overwhelmed her and she lay down on the floor, quietly crying herself to sleep.

She awoke with a start to the sound of screaming. She sat up with a cry, the memory of where she was flooding back to her. "What's going on?"

"The warden is making his nightly round, checking up on everyone."

Her stomach rumbled noisily. Embarrassed, she pressed her hands against it.

"If you are hungry, you had better tell him."

She rose and flew to the door and began to pound on it. She heard heavy footsteps coming and they at last paused before her door.

"Please," she called. "May I have some food?"

A startled voice asked, "You're still alive, Lady?"

"Yes, but I am terribly hungry."

There was another pause and then she heard footsteps hurrying away. She sagged against the door in frustration. "So, they mean to starve us to death?"

"One of us, at any rate."

Before she could ask him what he meant, the footsteps returned.

"Lady, are you still there?"

"Yes, yes," she cried.

A plate was shoved underneath the door and she dropped to grasp it.

"Thank you," she answered.

"You're welcome," came the mumbled reply. Then the warden's footsteps hastened away and she and her cell-mate were again alone.

"Do you want some?" she asked.

"No, thank you."

"You must keep your strength up," she insisted.

"No, please, I ate while you were sleeping."

She nodded and took her plate back to her corner. It was a meager meal of cheese and a hard roll, but it tasted better than any food she remembered. When she had finished, she put the plate down.

"Slide it back under the door so they'll know to bring you more tomorrow," he told her.

She got up and placed the plate under the door and shoved it through to the other side. Then she sat down and leaned with her back against the door. The air in the room was foul and dank and reeked of something that she could not name. She had noticed that what came under the door was slightly fresher.

It occurred to her she hadn't introduced herself.

"My name is Carissa," she said.

"I am Gabriel."

PRAGUE, PRESENT DAY

Wendy dropped the pages with a gasp and stared at Susan, reeling from the shock. "Gabriel?" she asked. "As in, *Gabriel*?"

"I figured it must be. After all, he was the one who gave me the diary. And the first time we met he said something about calling him uncle."

"He said I looked like her."

"He's right. And he didn't just see her portrait, like I did. He knew her."

Wendy pressed her hands to her forehead. "It's all too much."

"It seems that our family history is entwined with Raphael's," Susan said, sucking in her breath sharply. "If you can call a vampire's sire 'family.'"

"But how? Why? I don't understand."

Susan picked up the parchment and handed it back to her. "Neither do I. I think that's why we need to keep reading."

Wendy reread the sentence. "'He said his name was Gabriel.'"

FRANCE, AD 1198

"Pleased to meet you," Carissa answered and Gabriel laughed grimly.

"Does your father have nothing to say about your imprisonment?"

"My father died a few months ago."

"And you were his only heir?"

"Yes. The king chose my husband."

"And along with you he received your father's lands and title, no doubt."

"Yes," she admitted.

"Then all he had to do was get rid of you and he could have everything he wanted."

Tears began to stream down her face again. "I just can't believe he planned this. He is a good man."

Gabriel snorted. "It is my observation that the 'good men' of this world are often the worst of the scoundrels."

"How can you say that?"

"Experience, lots of it."

"My father was a good man," she protested.

He sighed. "I do not doubt that he was. But, I assure you, he was one of the exceptions."

"I believed my husband was a good man."

"What made you think that?"

"He is very righteous. He's the youngest magistrate in France."

Hard, bitter laughter echoed out of the darkness. "He's part of this abomination called the Inquisition?"

"He protects France from heretics and evil people."

"Don't you mean he protects France from people like you and me?"

She shook her head slowly. "You must be right. When he brought me before the other magistrates, he accused me of being…" She drifted off, unwilling to say it.

"What?"

"A witch," she answered.

Another hard laugh issued from Gabriel's direction. "Probably too embarrassed to admit that he thought he'd been cuckolded. Either that or he was planning to get rid of you all along."

She shivered. "I just wish I knew why he did this to me."

"Why don't we ask him?" Gabriel said, his voice suddenly sounding deep and menacing.

"I don't think he'll be coming here to visit," she said bitterly.

"I wasn't implying that he would. I think, we should go see him."

She turned sharply toward him. "How?"

"We escape."

"Is it possible?" she asked, hope touching her for the first time since her wedding vows.

"It is."

"Then why haven't you done it already?"

"I couldn't do it by myself. Will you help me?"

Her heart began to race. She looked around at her cell, the one that the man who should have been her protector, her defender, had put her in. A wave of hatred unlike anything she had ever known swept over Carissa. For the first time in her life she wished for someone's death, craved it, with all her being. Her husband was the embodiment of everything evil to her and she couldn't believe that she was his wife, bound to him still. "God have mercy upon me," she whispered. Then she made a decision. She vowed that she would not die there in squalor and dark and dishonor.

"Yes," she said. "I'll do anything."

CHAPTER TWELVE

*O wretched man that I am! Who shall deliver me from
the body of this death?*

—Romans 7:24

TURIN, PRESENT DAY

Gabriel awoke with a start and after a second was able
to get up. He moved over to stand above Raphael
who was glaring daggers at him. A sound outside alerted
Gabriel and he bent down and picked up the younger vampire.

"We need to leave now."

Carrying him he made his way upstairs as swiftly as
he could. The priests were setting up for an evening mass.
Gabriel waited a beat and then made it out the door with
no one seeing him. Once outside he felt Raphael spasm as
the paralysis passed and he dropped him on his feet.

"You couldn't wait another fifteen seconds?" Raphael
said, glaring.

"Not under the circumstances," Gabriel said. "Let's
move."

"Hold on," Raphael said, pulling out his phone.

"Did she call?"

Raphael nodded and played the message. When it was finished he glanced up uncertainly at Gabriel. "It seems like a long shot."

"I agree, but perhaps Richelieu has more information than we do."

"Any chance he'd want the spear because it might have belonged to Constantine the Great?"

Gabriel stared hard at him until Raphael bared his fangs at him. "What?"

"You're asking me? You're the one who cursed him. You tell me if that's something that would interest him."

"Constantine was the first Roman emperor to convert to Christianity. And Roman emperors were like world rulers back in the day. I guess the symbolism would appeal to him."

"You guess?"

"I didn't get to spend as much time with him as I should have. Not unlike someone else."

They started walking toward the airport.

"What can you tell me about him that I don't already know?"

"I'm guessing you already got the obsessive, control freak, megalomaniac part."

"Yeah. Hard to miss."

"He believed in consolidating power in one ruler."

"Back then the king of France. He thought he was the only person who could save the world. What else?"

"He loved the arts. Even though most of the religious establishment thought that theater equaled heresy he loved it. That and art. He was a great patron of both."

"So, the spear could interest him because it's purported to have a nail that may have the blood of Christ on it, it's said to be the spear of a great Christian emperor, and it's certainly an antique, a cultural treasure if nothing else. Does that about sum it up?"

Raphael nodded. "Maybe it's not such a crazy idea that he'd try to snatch it after all. We better get to the airport faster. Who knows what kind of flight we're going to get and minutes could count at this point."

A short while later they were sitting in the airport, waiting for their plane.

"Not a direct flight to anywhere we have to go," Raphael muttered.

It was true, to get to Vienna before dawn they were going to have to fly through Munich.

To distract himself from the unpleasant thought of being trapped on a plane, he watched in amusement as people steered far away from the two of them. They were isolated in their section of the waiting area. He wasn't sure how, but from the look on Gabriel's face he was pretty sure his sire was causing the phenomenon.

"You'll have to teach me that trick," he finally said.

Gabriel flashed him a fangy snarl, clearly irritated at the interruption to his thoughts.

Which were clearly about Carissa.

Raphael blinked in surprise. Had he just read Gabriel's mind as the other so often did to everyone else? He didn't know. But the sudden certainty that she was in his sire's thoughts was strong enough he was willing to bet his life it was true.

Next to him Gabriel snarled again but Raphael ignored

it and tried to focus, to think. There was nothing else to glean, though.

"The Imperial Treasury is going to be much harder to get into than the chapel was."

Raphael felt a rush of disappointment. Had Gabriel been thinking about that and not Carissa? He shook his head. He had never understood why some vampires had abilities that most did not.

"What do you suggest?"

"There will be guards and security cameras, not to mention electronic security measures. If we cut the power that will raise the alarm."

"If we walk through an infrared beam that will do the job just as quickly."

"I think it's inevitable that we're going to alert security to our presence," Gabriel said. "Because of that I say we forget about stealth and trust in speed."

"You mean just crash in?" Raphael asked.

"I thought you'd like that," Gabriel said, closing his eyes and tilting his head back. To the casual observer he would look like he was sleeping, but Raphael knew better. Gabriel was thinking, planning.

His phone rang and Raphael reached for it.

"You should talk to her," Gabriel said without moving.

He was right, it was Susan calling. "Hello?"

"I'm glad you answered."

He could hear the relief in her voice.

"Did you get my message?"

"Yes, I did, thank you. We're on our way to Vienna now. In fact, our plane is about to board."

"Oh."

"Is everything okay?"

"Fine."

"Good. I'll call you later."

He hung up.

"Coward," Gabriel muttered.

"Realist," Raphael snapped. "Beauty and the Beast is a fairy tale. This is not. I won't change from a beast into a prince at the end."

"It's your story. It's time you take some responsibility for it."

Raphael glared, too furious to come up with an answer. He forced himself to look away and tried to clear his thoughts.

When they were called to board they made their way to their seats. They were in first class this time and he sprawled in the chair.

"Would you like something to drink before takeoff?" a pretty, dark-haired flight attendant asked.

He gazed for a moment at the pulse in her throat.

More than you could possibly imagine, he thought. He forced himself to shake his head and she moved on.

The flights were an agony of time crawling by but finally they landed. They made their way to the Hofburg Palace. Standing on the street staring at the sprawling structures Raphael was reminded a little of Prague Castle. They both had had so many additions and buildings added on to them over the centuries that they no longer served just a single purpose.

The Hofburg Palace now included a chapel, various living quarters, museums, the Imperial Library, the national theater, and the Hofburg Congress Center. There were even horse stables and a riding school. The prize they were after was housed in the treasury, the Schatzkammer.

"You got a map?"

"I was here once. I've been reviewing the layout in my mind."

"So, where is it?"

A sudden, shrill alarm pierced the night.

"He's here," Raphael shouted and leaped forward.

Raphael flew across the grass toward the buildings. Lights came flooding on and he veered away from them.

Think, where would he run to?

He skirted around the massive structure, heading for the source of the alarm. Had Richelieu tripped it on his way in or his way out? It didn't matter. Either way he had to escape. He must have a plan.

Raphael could hear men shouting now. Floodlights were blazing on everywhere, more sirens started up. He swept the wall with his eyes, wishing he knew what he was looking for.

He didn't know if Gabriel was behind him and he didn't have time to find out. He just had to—

Suddenly his eyes spotted a patch of dark among the lights. One of the lights had been smashed. He veered toward it just in time to see three figures run out of a building. They moved so quickly they had to be vampires. Each of them held something in their arms as they ran.

They were too far ahead of him. He couldn't catch up. He reached down deep and found more strength and leaped forward. His fingers brushed the back of one guy's shirt and he veered to the left. Raphael followed. His foot slid on something on the ground. He fell forward. Before he hit the ground he reached out and grabbed the other vampire's ankle, tripping him. The vampire hit the ground with a grunt and Raphael scrambled forward and straddled him. He saw a blur flash past him and he hoped it was Gabriel. He yanked the vampire's head to the side and hissed when he realized it wasn't Richelieu. He did recognize the vampire as one of the ones who had been in Richelieu's throne room when he had been there.

"Tell me where he's going!"

The vampire spat in his face. When he reached up to wipe his eyes the vampire twisted and grabbed his head. Raphael bit his arm and shoved his thumbs in the vampire's eyes.

The creature screamed and clawed at its face.

Raphael could hear shouts coming closer to them. In a moment they would be discovered. There was no time to get information, and he could not release his captive to attack him. He made the kill quickly.

As the creature disintegrated Raphael checked the package he had been carrying. He shook with rage when he discovered it was a crown and not the lance they were hoping for. He jumped to his feet and left the crown in the pile of ash. He took off in the direction the others had gone. Had they stolen other treasures to disguise their true goal or had they stolen them so that the other two could play decoy?

He ran through the night and after a minute stopped. He turned, but the smell of vampire had been dissipated by the blowing winds. He had no idea which way the others had gone. Richelieu would likely have made his way toward the airport. No doubt he had a private plane there, though. He could be gone before they got there.

A soft sound caused him to spin back around. It was Gabriel, his clothes tattered, smoke curling up off him.

"What happened?"

"I caught the one and the other took the opportunity to throw a Molotov cocktail at me. I got the fire out, but it killed the other vampire before I could ask him anything."

"And the third one?"

"Gone."

"Any chance the dead one was carrying the lance?"

"Crown jewels."

"Mine, too. What do we do now?"

Gabriel came to a stop before him and he looked at his sire in horror. The singed flesh was already healing but there was a dazed look in his eyes that frightened him.

"What's wrong?"

"I reached into the vampire's mind."

"The dying one?"

Gabriel nodded. "I saw his thoughts as he died."

Raphael couldn't imagine what it would be like to be in the mind of such a vile creature as it burned to death.

"There were two places he kept thinking of in relation to Richelieu."

"Where?"

"Bruges in Belgium and Oviedo in Spain."

They started walking in the direction of the airport. Beside him he could hear Gabriel breathing, which he usually only did when he was about to attack. It was unnerving but slowly it stopped. He glanced sideways and saw that the wounds had healed.

After a couple of minutes Raphael still hadn't been able to decide which of the two destinations they should try for.

"There's only one solution, we need to split up," Raphael said.

Gabriel curled his lips. "I don't like it. Either of us could be walking into a trap alone."

"I know, but I think we have to risk it."

Raphael hoped his sire would go for it. It was the best plan, the smartest use of their resources. It didn't hurt that it was the plan that got Gabriel far away from him and hopefully out of his head. It didn't matter how much time passed, he could never envision them becoming friends like Paul and Gabriel were.

No, to him, Gabriel would always be the monster that cursed him. And there was no making friends with that.

We sound like some twisted Odd Couple *sitcom. Could two monsters travel together and not rip out each other's throats?*

"Pretty sure I wouldn't want to be either Oscar or Felix in that scenario," Gabriel said.

Raphael folded his arms across his chest. "At least I'm keeping up with the times, like you've been lecturing me about."

Gabriel rolled his eyes. "That television show is four decades old. If that's your idea of current you're in worse shape than I thought."

"Leave me alone."

"Gladly. You take Belgium and I'll take Spain."

"And I'll get to Paris before you," Raphael said grimly.

"That song is nearly two centuries old," Gabriel noted. Then he turned on his heel and vanished into the night.

Raphael stood, spooked by just how quickly and utterly the other vampire disappeared. He searched the darkness for a moment, but there was nothing there.

"Okay, Belgium it is."

PRAGUE, PRESENT DAY

They had taken a break for dinner and while she was eating her sandwich Susan surfed the web. She was still irritated that Raphael had ended their call so quickly. She hated feeling like she was being shut out.

"What are you doing?" Wendy asked as she came downstairs from having seen David.

"Looking up other relics. Trying to figure out where Richelieu is going to go next."

"Any luck?"

Susan shook her head and sat back with a frustrated sigh. "There are just too many possibilities. And that's if you only count Europe."

"You think he'd go to a different continent?"

"If it served his purposes I think he'd find a way to get to the moon," Susan said glumly.

Wendy rubbed her shoulder. "Do you want me to look for a while?"

"No. I want to get back to the story."

Susan stood up and tromped over to the couch.

Wendy sat beside her, unfolded the pages carefully, and began to read. " 'I think the warden is surprised that I am still alive.' "

FRANCE, AD 1198

The warden slid the latest tray under the door. She suspected from the smells around dinnertime and the complaints she could hear coming from other cells that he had been giving her better food than the others. It was a small kindness she was immensely grateful for.

"Thank you," she answered like she always did, her tone light.

"Are you all right?" he asked.

"As well as can be expected," she answered.

"Are you, er, alone in there?" he asked.

She hesitated for a moment and then she answered truthfully, "I haven't *seen* anyone else."

"Good night," Marcelle said before hurrying off, his footsteps retreating quickly.

"How do you feel?" Gabriel asked after the warden had left.

"Good," she answered. "Why?"

"Because you have been here four days now. Your body should have replenished the blood you lost that first night."

"I wouldn't know," she answered truthfully. "I have not studied the body."

"There are few who have, at least, satisfactorily." He paused before continuing, "Would you mind parting with some more of it?"

She peered into the darkness, wishing she could see him, watch his expressions. It had indeed been four days and she felt stronger than she had when she arrived. She knew little more about Gabriel, though, than she had then. She had noticed one thing, though. He didn't eat.

"Why do you want it?" she asked, a terrible suspicion forming in the back of her mind.

"I would prefer not to answer."

"You said that my blood could save you. How?"

"Again, I would rather not say—just yet."

"In the past few days I've told you nearly everything

there is to know about me, and yet I still know almost nothing about you."

"That is true."

"Well, you can see then, that I have a decision to make. You say that we can escape, yet you do not say how. You say that you need my blood, but you won't say why. Either I can decide to trust you completely without question as I was raised to do, or I can refrain from helping you until I know exactly who you are and what you intend to do."

He laughed grimly. "Something your husband's actions have pushed you to."

"Yes, I am not as trusting as I was a week ago," she admitted. It killed her, but it was true. She was even suspicious of the motives of the warden, hence the reason she lied to him about being alone in the room. Well, technically she had not lied—she had seen no one. She sighed, afraid that the distinction was too fine to save her a scolding from a priest.

"You are right, you do have a big decision to make."

"You could help by being more forthcoming."

"I'm not sure that would help much," he whispered and she could not tell whether he was talking to her or himself.

"Try, please," she said, her voice softening.

"I need to regain my full strength to help us escape. I need the blood to help me do that."

"Are you some sort of witch?" she asked, her heart beginning to pound. "Do you worship false gods, do you need the blood for some sort of ritual?"

"No," he said, sounding tired. "The only God I know is the one you worship." He sighed. "And could you please calm down? The sound of your heart beating that fast is distracting."

She moved back. "It is not natural that you can hear my heart beating."

"I am not exactly a natural creature."

"Then why should I trust you?" she demanded.

"Because I want to help you."

"How can I know that?"

"Take my word for it."

"Last time a man gave me his word he vowed to cherish me and hours later he had me thrown into this place. How can I trust you?"

"You just can," he said, his voice rising in irritation.

"Why?" she demanded.

"Because although I am chained to this wall, the chains are long enough that I could have killed you already had I wished!"

Suddenly there was a blur of movement and a figure lunged out of the shadows toward her. She screamed and threw her hands up to block it. There was a loud clatter, and the figure disappeared back into the dark. Panting in terror, she looked down at her feet and saw the bowl into which she had first squeezed her blood.

I decided that night to trust him and he has done nothing to betray me since, she thought to herself, painfully aware that he had stood but inches from her and she had still not managed to get a glimpse of his face.

Her knees buckled and gave way beneath her. She collapsed on the ground next to the bowl. She stared at it idly. Such a small thing he was asking for really. Something she would never even miss.

She scratched at the scab on her hand, tearing it back open. "How much do you need?"

"More than last time."

PRAGUE, PRESENT DAY

Susan's phone rang and both she and Wendy jumped.

"It's Raphael," she said as she saw the screen. "Hello? Is everything okay?" she asked quickly.

"They got the lance. At least, we're pretty sure they did." He sounded exhausted and upset.

"'They'?"

"Yeah, Richelieu's brought along some of his entourage for this little hunt across Europe."

"Any idea where they're going next?"

"Just a couple of cities. Bruges in Belgium and Oviedo in Spain."

She stood up hastily and walked back over to the computer. "I think I recognize those names. I was doing some research earlier."

"What can you tell me about Belgium?" he asked.

She sat down and pulled up one of the websites she'd been looking at earlier. "It says that the Basilica of the Holy Blood is supposed to have a vial containing Jesus' blood. The blood is in the upstairs chapel. The vial was brought back by Thierry of Alsace, Count of Flanders, who apparently found it during the Second Crusade."

"You're kidding," he said, his voice sounding strange to her.

"No." She could feel excitement rising in her. "Do you think this could be it?"

"I don't know. But if I'm lucky maybe I can make it before sunrise."

"Be care—"

He had already hung up.

I guess he didn't want to know about Spain, she thought.

"You okay?" Wendy asked.

"I can't take much more of this waiting."

Wendy indicated the pages she had been reading from. "I think Carissa agrees with you."

FRANCE, AD 1198

Carissa had passed nearly a fortnight within the darkness. She shivered with cold and drew her knees up to her chest, wrapping her chemise tighter about her. Jagged stones dug into her back and she tried in vain to find a more comfortable position.

She thought of the warmth and comfort of her bed at home and sighed in misery. She didn't know if she would ever see it again. She wondered what Fleur must be feeling and prayed for her cousin that she might be kept safe. She thought of each of the servants at home and prayed for them all, wishing for them better fates than her own.

And last she thought of her horse, Dancer. She wondered if anyone would ride her beautiful mare now that she was gone. She closed her eyes and imagined she was again on her back, free with the wind in her face.

She reached for the cross that used to hang around her neck, but she grabbed only air. A wave of hatred washed over her. Of all the things that he had taken from her, that seemed the cruelest. It was the one thing in which she could have found comfort.

She heard Gabriel stirring in the darkness and she

opened her eyes as the bowl slid across the floor toward her. She sighed as she sat up. This would be the fourth time that she had poured her blood into the misshapen vessel.

She sliced her palm back open and began to squeeze blood into the bowl. As she watched the drops of blood ooze out from between her fingers by the faint light from under the cell door she vowed that someday she would pry her cross from the devil's dead fingers.

CHAPTER THIRTEEN

*"Now therefore forgive, I pray thee, my sin only this
once, and intreat the LORD your God, that he may take
away from me this death only."*

—Exodus 10:17

BRUGES, PRESENT DAY

Raphael felt like he could never escape the Crusades.
Particularly the second one. It seemed incredible to
him that during the same crusade that he was entrusted
with a relic someone else was carrying around a different
relic. A vial of blood. Was it even possible?

Had it been an accident that Gabriel sent him to Belgium and not Spain? Had he known the connection the
relic had to the Second Crusade?

I'm being paranoid, he whispered to himself.

But his sire was still a mystery to him in so many
ways. During the crusade, Gabriel had been an adviser to
the king. He was already a vampire at that point, though
Raphael did not know when he had been cursed. He had
always assumed Gabriel was serving as a military adviser,
but never knew his motive. What if he had been helping

the king in his quest for the relics? The knight, Jean, had presented the relic that had later been entrusted to Raphael. Had the king sought out other relics? Were others seeking them, too?

The Holy Land. That's what the Crusades had been all about. How much of it had been the result of careful planning by Gabriel and others? Was the gloss of years and distance making him see things that weren't there?

He shook his head. It was pointless thinking about the past. What mattered was the here and now. Particularly if he had a shot at killing Richelieu.

He had carried the guilt of unleashing that particular monster on the world for a long time. When he had cursed him he believed that he was creating another vampire, another in need of salvation. But something in Richelieu was fundamentally broken, damaged. He was beyond repair. Instead of mellowing with time he just became more obsessed.

Raphael hadn't known that there were rumors about others who had been cursed and failed to respond in the expected way. Only a couple through all the millennia. *I couldn't have known what would have happened*, he told himself for the thousandth time.

And just like all those other times it still didn't matter.

Somewhere out there Richelieu was planning, scheming. Raphael needed to put him down like the rabid creature he was before he could do any more harm.

Please let me find him instead of Gabriel.

He stopped in his tracks. It was a prayer that had just escaped him. Paul and Susan were rubbing off on him. Still, he didn't regret it. He just hoped if God heard that He cared to answer.

Bruges was turning out to be an interesting place, criss-crossed by canals. The Venice of the North he had once heard someone say, though a lot of places claimed that ti-tle. The city had kept much of its medieval architecture and character and as he moved through its streets he felt more at home than he could remember feeling anywhere recently.

He took several wrong turns but finally found the Basil-ica of the Holy Blood. Susan had said that the vial was housed in the upstairs chapel.

The sun would be up soon, but he should have time to discover if the relic was real and hopefully to find and de-feat Richelieu if he was there. He approached the front of the basilica and discovered that a door was already opened.

Was it used by a priest or was it a sign of an intruder?

He eased through and quickly found the broad stairs that led upstairs to the chapel that housed the relic. Though the entire structure was much smaller than he would have ex-pected, it was no less ornate than its larger cousins.

He passed down the center aisle moving swiftly by the rows of chairs. Stained-glass windows on either side glowed with the coming light of dawn. A massive mural covered the wall behind the altar. And to the side was an alcove with an-other altar. He felt the relic should be in there.

And then a silver chest drew his eye. It was exactly the kind of thing that would be used to house a relic. He moved swiftly to it and then hesitated for a moment. He wished Paul were there and fear pricked at him. What would happen if he touched it?

There was only one way to find out. He reached out and opened the chest. Inside was an ancient-looking glass vial, the kind the Byzantines used for perfume, enclosed in a larger glass container whose ends were capped with gold crowns. It was magnificent looking.

He reached out his hands and felt...nothing.

It was fake. He closed his eyes in frustration. He had allowed himself to hope, just a little bit, that it might be real. That he'd finally have something with which he could fight. He cursed in frustration, for the moment not caring where he was or who might hear him.

That only left two questions: Had Richelieu been here already? If so, had he swapped out the real relic for this fake? If he had that meant that he had the blood of Christ in his possession.

What if he's consumed it already? he thought, panic rising in him.

Raphael turned and came face-to-face with an ancient-looking priest. The man was wizened and stooped and had the saddest eyes he had ever seen. Raphael should have heard him coming up behind him, but he had been too intent on what he was doing.

It could have gotten him killed.

"Please, sir, you must stop him," the priest said in halting English. Raphael kept a close eye on the rosary that the old man clutched in his shaking hands. The last thing he needed was to be burned by a cross while inside the church.

"Who?" he asked, carefully, taking a step back.

"The monster who stole it," the priest said, pointing behind Raphael with a long, bony finger.

"How do you know?" Raphael asked in amazement.

The old man made a fist and put it over his heart. "I felt it in here the moment it had left the building."

"Did you see who took it?" he asked.

"No, but you find him." It was a command not a request.

"I'll try," Raphael said, easing around the old man.

"You do more than try. You bring it back to us. You find it and bring it back, vampire."

Raphael jerked at the word and stared incredulously at the old priest. He backed up several more steps and glanced around cautiously.

"You know what I am?"

"Of course. I can feel you."

A thousand questions crowded Raphael's brain. He had met people like Susan before who could sense the presence of good and evil, natural and supernatural. But never before had he encountered someone who could sense vampires specifically.

There was no time for questions, though. He had to go or risk missing Richelieu again.

"You promise," the old man said.

"I'll make sure it finds its way back here," Raphael said. It was the best he could do. He would tell Gabriel and hopefully somehow, someday the relic would come home if Richelieu hadn't already destroyed it.

He headed for the exit but turned back. "How long ago did you feel it leaving the building?"

"Less than five minutes before I saw you."

Raphael blinked. Five minutes. He turned and sprinted outside. There were only moments until sunrise. Richelieu would have had to go to ground somewhere. He wouldn't have had time to make it to the airport.

Where? Where would he go to hide and sleep for the day?

Raphael's mind churned even as he burst outside. The

sky was light, the sun starting to tip above the horizon. And he felt the pull of sleep.

But he forced himself to keep running. The area was too populated. There were too many people that would be around during the day.

Keep moving.

And then he saw it, an old building that looked dilapidated and abandoned. It was the perfect place to hide. He climbed through a broken window. The sun was coming and he staggered, fighting its pull. He found a stairway leading down to the basement. Dust on the stairs had been disturbed and he raced down.

Once he reached the bottom, he turned, eyes piercing the darkness.

He has to be here.

He heard a hissing sound behind him and he spun. There, lying on the ground, was a vampire wearing a long, gray trench coat. A box was cradled at his side. Rage washed over Raphael. It wasn't Richelieu. Richelieu had sent one of his minions, probably going to Spain himself, Raphael realized in despair. He crashed to his knees, reaching his hands toward the other vampire's throat. He could see the other moving sluggishly and felt fingers pressing around his own throat before he collapsed and sleep claimed him.

OVIEDO, PRESENT DAY

Gabriel awoke with the setting of the sun. He waited a few minutes and then called Raphael. He hated cell phones. He hated all phones. Although he would never have admitted that to Raphael. The more technology mankind had the more dangerous it was for his kind. Still, in this case it was a necessary evil.

It went straight to voicemail. "Call me," he growled.

He hung up, resisting the urge to throw the phone against the stone wall just to watch it shatter. Dreaming of Carissa always made him angry.

But even as he exited the hotel in the heart of Oviedo he couldn't help but think about her. Being near the girl Wendy stirred his memories. Carissa had been so beautiful, even when trapped in that stinking cell.

FRANCE, AD 1198

Gabriel watched Carissa as she squeezed her blood into the bowl. He licked his lips in a frenzy. He was nearly overwhelmed by the scent of her skin and the pounding of her blood in his ears. It took every last bit of willpower he had to leave her alone, unscathed.

When she was done, she slid the bowl across the floor to him without comment. He snatched it up and drained its contents in several quick gulps, savoring the warmth of it as it trickled down his throat. He could feel its life seeping into his body, strengthening muscle and bone. She had filled half of the bowl this time and he felt better than he had in a long time.

"Would more help?" she asked quietly.

"No, this is fine. It is not the amount that is quite so important as the frequency."

"I could give you more tomorrow."

"No, I cannot regain my strength at the cost of yours.

Every four or five days should be adequate. That way when we escape, we will both be ready."

She nodded and retired to the corner that she had claimed as her own. She looked weary, though her spirit was stronger than when she had arrived. He wished briefly that he could have met her before she learned the meaning of betrayal.

He shook his head. It was foolish to entertain such idle thoughts. Better by far to focus on how exactly they were going to escape. He began to again test his restraints, link by link. When he reached the chains that bound his left leg to the wall he stopped at the fifth link. It was weaker than the rest. He began to pull upon it, his arms stronger than they had been in decades.

The metal groaned beneath the strain. Slowly it began to twist and at last with a roar he was able to pull it apart. He let the chain fall to the ground triumphantly.

"What is it?" Carissa asked, sounding frightened.

"I was able to free my left leg," he told her.

"Wonderful," she said, although she still sounded apprehensive.

"It is," he assured her. "This is the closest I've been to freedom in fifty years."

"How old are you?" she asked.

"How old do you think I am?" he countered.

"Well, from your voice I would have guessed younger. However, if it's true you've been a prisoner for fifty years, and given that you remember what freedom is, you had to have been at least five when you were imprisoned. So, fifty-five, maybe a little older?" she asked.

He laughed. "Clever reasoning. What would you say if I told you I was closer to five hundred years old?"

"I would say you're either crazy, joking, or not human," she said with a laugh.

"Let me give you a hint, I'm not crazy."

"So, joking it is," she said. "How old do you think I am?"

"Nineteen."

"Ha, you are wrong. I am actually nineteen hundred."

"Very funny," he answered, enjoying the banter.

He finished testing the chain binding his right leg and finally had to give up. Still, freedom was close, he could feel it.

"Yes, I watched as Rome burned, and I studied poetry with Homer," she continued.

"Ah, Homer," he said. "I remember when I first read the Iliad. 'Many a brave soul did it send hurrying down to Hades, and many a hero did it yield a prey to dogs and vultures.' So artful in his use of language."

He became suddenly aware that something had changed. Carissa's heart had begun pounding again and he thought he caught a whiff of fear rolling off her. "What is it?" he asked.

"You couldn't have read that when you were five," she whispered. "And you certainly weren't able to read a copy of it in here."

He had given himself away. Then again, maybe he had meant to. He stood slowly, even as she did.

"Carissa?" he said quietly.

"What are you?" Carissa breathed.

He made a clucking sound with his tongue. "I think you already know the answer to that."

She stepped forward, even though clearly everything within her screamed at her to stay away.

"Show yourself."

"You don't want me to do that," he said, his voice somewhat threatening.

"Yes, I do. Step into the light." She took another step forward.

He stood before her in the space of time it took her to blink.

She stared at him wide-eyed. "You have the face of an angel."

As though in a dream, she moved her hand toward his cheek.

"You look so young," she murmured.

He could read her mind, felt her needing to touch his face, to know that what she saw was real and not some kind of hallucination.

"Not crazy," she whispered. "And not joking."

"Not human," he said, catching her hand in his own.

"Then what?"

He kept hold of her hand, refusing to let her move. Instead he took a step closer, so that he loomed over her. "I think," he said slowly, "you know the answer to that."

He enunciated every word, giving her a clear glimpse of his predatorlike fangs.

"Demon!" she gasped, pulling backward suddenly, frantically.

He released her hand and caught her by both shoulders. He leaned closer and by the way her face twisted he could tell that she could smell blood—her blood——on his breath.

"Carissa, I am not going to hurt you, but you have to trust me."

"You're a—some kind of monster."

"You knew that days ago. This has been nothing but a game that you and I have played. You wanted to know, now you do. I will answer all your questions, do what I can to allay your fears, but we have to work together."

"I can't."

"You can, Carissa, and you will, otherwise I will have to kill you, because I can stay here no longer."

He meant it, too. He had been trapped in hell for fifty years and if he didn't act soon there was no telling how much longer he'd be trapped, how many more people he'd be forced to kill. One life sacrificed to save that was worth it. Even if it was hers. Even if he would hate himself forever for killing her.

"This is what he meant to happen," she muttered, her face draining of all color.

"Carissa, stay with me," he said. But she was beyond hearing him. He caught her as she started to fall.

Gabriel listened as the guards performed their nightly rounds, feeding prisoners, changing torches. At long last things quieted down. He could hear the heavy steps of the warden as he started his rounds.

He glanced down at Carissa. She lay, sleeping, and he knew that she would not waken by the time the warden came by. She looked so peaceful. But for the steady beat of her heart, he might have thought she was dead.

At last the heavy footsteps stopped before their door.

"Lady, are you there?" the warden called.

Gabriel debated waking her. She needed the food as badly as she had needed the sleep.

Still, he had not wanted the warden to have proof that

he was still alive. He weighed his choices and at last he made a decision. "She is asleep," he said.

After a moment the warden asked in a trembling voice, "You're still alive?"

"We both are," Gabriel answered.

There was a stunned silence and then a plate of food was slid just beneath the door. The footsteps disappeared at a rapid rate and they were again alone.

She woke up in his arms. With a start she tried to pull away, but he held her too tightly. She lay still, and he could feel terror filling her. Her cheek was against his shoulder and her arm was around his waist. He knew her thoughts. She had no idea how she had gotten where she was and her chemise offered her little protection.

"Are you feeling better?" he asked.

She jumped and then lay still, too afraid to answer.

"You fainted. After a while I became worried about you because your body went into shock. You were shaking and I was afraid you would hurt yourself on some of the more jagged stones in the floor. I offered you what little protection and warmth I had. My body is only warm after I've fed. Even now my skin has cooled again, but for a brief time I had something to offer you."

"I am warm where our bodies are touching," she said, licking her dry lips nervously. She tried again to pull away, but he still held her tight.

"I have never slept with a woman in my arms before," he said in a conversational tone.

Again she licked her lips. "Oh. Then I take it you were never married?"

"No. The darkness took me before I had the chance to marry."

"I'm sorry," she answered.

"I never really was," he said. "But then, my kind seek a different kind of—intimacy."

She stiffened.

He chuckled softly. "No, I didn't harm you."

"How long have I been asleep?" she asked hurriedly.

"About two hours. Rest now, you need it."

"Will you let me go?"

"No, I will not. Not until morning. I don't want you trying to hurt yourself, or me."

"I've never slept in a man's arms," she admitted.

"I know," he said softly. "Now, sleep."

He let his words wash over her, mesmerizing her lightly so that she would rest.

He lay for a while listening to her breathing, so gentle, so shallow. Everything about her seemed fragile, yet inside he could sense her strength, and it was asserting itself more by the day.

He didn't know what had possessed him to make her stay with him until the dawn. She was no longer in shock and no more a danger to herself. She couldn't be a danger to him, even if she could have found a weapon in the cell to use upon him. His senses were far too attuned to allow her to sneak up on him.

He closed his eyes and willed himself to stop analyzing his behavior. As he drifted off to sleep he lamented for the first time that he had never married.

CHAPTER FOURTEEN

The last enemy that shall be destroyed is death.

—I Chronicles 15:26

Raphael could hear his phone ringing. And then his sight returned to him. He was lying, limbs still locked in sleep paralysis, his hands wrapped around the throat of the vampire who had his own hands around Raphael's throat.

A surge of panic swept through him. The other vampire was awake, too, straining to move just as he was. He could see his own rage and fear mirrored in the other's eyes.

As each second ticked by he fought to overcome the paralysis, hoping his enemy wouldn't be able to move first. He felt the other vampire's body spasm and at the same time the paralysis released its hold on him. He leaped with a roar, crashing down on top of the other.

They thrashed around on the floor, each struggling to get the upper hand. They crashed into a pile of old chairs.

Raphael reached out his hand and snapped off a wooden leg.

He twisted, trying to angle it for the other vampire's heart and felt stabbing pain in his back as the other did the same to him.

I'm going to die here, the thought flashed through his mind.

And Susan will never know what happened to me.

With a grunt he flipped onto his back, bringing the other vampire down on top of him. The other lost hold of the stake and Raphael felt it wedge itself farther into his back. But his own hand was free and he buried the stake he held in the other's chest.

He missed the heart and he strained to move the stake sideways in the vampire's chest. He could hear ribs cracking. The other vampire screamed and tried to leap up, but Raphael held him tight with his free hand.

And then he felt the stake pierce the vampire's heart.

And a moment later it was over.

Raphael sat up and contorted his body until he could reach the stake lodged in his back and yank it out. Within seconds the wound had healed. He grabbed the box and a shudder went through him.

Carefully he opened the lid and looked at the contents. A vial, identical looking to the one back in the church. But this one had power coming off it.

The blood of Christ, he realized in awe.

I should take it for myself.

No sooner had he had the thought than he slammed the lid of the box shut. He shook like a leaf. The power of God. It was an awesome temptation to him who had once fancied himself a god.

He felt sick inside, like something was struggling to crawl out of him.

Why shouldn't I have it?

He fell on his knees and began to retch. He set the box down. Something was happening to him, changing. Suddenly he knew that the choice before him was the most important choice he had ever made.

He could fulfill the promise of his youth or allow himself to be redeemed. Both choices terrified him. Bloody tears streamed down his face.

And then he saw Susan, standing in front of him, her face bathed in angelic light. And he knew what choice she would have him make. He only wondered if he was man enough to make it.

He didn't know how long he stayed like that but when he finally rose to his feet he knew that things were far from decided for him, for his future. But he did know that he needed to keep his promise and return the blood to the church from which it had been taken.

It was just a minute's walk back to the basilica. The same door was open and he walked slowly inside, looking around. He made his way upstairs, the box containing the vial in his hands. At the very front of the chapel he saw a solitary figure, kneeling in prayer.

He approached quietly until he stood just behind the old priest he had seen that morning. The man crossed himself and then stood slowly and turned to face him.

"You knew I was here," Raphael said.

The man nodded. "I prayed you would return the holy blood tonight."

Raphael held the box out to him. "Your prayers were answered," he said, feeling odd.

The priest took the box and opened the lid. A look of reverence lit up his face. Raphael felt humbled that he had been the instrument of this man's prayers. Did God really work that way?

"Thank you, my son," the priest said, placing a hand on his shoulder. "You have done a great thing tonight."

"You're welcome," Raphael whispered. "Please, make sure that you have some crosses put around the box. At least make it harder for the next vampire who decides to come after it."

The priest nodded. "And now I fear that you must go. There are others that need you."

"Yes."

"But I will give you a blessing first."

Raphael could barely stand still as the priest blessed him and his journey. He flinched as the old man made the sign of the cross over him, but apparently it took contact with an actual cross to burn him. At the end he bowed and left the old man to return the relic to its resting place.

Outside in the night air he checked his phone and saw that the call he had missed came from Gabriel. He hadn't left a message. Raphael called back.

"I stopped the theft here in Belgium. Heading to Paris now."

OVIEDO, PRESENT DAY

Gabriel couldn't shake the feeling that he was being followed. He twisted and turned, taking side streets, and circling back around. He didn't see anyone out of the ordinary and he couldn't catch any scent of a vampire. Still, his instincts told him that there was someone watching him. He stopped and made some makeshift stakes out of discarded wood in a dumpster. He tucked them into his trench coat and then kept moving.

He didn't like it. He also didn't like that it was delaying his arrival at the cathedral. The cathedral was supposed to have five of the thorns from the crown of thorns. He had gotten the message that Raphael was heading to Paris. He should have already been on his way as well.

Years of hunting had taught him to be patient. But there was a time to be patient and a time to act and unfortunately it was all dependent on how much time one actually had.

He felt like theirs was running out. It was either leave and try again the following night, losing precious time, or go ahead to the cathedral.

He turned his steps to the cathedral. When he got there he circled around the building twice, searching the shadows for something, anything. The main spire soared four stories into the air. He briefly considered climbing on top of the cathedral to get a better view of the surrounding area.

He could practically hear a clock ticking in his head. No time to stop.

He moved around to the side of the building and found one of the service entrances. He forced open the door and stepped swiftly inside.

He was a dozen steps into the cathedral before he realized why he hadn't been able to sense any vampires outside before. They had all been here waiting for him.

PRAGUE, PRESENT DAY

David woke and for the first time did't feel like he wanted to scream from the pain. He turned his head and was disappointed to see that Wendy wasn't sitting, watching him. He had grown used to having her there.

He pushed himself up to a sitting position. It hurt, but it didn't make him feel like he wanted to pass out. There was aspirin and water on the nightstand next to him and he swallowed both gratefully.

He wasn't sure if it was day or night. Then he realized with a grim smile that he didn't even know what day of the week it was. He swung his legs over the edge of the bed and pushed himself to a standing position.

So far, so good, he thought. He made it out of the bedroom and into the neighboring bathroom. When he came out Wendy was waiting for him, arms crossed over her chest. "You shouldn't be up," she said.

"Well, I had to come find my nurse," he said, smiling in what he hoped was a way that would get him forgiven.

She seemed to soften at that. "Let me help you back to bed."

"Actually, I've had enough of that bed for a while. I'd love it if you helped me downstairs."

She looked like she was about to argue with him.

"Please. I promise I'll be good. I'll just sit on the couch and maybe have some more soup."

"Okay," she said, relenting.

He put his arm around her shoulders but didn't put much weight on them. Slowly they walked toward the stairs. When they passed the room next to his he glanced in.

"How's Paul?" he asked, lowering his voice.

"No change," Wendy said. "Susan checks on him every hour, but there's nothing. He hasn't moved. He hasn't started to heal. Nothing."

"That makes no sense."

"The other vampires didn't know what it was about, either. They just thought he should have died from the wounds he sustained."

"I'll send up some more prayers for him."

They made it to the stairs and went down carefully. Each step jarred his ribs but he refused to let Wendy see how much he was hurting. The last thing he wanted was for her to banish him back to the bedroom. He was tired of feeling like an invalid, tired of feeling like he was out of the loop.

When he made it to the couch he was relieved to be able to sit down. Susan came out of the kitchen with a bowl of soup, which he took happily. "What have you heard from Gabriel or Raphael?" he asked.

Her mouth tightened and her eyes darkened. "Nothing," she said.

Clearly she was sick of being out of the loop, too.

"So, what have you two been up to while I've been out of it?" he asked.

It was surreal. It was the first time the three of them had just been able to sit down together. There was no fight to rush off to, no huge revelations. It was the first normal moment they'd ever had together.

He smiled. Of course, trapped in a house with two women he barely knew but had fought vampires with and a half-dead vampire monk upstairs wouldn't be most people's idea of "normal." It sounded like a bad sci-fi TV show. Or maybe it was the newest reality craze.

"What?" Wendy asked, smiling back at him.

"Nothing. Just enjoying the moment," he said.

"We've been reading the diary of our great-great-et-cetera aunt," Wendy said.

"Learn anything interesting?" he asked, lifting a spoonful of soup to his mouth.

The two women glanced at each other and then burst out laughing.

"What?" Clearly there was a joke he was missing.

"We've learned lots of things," Wendy said with a grin.

"Like men can be jerks," Susan said.

"And liars," Wendy added.

"Or monsters," Susan kept on.

"Or out to steal your land."

"Or just after you for your blood."

He held up a hand to stop them. "Do I want to know?"

They both started to giggle. He couldn't help but join in and even though it hurt his ribs the more he laughed the harder he laughed. And it felt so good.

Soon they were all laughing so hard tears were rolling down their cheeks.

"Wait!" he gasped, "Just tell me. Does it have anything to do with vampires?"

And then there was more laughing, which was even better. Wendy picked up a pillow from the sofa and hit him in the shoulder with it.

"No fair beating up a wounded man," he said.

"Hah!" she shouted and hit him again.

He picked up another pillow and prepared to defend himself. "Did anyone ever tell you that you hit like a girl?"

"Very funny!" she shrieked as she pummeled him again.

He turned so she could only hit him in his good side. It was probably stupid to engage her, but it felt so good to be silly, to be fighting without fighting, to wield a pillow instead of a stake.

And besides, she looked so cute when she was whacking at him, how could he stop her?

Susan's phone rang and they all jumped. She snatched it up from the coffee table. "Hello?" She listened a moment.

"Okay, and you?"

David and Wendy exchanged glances as they tried to figure out who was calling her.

"What!"

Trouble. David tensed, ready to spring into motion. Was it Raphael? Had they found something? Was he in trouble? Were vampires headed their way?

Wendy reached out, grabbed his hand, and squeezed it hard. He rubbed the back of her hand with his thumb, trying to calm both of them down.

"What happened?...Did they find out who did it?...Oh no."

A chill hand wrapped itself around David's heart.

"Oh you did, thank you."

More silence as Susan listened, eyes wide in shock.

"No, I don't know. I mean...Of course I'm coming home. I just can't...Yes. Yes, Wendy is with me. She's fine. Okay, we'll call later."

Susan hung up the phone and passed a hand over her face.

"What is it?" Wendy asked, her voice high with fear.

"Someone broke into my apartment. They trashed the place."

CHAPTER FIFTEEN

The sting of death is sin; and the strength of sin is the law.

—I Corinthians 15:56

G abriel was surrounded. There were ten vampires staring at him, eyes glowing in the darkness of the cathedral. Every one of them held stakes.

He began to breathe deeply, sucking in great lungfuls of air.

"Where's the other one?" a tall vampire with a Slavic accent asked.

They're just as in the dark about our movements as we are about theirs.

"Where he can do the most damage," Gabriel growled.

"Pity he's not here."

Gabriel eyed each of the vampires in turn, taking stock of them. "He'd just spoil my fun."

Five of the vampires laughed. Two looked like they were ready to turn tail and run already. That left three who stood, silent, waiting. They were the dangerous ones. If he killed one of them fast it would terrify the others. There! One of the three was huge, easily seven feet tall with heavily muscled arms. The others stood a respectful distance from him because he looked like a massive and powerful brute.

Fools. Most of them hadn't realized the cardinal rule, the thing that determined all vampire fights. He turned back, facing the spokesman, the hulking vampire only barely visible in his peripheral vision.

In a fight with vampires it wasn't about being the strongest.

It was about being the fastest.

He seized one of his makeshift stakes and hurled it to the side. Before any of the others could even move their Goliath crumbled to ash. Unlike the others, Gabriel didn't watch it happen. The instant the stake left his fingertips he threw himself forward. He grabbed the spokesman's arm and twisted it, plunging the other's stake into his heart.

Gabriel dropped to the ground and swept out the legs of one of the other dangerous vampires who reacted a hair too slowly. And as the vampire fell forward he landed on another of Gabriel's stakes.

Three dead in three seconds. The ones he had marked for cowards turned and fled as he suspected they would. That left five. Those who had laughed at him leaped forward, stakes extended.

Gabriel jumped into the air as high as he could and beneath him two of his surprised attackers staked each other. He crashed down on top of the third, breaking his neck. He grabbed his head and finished the job, ripping it off the creature's body.

Two left.

Fire exploded between his shoulders as one of them plunged twin stakes into his back, each barely missing his heart. He snarled and whipped around.

The vampire standing there slashed at him with a knife. Gabriel jumped back but not quite fast enough. The tip sliced across his throat and blood began to flow out, coating his shirt in an instant.

The pain was crippling and he felt himself weakening as the blood drained. Black spots began to fill his vision. Vampires could be incapacitated by blood loss and he was almost there.

A whisper of sound behind him alerted him to the presence of the other vampire. He spun, grabbed the creature's wrist and sunk his fangs in.

The vampire shouted, clearly stunned, and hit him with his free hand. But Gabriel hung on doggedly, trying to drink blood as fast as it seeped from his body. It was vampire blood, stale, dead. But it would help save his life.

And when he sensed the other vampire taking another swing at him with a stake he fell backward, pulling the vampire he was feeding on with him. The stake meant for him drove through the other vampire's forehead.

Gabriel used the vampire who was too weak to fight anymore as a human shield as he continued to drain him of blood. He could feel his throat beginning to heal, fire tracing along the wound.

And then the vampire he was feeding on turned to ash in his mouth as his comrade staked him to get to Gabriel.

Gabriel spat the ashes out of his mouth and punched upward with his fist, momentarily crippling the other vampire. And that moment was all he needed as he yanked the stake from the vampire's hand and killed him.

Before it had really begun the whole thing was over.

Gabriel lay panting in a pool of his own blood, his vision still swimming with black spots. As the tissue and muscle and skin knitted itself back together he groaned in pain.

Finally he rolled over and pushed himself to his knees. He tried to stand, but his shoes kept slipping on the wet floor. When he was standing at last he was weaker than he'd been in centuries. His hand shook as he wiped some of the blood from his face.

He looked around, sorry for the mess that he was going to be leaving.

It looks like something was sacrificed in here, he thought hazily and then almost laughed. Richelieu had sacrificed eight of his men.

He stepped carefully out of the circle of blood and ash and moved toward the front of the cathedral. He was walking heavily, dragging his feet, every step an effort. The arched ceiling caught the sound of his footsteps and echoed them around the room until the sound filled his ears. He struggled to focus. There was something he needed to find. Something with blood.

He made it to the front of the cathedral and stood before the altar. He took a step and his knee gave way beneath him. He caught himself on the altar and pushed himself up off it.

A proper altar, soaked in blood just like the old days.

But that wasn't the blood he was looking for. He moved slowly, eyes half closed. He was trying to sense . . . something.

And at last he knew he was too late. He could feel the remnants of the power, like an echo. Someone had taken it already, but how long before?

He stumbled. He couldn't worry about that right now. He just had to get out of there.

And he had to find someone to eat.

PRAGUE, PRESENT DAY

"Oh my gosh! Was anything taken from your apartment?" Wendy asked.

Susan shook her head. "They're still trying to sort that out. They can't be completely sure without me looking it over."

"What are you going to do?" David asked.

"What can I do?" Susan asked, her eyes helpless looking. "I can't go home, not now. Not yet, I mean. Why would someone do that?"

"Could it have been one of those Raiders looking for you?" he asked.

She put a shaking hand over her mouth. "Do you think so?"

"Are my parents in danger?" Wendy asked, eyes wide and terrified.

David took a deep breath. "Let's not panic. Maybe this has nothing to do with anyone else. Maybe it's just a random burglary."

Tears shimmered in Susan's eyes. "I don't know if that makes me feel any better or not."

He nodded. "I know, random stuff sometimes just seems worse."

"What else did they say?" Wendy asked.

Susan sighed. "It was your mom. She told me that she had mailed out the package I asked her to and that I should be seeing it any day."

"Where did she send it?" David asked. "She didn't have this address, did she?"

"No. I don't even have this address," Susan said. "I have no clue where we are."

"Me either," Wendy admitted.

"So, where are you supposed to pick this package up at?"

"A lawyer's in the city."

"How do you know a lawyer in Prague?" David asked.

Wendy cast him a pitying look. "I think we need to catch him up to speed."

"Please do," he urged. "Apparently I'm farther out of the loop than I realized."

They spent an hour telling him everything. He asked to examine Susan's necklace and as he held it in his hand he turned it over and over wondering what secret it possibly held.

"And your grandmother said that a key ring she gave you could help unlock the secret?" he asked.

"Yes, that's what the letter she left said."

"But she didn't tell you what the secret was?"

"No, she wanted me to read the letter from Jean, the French knight who found it, for myself. But I can't read French and it was stolen along with her letter when I got back from France."

"I would give just about anything to have been able to read Jean's letter and find out what the secret is," Wendy said.

"Me, too," David said. "But I guess we'll never get that chance."

"What do you think the secret could be?" Wendy asked him.

He shrugged. "I don't know. Maybe there's a secret compartment in it. Some old-fashioned jewelry had compartments you could hide things like poison in."

He handed it back to Susan who put it back around her neck. "But what poison could be effective against a vampire?" she asked.

"I don't know, but maybe it's tied in some way to garlic. That stuff really incapacitates them."

"Even if it were something like that," Wendy said, "do you think it would still be good? I mean, like old perfume turns to sludge in bottles and becomes unusable."

"I guess it would depend on exactly what it was. If it was in powder form, though, it might have survived that long."

Susan stroked the cross while they discussed it. "Maybe when the key ring arrives we'll be able to figure it out, get some answers."

"Answers would be nice," David said with a smile. "I think we all could use more of those and fewer questions in general."

"Amen," Wendy murmured.

"Now, how about we read some more from that diary?" David suggested. "After what you've told me, I'm eager to hear more myself."

They all settled into place and Wendy carefully unfolded the parchment papers that had been inserted into the diary.

"'My terror of him was great, but of staying in the prison greater.'"

FRANCE, AD 1198

Carissa woke slowly, aware that something was amiss. She opened her eyes and saw Gabriel. Her memories came flooding back. Terrified to wake him, she lay still.

Gabriel stirred beside her and she held her breath. There was no hiding from him, though.

"How do you feel?" he asked quietly.

"Better," she admitted.

"Good," he said, unwrapping his arms from around her. She sat up quickly, but didn't move away from him.

He smiled slowly and she got a good look at his fangs. She shivered and wrapped her arms protectively around herself.

"Last night when I first saw you, I thought you were an angel."

"An angel of death, perhaps," he replied. "I dwell in darkness."

"And yet it was Lucifer, the angel of light, who fell," she mused.

She could not help but think of her husband, a man who appeared so good, yet treated her so harshly. Then there was Gabriel, a monster, who treated her well. She shook her head, wishing she understood.

"There's food for you," he said, interrupting her thoughts.

She turned and stared for a moment at the plate before moving slowly over to it. The roll was hard but she nibbled at it thoughtfully. She could feel his eyes upon her and she tried not to let him see her fear.

She risked a glance in his direction and was taken aback to find he had disappeared. She spun quickly toward the shadows, eyes probing.

"I'm still here," he said.

She stiffened. She hastily finished her meal and shoved the plate under the door. She then retreated back to the corner she had come to think of as hers.

Silence hung dark and thick between them, and she tried to make herself still. She tried to breathe shallowly and keep her heartbeat slow.

"Do not be afraid," he said, suddenly enough to make her jump.

"How can I not be?" she squeaked.

"Ignorance breeds fear, knowledge sets you free. Ask what you will."

"Are you really five hundred years old?"

"Yes," he said. "Are you really nineteen hundred?"

She laughed, caught off guard by his humor. "No, I'm not."

"I didn't think so," he said. "You are far too sweet to be so old."

"You are funny."

"You have a wonderful laugh. It's light, airy. It reminds me of springtime. And in this place of death that's quite an accomplishment."

"Why are you here?"

He paused. "I understand why you would want to know that. Unfortunately, it is the most painful question you could have asked me."

"I'm sorry," she said, but she didn't retract it.

"You think you are the only one who had lands and riches envied by others?"

"You, too?"

"But of course. They needed to remove me for a time so that my lands would be forfeit. The Bishop of Avignon helped to plot against me."

"But, as a prisoner, are they not forfeit already?"

"No, because they have not declared me a prisoner. Officially, I do not exist, and unofficially they use me to help them dispose of other inconvenient prisoners."

"But given what you are, surely they could show a cause for executing you?" she asked, stunned by his admission.

"Yes, but then the church would have to admit that abominations such as myself exist and then they would have to explain them and the whole countryside would be in an uproar, blacksmiths staking butchers and butchers beheading tavern wenches. It would turn into a bloodbath. The clergy have a hard enough time keeping peace. No, far better to keep it quiet and allow things such as me to exist in rumor, legend."

"How did they find out about you?" she asked. Given his age he must have learned to be careful. What, then, had happened to him?

"It is the job of the magistrates to listen to rumors, whispers in the night whether they are true or not. As it turned out, a loyal servant wasn't quite so loyal."

"How did they capture you?"

"I was betrayed," he answered grimly. "The same one who let slip my existence helped them come for me. They came in the daylight when I was sleeping, hours after I had fed. In those days I slept deeper, I was accustomed to the servants moving around in the daytime while I slept. They came with chains and crosses, torches blazing. By the time

I knew what was happening, half my body was scorched by the fires. I was tried and convicted within an hour and put here."

"I'm so sorry. What happened to the servant who betrayed you?"

"Andrew lives, or, at least, he did. I imagine death has taken him by now. I had to give up that dream of revenge years ago."

"That's what kept you going? Dreaming of revenge?" she asked, intensely curious. She had to admit, her own thoughts of revenge burned brightly in her mind and kept her going when all else failed.

"I spent twenty years plotting against those who caged me. The next ten years I spent despairing that I would never escape. The last twenty passed in a blur, knowing that there would be no one left upon whom I could exact my revenge if I ever did manage to escape."

"How are we going to get out of here?" she asked.

"Soon, I will have enough of my strength back that I will be able to break these chains. Then we will wait until the warden begins his evening rounds. I will rip the door off its hinges, and then set it back into the wall. The sound should be covered by the screaming of the other prisoners. Then we will wait an hour after the warden has retired and we will sneak out. He is the only one who comes to this far cell, and he will not return again for another eight hours."

"And then what?" she asked, eager to fix her mind on what little hope she could find in his words, in his plan.

"We will travel by night, stopping during the day. Once we get far enough away we will be safe."

"How do you know?" Safety that she had taken for

granted now seemed like an elusive thing and she wondered if she would ever truly be safe again.

"Because most people never travel more than twenty miles beyond their birthplace. We will not be recognized farther away than that."

"If we travel by day as well, we can get away faster," she said.

"I cannot travel by day, except for a few minutes immediately after I've fed."

"How many minutes?" she asked.

"Fifteen minutes, a half hour at most."

"And then what happens?"

"My body is set ablaze and turns to ash within seconds."

His answer shocked and frightened her. She pressed a hand over her heart.

"Then we shall travel by night," she said at last.

Carissa stared at the scab on her palm. Just when the wound would begin to heal, and the pain would go away, it would be time to tear it back open to feed the beast whose fate seemed tied to her own. As she picked at the scab she reminded herself that although Gabriel was both witty and worldly, he was still a creature of darkness who would likely turn upon her once they made good their escape.

He had an interest in keeping her alive while they were imprisoned, he had said so himself. It was the frequency of the blood that was important, not the amount. Once he was past these prison walls and no longer solely dependent upon her, he would likely kill her.

It was up to her, then, to be faster, cleverer, and think of a way to part company with him as soon as they were free.

A dozen times she had thought of telling the warden what Gabriel was planning and a dozen times she had stopped herself. She wished to be free as much as he did and this seemed like her best chance as well. Also, the idea of betraying him as she had been betrayed was, at the last, unthinkable.

"What is wrong?" he asked and she forced herself not to stiffen or betray her thoughts in any way. He was remarkably intuitive and she did not need to further disadvantage herself by letting the conscious and unconscious movements of her body betray her.

"It's frustrating to keep ripping the wound open just when it heals."

"I am sorry," he said and she almost believed him, so sincere was his voice. Trust was a thing she had left in her marriage bed, though, and she doubted she would ever return there to reclaim it.

"It's not your problem," she lied.

She hooked a fingernail under the scab and ripped. Liquid fire coursed through her hand and she hissed sharply against the pain. She held her hand above the bowl and let the blood trickle out. She watched as the dark liquid splattered onto the metal. It seemed like her whole life revolved around blood, first not enough and now too much.

When the stream slowed and began to congeal, she squeezed her hand into a fist, her nails digging into the open wound. A fresh stream splashed down. She thought of the cross and the blood that had been spilled there. Christ had given His by choice, though, and she out of necessity. He to die to save others and she to live in order to kill others. Well, one other at least. She squeezed her fist harder, the pain hardly noticeable as she fixated on her hatred.

The blood began to flow faster and faster and she did not notice. Instead she pictured her betrayer's face as she killed him—ran him through with a sword, or even poisoned him to death.

"Carissa, that's enough. You have to stop," she heard through the haze of her hate.

She wouldn't stop, not until the man was dead.

"Carissa!"

With a start she noticed that she was shaking uncontrollably and the bowl was nearly full. She forced her hand open, the muscles cramping. She picked up the piece of cloth she had ready and wrapped the wound tight. She stared for a moment at her blood, steaming slightly in the cold and then rose to her feet. Carefully, unwilling to lose a drop to the uneven ground or her own shaking hand, she carried it to the darkness and set it down before backing slowly away.

She didn't get far, though, before she collapsed on the ground. She was tired, so very tired. Hatred took a lot out of a person. After a minute she heard the deep groaning of metal and the clanking of another chain hitting the ground. Then Gabriel was beside her.

His voice was a deep growl. "You should not have given me so much. Did you not hear me when I told you to stop?"

She was too cold and too tired to argue with him. Instead she curled up into a little ball and asked, "Did you get another chain undone?"

"Yes, the other leg and my left arm. That just leaves one."

"Good," she said, drowsily. She knew she shouldn't let him so close to her so soon after he had fed. The bloodlust was probably still upon him and she could still hear him breathing, but she didn't care.

He lay down behind her and wrapped his arms around her. She lifted her head slightly so he could slide his shoulder underneath and then she fell back against him. His body was warm, very warm, but it, like her blood, couldn't last forever.

She didn't know how long she slept, but she remembered Gabriel putting a wet cloth on her face and talking to her, though she couldn't quite hear what he was saying. She also remembered nibbling on some cheese, but it had made her stomach turn. She did remember that at some point his body had grown cold, his hand like stone against her cheek.

When she woke up, her head was on his leg and she was looking up at him. A look of relief passed over his face. He mopped her brow with a wet cloth.

"No more chains?" she asked, noticing that his right hand was unfettered.

"Not for three days now," he said quietly.

"Three days?" she asked, trying to push herself up.

He held her shoulders down, though. "Rest, you've been through a lot."

"What happened?" she whispered.

"First, you gave too much blood and it weakened you. Then, I noticed the next morning that the wound had turned bad."

"You could see it?" she asked.

He shook his head. "I could smell it."

"Am I okay?"

"You are now," he said, looking grim.

"What did you do?"

"I sucked out most of the bad blood."

"You . . . you . . ." She lifted her palm and gazed at it, unable to complete her sentence.

"I took no pleasure in it," he said darkly. "Blood like that is not appealing to my kind. It makes us ill. I spat out everything I could."

She let her hand drop and stared up at him. "You've been free all this time?"

"Most of it," he affirmed.

"Why did you stay?" she asked, bewildered.

He averted his gaze for a moment and she waited, stunned, for his answer.

He finally answered without looking at her. "We agreed to go together."

She began to cry, unable to stop herself. Could she have so misjudged him?

"Shh," he told her, "you need to rest and regain your strength."

"When can we leave here?" she sobbed.

"About a week."

"A week! That's a lifetime!"

"No, it isn't. Trust me."

Carissa spent the next three days with her head on Gabriel's knee. Occasionally he would rise to pace about the cell, but then he would return and offer her his knee once more.

She watched him and she knew that it was the most he had been able to move in half a century. She tried to imagine what he must be feeling, but found herself unequal to the task. She knew he was anxious to go and she did not blame him. Every morning when she awoke she was still surprised to find him there.

On the fourth day he finally allowed her to stand and she joined him in walking around the cell. She glanced down at her hand as she walked. The pain was again gone, the wound healed over.

"Won't you need some more blood before we leave?" she asked.

He shook his head almost imperceptibly. "No, I shall be fine."

"What's it like?" she asked after a moment.

"What?"

"Being a demon?"

"I'm not actually a demon," he said.

"Then what are you?"

"Some call us 'upir,' others 'the undead,' 'drinkers of blood.' We call ourselves 'vampires.'"

"What is it like being a vampire?"

"It's like spending every moment consumed by passion and unable to control it."

"I would imagine that would be nice."

He stopped midstride and turned to loom over her. She recoiled. His eyes were gleaming and his fangs were showing. "Quite the opposite, actually. Say, for example, that you had a passion for spiced pears. Now imagine hunting them down and eating them all day, every day. You can't stop yourself. You eat until you are sick. You eat until you think you should die, but you cannot die. Instead, you just keep eating, until all you do is eat spiced pears and vomit."

"That would be terrible," she whispered.

"Exactly. Whatever your passion is, it consumes you, until you can do nothing else but destroy your life and the lives of those around you. Now imagine that in addition to this great passion, whatever it is, you have another passion, a thirst for blood. Take the noblest person on the face of this earth, turn them into a vampire, setting their passions free and removing all their sense of reason and restraint, and they will rain destruction upon everything in their path, even that which they love."

"But, why?"

"Because it is a curse. Those like me are given unnatural long life in order to truly understand, through time, the sins of their past. If one lives long enough, he eventually regains the ability to reason, to repent, and he learns to control that which has always held sway over him."

"His passion," she murmured.

"His passion," he affirmed, leaning close to her.

"And what is your passion?" she asked, forcing herself to stand her ground.

"You might as well ask me what my sins are, though I shall not tell you. I was a creature of darkness even before I was forced to dwell in it," he hissed.

Then he turned and paced away. She stood, unnerved and not knowing what to say to him.

"If passion holds so much sway over you, then you must not be able to love another, to be with them," she said, before she could stop herself.

"We may love."

"But would it not be difficult to be that close to another and not..." She stopped, at a loss for words.

"Very difficult," he growled, standing suddenly right before her.

She blinked. She had not even seen him move.

"Then again, it is difficult for me to spend each moment alone with you in this cell. Any time I am close to a person, even just physical proximity, it is difficult. Love is just a motivation not to act on our most primitive desires."

She stared into his eyes and knew that as long as she stayed with him, she could never be completely safe.

CHAPTER SIXTEEN

O death, where is thy sting? O grave, where is thy victory?

—I Corinthians 15:55

Carissa awoke on the fifth day feeling better, stronger. She walked for an hour around the perimeter of the cell, driven to keep going. When they made their escape she would need to be ready. She would run from the prison and the warden. If necessary, she would even run from Gabriel.

They spoke not a word to each other all day, but she often felt his eyes upon her. She pretended not to notice. She didn't know how to act around him. First he would frighten her, more than anything had ever frightened her. Then he would show her such tenderness and humor that he would set her completely at ease. It was exhausting.

At last when she lay down to sleep it was with a growing sense of excitement. One way or another, they would be leaving this place soon.

Oviedo, Present Day

As Gabriel stalked through the streets of the city chasing down his prey he felt the singing of his blood. It was so much better being the hunter than the hunted. It had been days since he had eaten and with the blood loss it had become crucial. With nowhere to find blood in the middle of the night he was going to have to drink from a human. It would be easy enough to find a willing donor, but Gabriel the hunter didn't want a donor. He wanted a victim.

He searched the streets until he found one. The man was a drug dealer, his pockets full of packets of cocaine. His breath reeked of the clove cigarettes he was smoking. And there was blood on his clothes.

From the glimmer he saw of the man's mind, there was blood on his hands as well.

A criminal. One who wouldn't be much missed. Gabriel was slow, stumbling. He knew he probably looked drunk. He let that work for him. He hailed the man, then walked up to him and put an arm around his shoulders.

"You looking for a fix?" the drug dealer asked him.

"You could say that," Gabriel said.

He bit the man who screamed and flailed for only a moment before collapsing into Gabriel's arms. He drained him dry and then dropped the body on the ground. He wiped his lips, feeling more alive than he had in a long time. The kill was exhilarating. It was the last thing a vampire could stop himself from doing, and the thing he craved to the end of his wretched days.

The blood was fresh and vibrant and he felt himself

wakening even as the monster inside him stirred. The blood was good, but no blood would ever taste as sweet as Carissa's.

Carissa shouldn't have had to live the life she had. That sentiment always came to Gabriel when he thought of her. He had been there for so many firsts in her life. Some had been good. Most had been horrible.

FRANCE, AD 1198

The sixth day dawned. Gabriel could feel the pull of the sun though he could not see it. Fifty years trapped in a cell hadn't changed that. With one day of captivity left he did what he had done every other day. He cursed the loss of another moon and cursed those who had bound him in this darkness blacker than night.

He stared at Carissa, watching the pulse at the base of her throat. Its steady beating called to him and he found it hard to ignore. A dozen times he had bent over her while she was asleep, his teeth an inch from her delicate skin. A dozen times he had stopped himself at the last moment, retreating in rage and frustration.

Even now he longed to take her in his arms, embrace her, and give her the kiss of death. He had killed many in his day and she would not be the last, he feared.

And then of course there were those whom he had killed and then brought back. He had only converted two, both arrogant, wanton creatures much like he had once been. One of them had taken his own life, after murdering his wife. Raphael was the other. Gabriel hadn't thought about him in many, many years. If he was still alive, he'd be surprised.

Carissa stirred, awakening, and he returned his thoughts to her. He wondered what future waited for her. What kind of life would she make for herself once she was free? Whatever it was, it was not going to be easy. A man alone could go somewhere new and remake himself. For a woman, it was not quite so simple.

She sat up suddenly, her hair falling about her. She turned and when she saw him she smiled. He smiled back, giving her the full-tooth grin. She didn't flinch. She was the only one in five hundred years who hadn't. Even servants who had been with him since they were children and knew exactly what he was flinched whenever they saw his fangs. He had never blamed them.

"Good morning," she said, sounding as cheerful as she would greeting him at a breakfast table in a great castle.

"And to you," he answered, shaking his head in wonder.

"A day and a half?"

"A day and a half," he affirmed.

There was a light in her eyes that hadn't been there yesterday and he could feel the excitement coming off her in waves.

She stood and began walking around the cell. Her step was surer than it had been the day before and he watched her carefully.

"What shall we do today?" she queried.

"Let's discuss the future."

"You mean, beyond tomorrow night?" she asked with a laugh.

"Yes. Within a week we can be far away from here. I will make a brief stop at my old home and then I'll be traveling on farther. What will you do?"

She stopped walking and he watched in fascination as

a transformation came over her. A shadow passed over her face, the light in her eyes died, and she clenched her fists at her side.

"Carissa?" he asked, prodding.

"I want to kill the man who put me here," she hissed at last.

"Are you sure?" he asked slowly. "Revenge is rarely all that one hopes it will be. You also run the risk of being captured again, and this time, killed."

"I don't care," she answered, a tear making its way down her cheek. "He took everything from me and I want to take everything from him. Besides, truly, what will I have in the outside world? Nothing. Thanks to him I don't even have a home."

Listening to her he knew with a rush of conviction that she would succeed in her goal. He also knew that she would certainly be killed. It wasn't his affair, best to leave her alone and not get involved. In his heart, though, he knew that wasn't what he was going to do.

"I will help you."

"You will?" she asked, turning eyes that burned upon him.

"Yes. You will need help to pull it off and make your escape."

She came and knelt down beside him. "Thank you," she said fiercely, putting her hand on his.

He lifted her hand swiftly and kissed it, then let it fall. "You are welcome," he whispered.

"Lady, are you there?" the warden called from outside the cell.

"I am here," Carissa answered.

There was something in the warden's voice that caught Gabriel's attention, a sadness he had never heard before.

A plate slid underneath the door and then footsteps headed off. Gabriel stared at the food on the plate with a feeling of misgiving.

"Mutton!" Carissa exclaimed as she picked up the meat that was still on the leg. The meat was accompanied by some potatoes and an apple.

"That's better food than what you've been getting," he noted.

"Yes, I wonder why?" she said, her voice contented.

Gabriel didn't like it. Something wasn't right. He stood and walked to the door, where he tested its strength. It groaned beneath his touch. He turned to look at Carissa as she was eating her dinner.

They should leave tonight, he could feel it. She needed another day to recover, though. He stood there, weighing his options. He closed his eyes sending his senses out, listening, feeling.

"What's wrong?" she asked, suddenly and loudly enough to make him wince in pain.

He turned to stare at her and made a decision. "We're leaving, now."

She gasped and scrambled to her feet, a mixture of fear and excitement on her face. "Why?"

"Something's wrong, I'm not sure what. I just know that we need to go."

She nodded. "I'm ready."

"Do everything that I tell you. This isn't going to be how I planned things and I must be able to count on you doing exactly as I say."

"I will," she promised.

"As soon as I open the door, run out into the hall and wait for me. Stay close."

He turned and faced the door, flexing his hands and arms as he did so. The sense of urgency was rising in him, becoming overwhelming. He placed his hands against the door and pushed. Wood groaned and began to splinter. The metal of the hinges screamed for a moment before tearing loose.

With a crash the door fell and slammed onto the floor. Carissa dashed past him, through the doorway and over the remains of the door. He followed her, kneeling to lift the door with two fingers and set it quickly back into place, leaning it slightly against the stone so it would not fall.

It would survive only a cursory inspection. Anyone taking a close look would be able to tell that something was wrong.

He grabbed Carissa's hand and began to run. Halfway down the hall, he stopped and kicked down a door. With a roar the prisoner inside rushed to attain his freedom. Gabriel and Carissa continued running.

He heard other footsteps approaching, the guards running to see what had happened. Before they came around the corner, Gabriel pulled Carissa into an alcove and flattened them both against the wall.

The guards came around the corner in a rush, dashing right past the alcove and heading for the prisoner down the hall. Gabriel heard the man's wail of despair as the guards captured him.

Pulling Carissa with him, Gabriel ducked out of the alcove and ran around the corner. Another passage opened up on their left and they took it. Another left and they were at the base of the staircase. He could hear shouting behind them, but it wasn't clear if their escape had been discovered yet.

At the top of the stairs they took the corridor to the right. They rounded the corner and came to a halt. There, blocking their way, stood the warden. Gabriel recognized him by scent as he had never seen the man's face. They locked eyes for only a second before the warden turned to gaze upon Carissa.

Gabriel tensed his muscles, ready to attack.

"Milady," the warden murmured, dropping his eyes and stepping almost imperceptibly to the side.

Gabriel stared at him in astonishment, unable to believe what was happening. Together he and Carissa walked past the man.

"Thank you," Gabriel whispered as they passed.

The man said nothing but nodded slightly.

Once past him they resumed their run. Another corridor opened up on their left. A waft of fresh air swept toward them. They turned down it and in a few steps had reached a door. Gabriel kicked it open and they burst outside. He blinked as his senses took in the smell of the fresh air, the sound of the wind in the trees, and the insects. There was so much space and for a moment it overwhelmed him. But he hadn't come this far to fail. They ran across the ground toward the great gate, being careful to keep in the shadows.

"Who's there?" cried a fearful guard.

Gabriel smashed him in the face with a raised fist and the man tumbled to the ground unconscious.

They stopped before the gate. "Get ready," Gabriel whispered.

He grabbed hold of the gate, closed his eyes and heaved. The metal rose slowly, too slowly. His mind screamed at him that they were out of time. At last he had pulled it up two feet. "Under!" he hissed.

Carissa dropped to the ground and crawled beneath the gate. Once she was on the other side he dropped to the ground, and holding the gate aloft with one hand, rolled beneath it. He stopped, focused all his energy and then let go of the gate, recoiling his hand at the same time.

The gate crashed down and they were both safe on the other side. Carissa stood slowly, trembling. He joined her in a moment.

"We're free," she breathed.

A sound reached his ears and he whipped his head to the side. He wasn't so sure they were free yet.

PRAGUE, PRESENT DAY

Susan realized that she was holding her breath as she listened to Carissa's account of her and Gabriel's escape from the prison. She let it out. "She got her freedom."

"But did she keep it?" David asked darkly.

"Both of you shush," Wendy commanded. "'We had made it outside the gates and I could taste the air and it was so clean and pure compared to that of the prison. It made me slightly dizzy and the joy I felt was unlike any I had ever known.'"

FRANCE, AD 1198

"Quickly!" Gabriel hissed as he yanked her into the bushes.

"What?"

"Ssh!"

She waited, for what she did not know. Her heart was

pounding loudly and she strove in vain to calm it for her sake and Gabriel's. Slowly she began to hear something else, a low dull roar that she at first thought was her heart. The sound was growing increasingly louder, though. After a moment she recognized it as the sound of horses.

She ducked lower into the bushes and grabbed Gabriel's arm. He closed his hand over hers, and the touch calmed her.

The horses were coming at a fast clip and Carissa wondered what their business was at the prison. At last they came into sight, five cloaked figures carrying torches.

"Open the gate!" one of the men shouted.

Slowly the portcullis began to rise beside her. The horses slowed to a trot and at last came to a halt not ten feet from her. The man in the lead turned slightly to speak to one of his companions and the light from a torch fell full across his face.

"It's him!" Carissa whispered before she could stop herself. For one brief moment she thought that it had all been some terrible mistake and that he was here to rescue her. She glanced at his companions. They were all soldiers, heavily armed. If he were coming to free her, he would not have needed such an escort.

Anger washed over her as she stared at the face of her captor. She wanted to confront him, to see the look on his face when he realized that she was alive. Then she wanted to kill him, to make him pay for what he had done to her. She took a step forward, but Gabriel grabbed her, holding her back.

"Later!" he whispered fiercely in her ear.

And then the devil turned suddenly, as though he had heard something. She held her breath. Just then, though, there was a hail from inside the prison wall and the portcullis finally rose high enough to allow the riders to pass through.

He turned back to the castle and touched his spur to his horse's flank. The five disappeared inside and slowly the gate was lowered back into place. Carissa thought she heard a second set of hoofbeats beating down the road toward them, but could see nothing in the distance.

"Now, go!" Gabriel whispered.

Then they were running. Carissa strained her ears, listening for the sounds of pursuit but heard none. After only ten minutes she was exhausted. Another five and she came to a sputtering stop, lungs burning, heart feeling as though it would burst from her chest.

"I can't, I'm sorry," she gasped as Gabriel turned to look at her.

"That's all right, I can," he answered. "Did your father ever give you a ride on his back when you were a child?"

"Of course," she said. "But I am a bit more than a child now."

He turned and knelt on one knee. She clambered onto his back, feeling self-conscious as her tattered chemise hiked up to her thighs. She wrapped her arms tight around his chest and leaned her head against the back of his shoulder.

"Hold on tight," he instructed. Then he stood in one smooth movement, slid his hands under her knees and began to run. She shivered where his hands touched her bare skin.

Suddenly he turned from the road and ran through the fields. He began to pick up speed. She gasped as her eyes blurred with tears. Objects whipped by, too quickly for her to make them out. At last he seemed to reach his top speed and she realized that they were traveling far faster than they could by horseback.

After a time, the moon came out from behind the clouds that had covered it. It was full and it cast its silvery light all about them. It was the brightest light she had seen in weeks and she squinted slightly at first.

She clung tight to him, though her arms began to ache. They slid farther and farther up his chest until they were clasped around his neck. Gabriel twisted and turned as he ran. She struggled to keep hold of him.

"Hang on!" he yelled sharply and she hunched down closer to him, locking her wrists.

Suddenly he jumped and for one moment she knew what it would be like to soar upon the wind like a bird. She cried out in wonder and joy. Then they landed, hard, upon the ground. She felt her teeth knock together painfully and fire shot up and down her arms. Gabriel staggered and fell to one knee before leaping back up and continuing on.

He moved slower now, about the pace of Dancer's canter from what Carissa could judge. They also seemed to be heading in a straight line. She struggled to keep her hold around his neck but it grew harder with each step.

After what seemed like an eternity, Gabriel came to a halt. Gratefully she slid off his back. When her feet touched the ground, she let go of him. Her knees wobbled and collapsed and she fell on her bottom with a grunt.

He turned and looked at her with a smile twisting his lips. The glow from the moon bathed his face in light and softened his features.

"If I were human you would have choked me to death," he commented, rubbing his neck. "It is lucky that I am not."

"I am sorry," she whispered ruefully, trying to massage feeling back into her hands and wrists.

"Here, let me help," he said shortly, kneeling before her.

He grasped her hands and began chafing them.

She closed her eyes and groaned gratefully. "Where are we?"

"About three miles away from an inn. If we walk we can reach it in about an hour."

"Sounds good," she said. "I'm not sure I can take another ride like that."

He smiled. "I think you did quite well. I fully expected you to fall off long before this."

"I'm ready," she said, after another minute.

He offered his hand and she used it to pull herself up.

They walked slowly and in silence. Carissa's body ached in places she had never known she had, and she had to will her feet to move. They'd only walked a few minutes, when she stumbled and fell with a cry.

"Are you all right?"

"Yes," she gasped. "But I think I twisted my ankle. Let me sit for a moment and I'll be fine."

"We don't have time for that. Here, let me help."

Gabriel bent down and picked her up.

She began to protest but the throbbing of her ankle made her think better of it. Instead she forced herself to relax in his arms. After a minute she leaned her head against his shoulder and closed her eyes.

CHAPTER SEVENTEEN

That as sin hath reigned unto death, even so might grace reign through righteousness unto eternal life by Jesus Christ our Lord.

—Romans 5:21

Carissa awoke with a start. They had come to a stop before an inn.

"Can you stand?" Gabriel asked.

"I think so," she answered nervously.

Very carefully, he set her down on her feet. She wobbled for a moment and then gained her balance. She followed Gabriel as he strode forward and knocked on the door.

It opened quickly and a middle-aged man stepped outside. He looked at the two of them with surprise on his face.

"Innkeeper," Gabriel said, his voice deeper than usual. "We pray thee lend your aid."

"What happened to you?" the innkeeper asked, plainly startled at their appearance.

Carissa stepped behind Gabriel, remembering herself and the state in which she appeared. As she looked more closely at Gabriel, though, she realized he proved an even stranger sight in tattered, ill-fitting clothes that reeked of the prison.

Gabriel continued speaking, his voice smooth and deep. "Our cursed horse took a fright several miles down the road and threw my wife into a thorn patch. I had to cut off her dress to free her and the beast ran off with the rest of our possessions. I'm afraid we have only this with which to pay you for your hospitality," Gabriel said, holding up a small gem that glinted in the light.

She wondered where on earth he had found the stone. Had he managed to bring it with him to prison or had he taken it off one of his nameless victims? She shuddered and tried not to think about it. Fortunately, it seemed to be doing the trick as the innkeeper seemed willing to take them at their word despite their impossible appearance.

"This will more than do, milord. Come in and I will see what me and the missus can do for you."

"Is there anyone about?" Gabriel asked, an anxious tone in his voice. "My lady does not wish to be seen in such a state."

"No, milord, they're all asleep for the night what's here. The last went off to his room a half hour ago. You can both come right in." To Carissa he added, "My wife has got a dress you can wear, my lady."

"Thank you," she murmured.

Inside they met the innkeeper's wife, a pleasant woman with a warm manner. She bustled forward after a word from her husband and took Carissa by the arm.

She clucked comfortingly. "You poor thing, let us get you cleaned up."

Carissa glanced at Gabriel who nodded encouragingly. She turned and let the woman, Martha she said her name

was, lead her away into a private room. She squinted her
eyes against the brightness of the candles that seemed to
glow all about. "You just relax here a moment."

Carissa sat down on a chair and was grateful for the
softness. It had been long since she had sat on anything but
a stone floor. She closed her eyes and willed the tension
from her body. She was just starting to get drowsy when
the innkeeper's wife bustled back in.

"I've filled a nice basin for you so you can wash up,"
she informed her. "You go ahead, and I'll bring you some
clean clothes."

"Thank you," Carissa said, tears stinging her eyes. She
rose and made her way into the next room.

Never had washing felt so good. She scrubbed and
scrubbed at her skin, fearing that it would never be free of
the dirt of the prison. She washed her hair, not caring that
it would not have time to dry before she went to sleep.

True to her word, the innkeeper's wife had laid out
clothes for her when she had finished. She dressed, enjoying the feel of the clean clothes.

At last, clean and hungry, she made her way downstairs. A man stood in front of the fire, hands clasped
behind his back. His ebony hair hung in a damp mass
down to the middle of his back. He was dressed in clean, if
ill-fitting, peasant's clothes. As she stepped into the room,
he turned and she recognized Gabriel with a start.

He gave her a tight-lipped smile as she entered the room.

"You look more comfortable," he noted.

"I feel better," she admitted. "And you, you look wonderful."

"It's amazing what half a century of dirt does to a person," he remarked.

She noticed in awe that he was speaking with his lips nearly shut, so that there was no glint of fang when he spoke. Before she could say anything, the innkeeper hurried in with steaming plates of food that he set on a small table. He left and returned moments later with tankards.

"Sit, eat, you must be famished," he instructed.

Gabriel gave her a strained look, but sat obediently. She took her seat and realized just how hungry she was. She eagerly picked up the leg of mutton and began chewing happily, closing her eyes to savor the flavor.

The innkeeper entered again with a plate of bread. "Eat up, young man, your wife's already got a head start on you," he said laughingly before exiting again.

She opened her eyes and saw Gabriel staring at her with a distressed look on his face.

"I can't—"

"Oh," she said, understanding.

She put down her mutton and cast a quick glance over her shoulder. She switched plates with Gabriel and then picked up his mutton and began eating.

"Thanks," he whispered, picking up her partially eaten mutton as the innkeeper reentered the room.

The man beamed at them both, stoked the fire, and then bustled off to the kitchen. Carissa ate quickly, switching their plates frequently. Every time the innkeeper reentered the room, Gabriel was sure to look as though he were just finishing a bite or about to take another.

After eating half of each of their meals, she began to get very full, but pushed herself on a little further. She ate another quarter of the food on the plate that ultimately ended up sitting in front of Gabriel.

By the time she was finished she groaned and pressed her hand to her stomach.

"I haven't had that much food in so long," she gasped.

"You shouldn't have eaten so much."

"What was the alternative if we did not want to raise suspicion?" she whispered.

The innkeeper appeared and came over to them. "Are you full already?"

"Yes, but it was very good," Gabriel said.

Dinner finished, the innkeeper took them upstairs to their room. They thanked him and then shut the door behind them.

Carissa crossed to the bed and sank down upon it. She fingered the fabric of her dress thoughtfully. "Is it even possible that I'm actually feeling overdressed?" she asked.

Gabriel smiled. "Ironic considering your panic at being underdressed just a few hours ago."

She grinned sheepishly.

"That's all right, the smell of soap nearly overpowered me," Gabriel assured her.

She barely choked back a laugh.

"We'll rest today and leave late tomorrow night," Gabriel said after a pause.

Her exhaustion finally caught up with her and she lay down. "I really shouldn't sleep in my dress," she muttered.

"Don't worry about it," he said, lying down beside her. He threw an arm over her. "We can worry about such things at a different time."

"We really shouldn't be sleeping in the same bed," she protested, feeling like she should at least say something.

"We really should if we're pretending to be married," he answered.

Makes sense to me, she thought, before drifting off to sleep.

She awoke suddenly, feeling cold. She shivered and pulled the blanket up under her chin. There was something wrong. She turned and saw that the bed beside her was empty. Gabriel was gone.

She bolted upright. Had he abandoned her? She forced herself to lie back down. Nothing would be gained by her waking up the occupants of the entire inn looking for him. She glanced toward the window and saw streaks of light in the sky beyond. Dawn was at hand, he couldn't have gotten far.

She closed her eyes and tried to go back to sleep, but her mind was racing. She had been so worried about the fact that she might have to escape from him, was it possible he had felt the same way? Had he worried that she would betray him?

Then she heard the door open. She lay still, eyes squeezed tightly shut. Was it Gabriel? The door closed and she didn't hear any other sounds. Someone sat down on the edge of the bed and somehow she knew it was him. He lay back down and put an arm over her.

His arm was warm and her heart skipped a beat at the realization. He had just fed! But on what or on whom? She shuddered in horror.

"What's wrong?" he purred.

"Nothing," she whispered hastily. "Just trying to get comfortable."

She wondered if he knew that she was lying.

Gabriel and Carissa rose before the sun and made their way downstairs. Once more Gabriel watched, amused, as Carissa tried to eat for both of them.

After the meal he addressed the innkeeper. "We need to rest today but would like to leave early tomorrow morning. Do you have a horse that you can sell us?"

The innkeeper nodded. "I've got a mare, not as young as she once was, but a good animal. She's in the barn."

Carissa could hear the slight hesitation in the other man's voice and see the regret in his eyes. He obviously cared for the horse.

"Thank you, we will see that she makes her way back to you once we've reached home," Gabriel said.

The innkeeper's eyes lit up in surprise. "Thank you, I'd be appreciative."

"'Tis no bother," Gabriel assured him.

The innkeeper bustled off and Gabriel turned back to Carissa. She met his eyes for only a moment and then looked away. It was kind of him to offer to return the man's horse. Still, one little kindness didn't change what he was. She wondered if he knew that she had known he'd fed.

"We'll leave about an hour before dawn," he told her. "I have some arrangements to make, but we should be safe here today. Just be careful who you talk to and what you say."

She nodded and he rose from the table. She watched him walk out of the room and breathed a sigh of relief when he was gone. She stood slowly from the table and walked outside where she knew she could be alone, well, at least away from Gabriel for a while.

The sun that shone down upon her was pale and watery. Still she had to squint against the brightness of it. She pushed her sleeves up to her elbows, noting with a grimace the bruises on her wrists where she had been clasping them around Gabriel's throat on their night run. She spread her arms wide, trying to soak up as much of the sun's warmth as she could.

She closed her eyes and let her mind go. She day-dreamed that she was back home, safe, and that everything had been just a terrible nightmare from which she was glad to have awoken. She imagined that she was standing out in the fields, watching Dancer race by.

It was all wonderful, and as she opened her eyes she re-alized it was also all gone, forever. Even if she survived Gabriel, the men that her husband would send to hunt her down, and her revenge, she would never again be able to return home, or know the simple pleasures of her girlhood.

It was true then, marriage had made a woman of her, though not in any way she could have imagined. Her childhood seemed a thing of the distant past and her future held no ease in sight.

She began to walk, taking grim comfort in the fact that she seemed no worse for wear from her night flight. Her steps were stronger, more sure and she walked around the inn, its small garden, the barn, and pens containing a few sheep and pigs. The innkeepers had so little, yet they were rich in comparison to her in her current state.

She walked into the barn where she found a lone horse. She was a small dun-colored animal, clearly past her prime. Her eyes were clear and gentle, though, and seemed to look right through her. She reached out and pat-ted the horse's soft nose.

"We raised her from a foal," Martha, the innkeeper's wife, noted. "Her name's Duchess," the woman added with a blush.

Carissa jumped, surprised to discover that she wasn't alone. She said softly, "And she is quite the lady."

"We've always thought so."

A surge of pity swelled in Carissa. "I promise we will treat her well and send her back as quickly as we can."

The woman gave her a strained smile. "That's what your man said."

"You don't believe him?" Carissa asked, curious.

"Pardon me, milady, I don't mean to question my betters, it's just, folks sometimes forget about promises made to innkeepers."

Carissa couldn't help herself. She strode forward and placed her hand on the woman's arm. "You have shown kindness to strangers in our hour of need and I shall not forget it. I will make sure that your horse is returned safely to you and someday, when I am able, I will do what I can to return the favor. There is not enough compassion in this world, it wouldn't do to hurt those still unafraid to show it."

She couldn't be sure, but she thought she saw tears glistening in the other woman's eyes.

"Thank you, milady."

"No, thank you," Carissa said.

"Well, look at me, making a fuss, when I should be helping you get ready for your journey," Martha said, voice husky.

"I believe my…husband…is taking care of everything," Carissa said, nearly choking on the word *husband*.

Martha sniffed, "Leave all the travel arrangements to menfolk and you often end up without the things you need most."

Carissa laughed, surprising herself with the sound. "I guess you're right."

"'Course, I am. Now let's go attend to some things," Martha said.

* * *

Carissa found that she awoke every hour during the night, heart racing. Each time Gabriel quieted her with a word or a touch and she fell back asleep, to dark dreams that terrified her.

At last she woke and found that he was standing in the middle of the room. Even in the dark she could see his eyes shining, catlike. "It's time to go," he told her.

She rose quickly, and was ready in a minute, having slept in her clothes. They made their way quietly down the stairs and out the back door. When they reached the stables, Duchess was ready and waiting for them.

"Who saddled her?" Gabriel questioned.

"For sure that would be me," Martha said, entering the barn behind them. "Made no sense to have you stumbling around in the dark looking for things that you didn't know where to find." The light of a lantern she was carrying shone upon her face and she winked at Carissa.

She gestured to a bundle tied onto the back of the saddle. "There's enough food in the pack to last you two days, more if you need it to."

"Thank you," Carissa said, reaching out to touch Martha's hand.

Martha smiled. "I only wish I could do more. Well, time's a'wasting. You two had better get started if you're going."

"Thank you," Gabriel murmured, checking the trappings. He mounted in one smooth motion, almost springing to the saddle. He reached down and pulled Carissa up effortlessly, to sit sidesaddle in front of him.

"Godspeed," Martha called as she untied the reins and handed them up to Gabriel.

"Bless you, milady, and your husband," Gabriel said before urging the horse forward.

Once clear of the barn, Carissa turned back to wave. Then they were on their way, the road stretching before them like a dark ribbon. They rode until the inn was swallowed up in darkness behind them and then Gabriel stopped the horse and dismounted.

"What's wrong?" Carissa asked sharply.

"It will be dawn in another half hour, but we could not risk waiting until tonight to begin our journey."

"So, what do we do?"

"I can move swiftly on foot and the mare will fare better with only your weight. I will go on ahead and stop when dawn breaks. I will find shelter either in the forest or some other place. Ride, trotting only half the time, and you will catch up to me at nightfall."

Fear twisted her stomach. She had ridden by herself on many occasions, but only on her own land, on trails she knew well.

As though reading her mind, he assured her, "You will be quite safe until then. Just stay on the road and keep coming. I will be waiting for you."

He helped her reposition herself so she was sitting in the saddle, astride the horse. Her skirts had not been designed for such activity and they hiked up to her calves. She tugged in vain at them, but it was no use. Gabriel handed her the reins, and then, without another word, he was gone.

She didn't even see him move, it was as though he simply vanished. She sat for a moment, blinking into the darkness and battling her fear. Behind her was the inn, a sanctuary. It could not remain a sanctuary forever, though.

For all she knew, soldiers were already on their trail and would soon reach the inn.

Taking a deep breath, she urged Duchess forward. They had only been walking a few minutes when the sky began to lighten. As the path grew clearer she urged Duchess into a trot. When the sun finally reared its head above the horizon, she felt her spirits lifting as well.

The countryside was beautiful, especially for one whose eyes had long seen only darkness. Duchess did live up to her name. Even her trot was gentle and stately. Slowly Carissa began to relax.

As the sun reached its peak, she followed the sound of water to a brook not far from the path. She stopped and dismounted, needing to stretch her legs. She let Duchess drink her fill, then tied her reins to a tree. Carissa pulled a small slice of cheese from the bundle and ate it as she walked.

After about fifteen minutes she remounted and prepared to retake the road. The icy hand of premonition touched her spine. Without knowing why, she urged Duchess behind a couple of trees and sat still, waiting.

A minute later she could hear the pounding of many hooves. Four riders, soldiers by their clothes, came into view and Carissa held very still. They thundered by, heading in the direction of the inn. Her heart began to pound, drowning out the sound of the horses. At last they passed.

She waited five minutes before urging Duchess toward the road. She looked down it both ways but could see no one. *What if they were looking for me?* she wondered. *I didn't think they could get word this far away so quickly.*

She turned her back toward the riders and touched her heels to Duchess's flanks. The horse jumped into a swift canter. Carissa wanted to get as much distance between herself and the soldiers as possible without overly tiring her horse.

She rode all day and just before sunset reached some woods. She was exhausted, half asleep in her saddle. Suddenly a voice called out to her and both she and the horse shied.

She settled the animal and did her best to bring her own heartbeat under control as she recognized Gabriel standing in the shadow of the trees.

"I thought you slept while the sun was up."

"I heard you coming. It woke me. I didn't expect you so soon," he commented.

She trotted off the road and pulled up in front of him. "I passed some soldiers around midday and I figured Duchess and I could manage to move a little faster."

He nodded and held Duchess as she dismounted. "I saw them this morning. We can rest up for a couple of hours and let the old girl here catch her breath. We'll move again once it's truly dark."

Carissa took the reins from him and followed as he led them back into the forest. At last she tied up Duchess and he removed the saddle. The horse snorted appreciatively and began to graze.

"She'll need some water soon," Carissa said as she flopped down with her back to a tree.

Gabriel led Duchess to a nearby stream and returned a short time later. He stowed everything away and then sat down next to Carissa. She was half asleep and barely felt it when he moved her head to rest on his shoulder.

CHAPTER EIGHTEEN

Now the brother shall betray the brother to death, and
the father the son; and children shall rise up against
their parents, and shall cause them to be put to death.

—Mark 13:12

The last of the light was fading as Gabriel roused
Carissa. Her eyes flew open and she stared at him for a
moment with an uncomprehending gaze. She sat up suddenly, as though overcome by some sense of propriety.
Gabriel bit his lower lip to keep from laughing or making
a rude comment.

She rose quickly, smoothing down her dress with nervous hands and he just watched her in amusement. She
disappeared into the forest for a moment and he gave her
her privacy. When she returned she looked more alert.

"How long was I asleep?"

"About two hours."

"It seemed longer."

"You must have rested well, then," he said with a smile
as he rose to his feet.

"How do you do that?" she asked.

"What?"

"Move like that, like it takes no effort."

He shrugged. "Because it doesn't, not really."

She looked like she was going to say something else, but instead she shook her head and turned to Duchess. She reached for the saddle, but Gabriel moved to intercept her.

"I'm not a weakling, I can handle a saddle," she snapped.

"I never meant to imply that you were," he said with a raised eyebrow. He stepped back and watched as she hefted the saddle into the air and then onto the horse's back. He could see the play of her muscles beneath her sleeves and hear the sharp intake of her breath.

She cinched down the saddle, and made sure everything was secure. After double-checking the girth, she mounted. That she did gracefully with a light step. She turned to look at him and there was a defiant gleam in her eyes.

"Coming?" she asked.

"I'll walk," he said, still trying not to laugh.

Fear touched her face and he hastened to reassure her. "I'll be staying with you, don't worry."

"I wasn't worried," she said.

He coughed so he wouldn't laugh. She glared at him. "I didn't think vampires coughed."

"Not unless we want to," he said, voice innocent. He moved to the horse's head and grabbed the reins beneath her muzzle. He whispered a few words to the animal to soothe her and then led them out of the forest and back to the path.

Once on the road Gabriel gave Duchess her head. The moon was already up and shining down brightly. Carissa urged Duchess to a trot and Gabriel matched the pace.

They traveled for several hours in silence, stopping briefly for Carissa to snatch a few mouthfuls of food and give the horse some more water. He could tell both Carissa and the horse were growing weary. Carissa was beginning to sway slightly in the saddle.

The night wore on and they continued, sometimes walking, sometimes trotting.

Finally Carissa said, "I think the horse is going to need to rest soon. It's been a long day for her."

"And for you," he reminded. "There is a monastery not far from here. We will find shelter there."

"Can you do that?" she asked.

"Yes, monks are always willing to help weary travelers."

"No, I mean you. Can you go to a place like that?"

He smiled to himself but said nothing. They should just make it before daybreak.

After another hour, Gabriel grabbed the reins again and led Duchess off the trail. They slid down a steep ravine, splashed across a narrow creek, and then climbed out the other side. The horse was breathing heavily and her sweat was dripping onto his hand when they reached the top.

"Just a little farther," he whispered to both horse and rider.

They topped a gentle hill and saw a cluster of buildings that composed a monastery. They approached and Gabriel could feel Carissa's relief. It was nothing compared to his because in the distance he saw an old friend, one he knew would help them now.

PRAGUE, PRESENT DAY

" 'I nearly wept with joy when the monastery came in sight because I believed that I had been delivered from death and evil and might find sanctuary not only from my pursuers but also from my rescuer,' Wendy read. She looked up.

"Why did you stop?" David asked.

"I think I know who..." She stopped herself. "It's just strange to think how long they've lived. How much they've seen. How much they must know. I never thought to ask...anything."

"It's not as if we've had the opportunity," Susan pointed out, stretching.

"Maybe that's why Gabriel gave you this," Wendy said, turning back to the pages in her hand.

FRANCE, AD 1198

Carissa breathed easier when she saw the buildings. She hadn't wanted to admit it, but she was exhausted and needed to rest.

The sky was beginning to lighten and she saw a monk, cloaked in a brown robe, kneeling beneath a tree, a wooden cross clasped between his hands and his lips moving in prayer. They approached quietly and then stood, waiting for him to finish. Carissa, mindful of the fact that riding astride the horse bared her legs, dismounted and straightened her skirts.

After a moment the monk made the symbol of the cross and rose to his feet, turning to them with a pleasant smile. The monk was older, with silver touching his close-cropped hair above his temples. His blue eyes crackled with the energy of a youth, though.

"Can I help you?" he asked.

"Is that any way to greet a friend?" Gabriel asked in a scolding tone.

"Gabriel!" the monk exclaimed, reaching out to him.

"Careful," Gabriel cautioned, moving to avoid the cross the monk held in his left hand.

They embraced, the monk carefully holding the cross away from Gabriel's body. When they parted the two men turned toward Carissa.

"Carissa, allow me to introduce Brother Paul."

Paul reached out and clasped Carissa's hand in both of his. "It is an honor."

"You're a friend of Gabriel's?" she asked, bewildered.

"That I am."

"But how is that possible?" she asked, thinking of all the years Gabriel had spent imprisoned.

"Ah, we are very...old...friends," Paul said.

She looked at him closely and he slowly smiled, revealing long, pointed fangs.

She couldn't restrain her gasp of surprise as he chuckled. She glanced down as he released her hand and her eyes were drawn to the cross he was still holding.

"Does that not burn you?"

"No, it does not."

"But, Gabriel said—"

"It does not burn *me*," Paul explained. She looked up at him. He continued, staring pointedly at Gabriel. "The touch of God harms only those who struggle against it."

Carissa stared at the two men and sensed that somehow this was an old discussion between them. Paul turned back to her after a moment.

"Come, let us retreat to the shelter of the monastery, the sun will soon be in the sky."

They began walking and Carissa gazed at Paul in curiosity. A hundred questions crowded her mind, each burning to be asked. First and foremost, though, she desired to know how he, a man of God, had become a vampire, a creature of darkness.

"I do not consider myself of the darkness, I consider myself one who cares for those who dwell in spiritual darkness."

"You read my mind!" she gasped.

He stopped walking for a moment and turned to her. He pinned her to the spot with his eyes as they searched her very soul.

Slowly he smiled. "No. It was the natural question for you to ask."

He resumed walking and she fell into step beside him, trying to ignore what sounded like stifled laughter coming from Gabriel.

"He has told you about our kind."

"Yes."

"And has he told you that before each of us were cursed we were slaves to our passions?"

"Yes," she said, wondering what each of their passions could have been. It was something that Gabriel still had not shared with her.

"He will tell you his when he is ready," Paul said, startling her again. "As for me, I had a passion for saving souls."

"A noble calling," she said.

"Not when your zeal leads you to try and convert others through the use of force and fear," he said, glancing at her. "My soul was so consumed with passion that there was no room left for compassion."

"Things are different now?"

"Time has a way of showing every man his folly."

They reached the monastery. The buildings were arranged around a central garden where rows of vegetables sprang from the earth. Bells began to peal out, their rich tolling breaking the silence.

"The end of morning prayers. Let us go and join in the morning meal."

Carissa and Gabriel followed Paul inside and joined a stream of men clad in brown robes walking at a stately pace into the dining hall. Paul seated them at the end of one of the long tables, slightly away from the rest of the brothers.

For one wild moment Carissa thought she was going to have to eat for all three of them. She was relieved when that proved not to be the case.

"Do you not have a problem hiding who you are?" she asked after a minute.

"One of the advantages to living in a monastery is that fasting is common. No one notices or cares when you do not eat," Gabriel said, winking at Carissa.

"This is true," Paul said. "The people here are focused upon God, not each other. It is far easier to pass by unnoticed than it is almost anywhere else."

As though to prove his point, he pulled a small drinking pouch from the folds of his robes. He filled his cup and then Gabriel's. He put the pouch away and the two raised their glasses to each other in a silent toast.

Carissa watched in morbid fascination as they drank. When they were finished they both wiped their mouths at the same time and she had to stifle a laugh.

"So, tell me, where have the two of you come from?" Paul asked quizzically.

"The prison," Gabriel answered grimly.

"Ah, that's where you have been all these years. How did they find you?"

"Betrayed."

Paul grunted understanding. "And they kept you alive?"

"They used me to dispose of prisoners."

Paul swore under his breath and Carissa flushed.

"And what about you?" he asked, turning toward her.

"She was falsely accused by her husband, a magistrate in the Inquisition."

The look on Paul's face was one of pity. "I am sorry for your pain."

She didn't know what to say. She could feel tears stinging the back of her eyes. She nodded, not trusting herself to speak. It amazed her that both men had chosen to trust her, believe her so quickly. It was such a contrast to that horrible night in front of the magistrates, when they had not even let her speak, had not cared what her side of the story was.

"Where are you going from here?" Paul asked, turning back to Gabriel.

"Home."

"Avignon?"

"Yes."

"That's quite a ways. You should take the river, it would be faster," Paul said.

"I had thought about it. However, it does present some unique challenges."

"I'll give you a robe, it will be easier for you to travel disguised as a holy man."

"And Carissa?"

"We will also have to do something about your clothes," Paul said to Carissa.

"What's wrong with them?" she asked.

"Nothing, but peasant ladies do not travel with their own personal priest. Don't worry, I think I can find something more appropriate," he said with a mysterious smile. "For now, though, I think the two of you should get some rest."

They rose from the table and Paul led them into the private chambers.

Carissa awoke with a start. She tiptoed out of her room and rapped softly on the one next to hers. After a moment she opened the door and discovered that the room was empty. Where could Gabriel be? She turned and walked down one of the halls, not sure where she was going. She ruled out the chapel and the dining hall and when she came to a crossroads she instinctively turned left.

She had nearly reached the end of that hallway when she heard low voices coming from one of the rooms. She froze for a moment, heart beginning to pound as she recognized one of them as Gabriel's. She forced herself to calm down, waited for her heart to slow and then crept closer. Her first thought was to boldly enter the room in search of him. Another, more cautious part of her urged her to go quietly, listening, because it would be to her benefit to learn what he had to say when she was not around. In her heart, she still didn't trust him entirely.

"I am sorry to hear of your troubles," Paul said. "I must say, it does explain quite a lot, though. I didn't think you would have left one so young running loose on his own."

"You encountered Raphael?" Gabriel asked.

Paul smiled. "Hunted him down is more like it. I'd heard of a young man, completely mad, who had managed to convince an entire primitive tribe that he was God."

"And?"

"I made sure he knew that wasn't the case," Paul said. "I set him on fire."

"So, he's dead then."

"No. I let him live."

"That was generous of you."

Paul chuckled. "It wasn't entirely his fault. Besides, we all go crazy when we're young."

There were a few moments of silence and Carissa moved closer.

"And what of the woman?" Paul asked.

"I don't know," Gabriel answered.

"You seem to be attached to her."

"I feel responsible for her. Without her help, I wouldn't have gained the strength I needed to escape."

"You would have found another way."

"Perhaps."

She moved closer still until she could see into the room. Gabriel and Paul sat together in chairs facing away from the door. She moved quickly behind a stone pillar where they would not be able to see her.

"You care for her, don't you?"

"Yes, even though we come from such different worlds."

"You started in the same one, that's all that matters."

"Is it?" Gabriel asked in her ear.

Carissa screamed and he clamped a hand over her mouth. She stood, eyes feeling like they would bulge from their sockets, and stared at him.

"Ssh, it's just me," he said, before releasing her.

She staggered slightly, putting her hand on the pillar for support.

"Won't you join us?" Paul asked, standing suddenly on her other side.

She glanced toward him and felt a rush of air behind her. She turned and Gabriel was gone. She twisted around and saw that he was once again seated halfway across the room. She turned back to Paul, but he was gone as well.

"Here's a seat for you," Paul called.

She turned again and saw him sitting by Gabriel, a third chair pulled up by theirs. She stood quivering as they stared at her, waiting.

Before her were two creatures of the dark the likes of whom she had been taught to fear. She had seen with her own eyes the destruction of which they were capable. Now they sat, waiting for her to join them, ally herself with them and their kind.

Behind her was an entire monastery filled with monks, all holy men and mortals. They would protect her if she went to them, stand between her and the two who were before her.

But had not holy and mortal men already condemned her as no better than these creatures? How long before the monks would discover that secret and turn upon her as well, decrying her as a Jezebel?

Both choices were fraught with danger, pain, and terror. In her heart, though, had she not already chosen? What else could have driven her from the safety of one of the monastery's bedrooms in the middle of the night to seek out a monster?

She took a hesitant step forward. The second was stronger, more confident. By the third she knew there was no turning back. She strode the rest of the way and, without hesitating, took the chair that was waiting for her.

After a moment she lifted her eyes to meet those of first Paul and then Gabriel. She wondered if they had any idea that a choice had just been made, and what it had cost her. Looking into their eyes, though, she detected sympathy and more than a trace of understanding.

She took a deep breath and asked, "So, what shall we talk about?"

CHAPTER NINETEEN

He that smiteth a man, so that he die, shall be surely put to death.

—Exodus 21:12

Carissa fingered the fine material of her gown. It was a pale blue embroidered all over with white flowers. It seemed like ages since she had worn something like it.

"You look beautiful, my lady," Gabriel whispered to her.

She glanced at him. He was covered from head to toe by a monk's robe. She bit back an urge to laugh at the absurdity of it.

She turned back toward the river. It was just a few minutes after sunset and in the fading light she could see the long, flat barge that would convey them toward their destination. There was a cabin toward the back of it that offered sleeping quarters for the owner or one of his customers.

The barge owner looked up as they approached. He mopped a hand across his forehead and squinted up at her.

"You my passengers?" he asked.

"My lady and I are in need of your services, yes," Gabriel answered.

Carissa did as she had been told to do. She scrunched up her face and turned to Gabriel and whispered, a little too loudly, "Are you sure he's reputable?"

The captain heard her and gave a short barking laugh. "Don't worry, I'll get you to where you're going."

"I'm sure that everything will be fine, milady," Gabriel said, in reassuring tones.

She turned back with a distrustful look upon her face. "If you are certain," she said, dismounting from her horse.

She handed the reins to Paul. The monk had promised to see Duchess safely back to the innkeepers.

The owner helped her onto the barge, which rocked slightly beneath her feet. Gabriel followed, grabbing her elbow to steady her and managing to do so without exposing his hand to the last of the sun's light. A minute later the boat pushed off and they were on their way.

The river barge moved lazily along the river and Gabriel became increasingly tense and irritable as they meandered along. Carissa didn't know exactly what the matter was with him but it made her nervous. She knew he had a drink bladder filled with animal blood but after a while she saw him toss it in the river while none was looking. When she raised a questioning eyebrow he whispered to her that it went stale.

She couldn't help but wonder what or whom he was eyeing for fresh blood. But she was so busy watching the boat crew she didn't really have time to worry about him, too.

The owner and captain of the vessel seemed like he was trustworthy, though he was almost certainly a smuggler when not more honestly employed. The two others, hired men, Carissa was not so sure of. They glanced furtively from time to time at Gabriel though they seemed to give Carissa no more notice than was to be expected.

She felt a change in the movement of the barge and glanced up. The horse had come to a stop and the barge had floated past the tired-looking animal.

"Swift water coming," the barge captain announced. He nodded at one of the two hired men. "You walk the horse along the path and meet us on the other side."

The man nodded curtly before making his way ashore. There he unhitched the rope tying the horse to the barge and tossed it back to the captain who plucked it deftly out of the air.

The barge began to move, the river grasping it and pulling it along. If the stretch of swift water lasted too long, the man and horse might not catch up with them until the next day. She didn't want to have to spend any more time on the barge than was necessary.

Carissa couldn't get comfortable. They had been on the barge two nights and she had just started to get used to its rhythm. Now that they had entered the swifter water, though, the boat moved differently. Gabriel hadn't seemed quite right to her either. He had acted distant, somehow distracted. It made her nervous.

She rolled from her side onto her back, no easy feat given the cramped quarters. She glanced over to his mat, his blankets were piled high on top of him. She longed to go to him. She missed the comfort of his presence, but knew that she dare not, lest the men on the boat begin to question the relationship between her and Gabriel. That would endanger them both.

Frustrated, she stared at the low ceiling and listened to the groaning of the wood as the water moved against it. It sounded eerily loud in her ears. It seemed like the prison had been quieter, even at suppertime when dozens were shouting, pleading for food and crying for death.

Gabriel still had not told her where they were going, something else which made her nervous. She trusted him, but not enough to follow blindly much longer. At least, she believed she trusted him, as much as she could anyone at this point. Still, why did she tense when he moved too quickly? Why did her heart begin to pound so loudly when he drew near and louder still when he was gone?

The night yielded up no answers and she resigned herself to sleeplessness. Suddenly, a new sound entered her consciousness. It was not the creak of the boat, the sound of the water, or the whistling of the men. It was a footstep and it was close by.

She lowered her eyelids to a slit. Better far to see when one was thought to be asleep. A shadow flitted, even darker than the blackness that surrounded the door. She let her eyes drift slowly away from it, knowing that she could more readily pick up the movement out of the corner of her eyes. It was a trick Gabriel had taught her and she had been practicing.

She held her breath the better to hear and then had the outrageous thought that with her breath stilled she was even more like Gabriel. Beside her bed was a lantern and she closed her fingers slowly and silently around the metal, gripping it tight.

The figure began to move and she realized that it was going to pass by her. She caught a glimpse of something raised in its fist. The man moved to stand before Gabriel's bed, so quietly that she could not hear him. Something in his stance spoke to her, told her that his intentions were murderous. Heart in her throat she rose out of her bed behind him, silent as the grave.

As he began to swing his arm downward toward Gabriel's sleeping form she lifted the lantern and smashed it down at the base of his neck as hard as she could. His head swiveled sideways and she heard a dull crunching sound before he fell. She jumped back as his body hit the ground where she had been standing and she bit back a cry.

Suddenly strong arms gripped her from behind and she tried to scream. Before she could draw the breath to make a sound, a hand clamped over her mouth. "'Tis me," a familiar voice whispered fiercely in her ear.

She let herself fall into Gabriel's chest, his arms about her the only thing that held her upright as she began to shake. After a minute he took the lantern from her trembling fingers and lit it. He bent down to inspect the boatman who lay still upon the floor. First he touched the man's throat, then slowly passed a hand before his mouth.

Carissa collapsed on her bed, covering her mouth with her hand and fighting a wave of nausea. Fierce waves began to pound the boat and Gabriel caught himself with a hand on her shoulder as he slowly stood.

"He's dead, neck broken," he pronounced shortly.

The boat rocked fiercely again and Carissa fell off the bed and onto her knees beside the body.

"Dead?" she asked, sure she couldn't have heard him right.

"Yes."

"I didn't mean to kill him," she gasped.

"I know, but it's as well that you did. He had come here to kill me," Gabriel said grimly, motioning toward the man's right hand. There, clutched in fingers that would move no more, was a long, wooden stake. "And then God alone knows what would have happened to you," Gabriel continued.

"But, you weren't in your bed."

"No, I suspected something and so I rose shortly after you lay down so that I could keep watch."

"But I didn't hear you," she accused, unable to think for the moment of the body beside her.

"I am not often heard when I wish to remain unheard."

There was nothing she had to say to that. Her eyes moved from him to the body of the man that she had killed. The boat bucked hard and she began to retch.

Gabriel just stood and watched her as she spilled the contents of her stomach upon the bottom of the barge. He said nothing and she hated him for it as she sobbed over the life that she had taken. She was a murderer. Everything that the boatman had been or ever would be meant nothing now, his life hollow, his death meaningless. She had killed him to save a monster who didn't even need saving.

At last she collapsed onto the floor and could not even find the strength to remove her hand from her victim's back. Before blessed black oblivion claimed her, though, she saw Gabriel's face floating above her and she spat at him.

PRAGUE, PRESENT DAY

"She killed a person," David said, the first of them to break the silence.

"She had to," Susan whispered.

Wendy felt chilled to her very bones. She looked at Susan and David. Interaction with vampires had already caused them to have to do things they normally never would have. She shuddered. How long before she was going to be caught in an impossible situation and have to do something she would have to live with for the rest of her life?

She felt a creeping sickness deep in her soul.

"I don't want to read any more," she whispered.

David reached out and stroked her cheek with his hand. "I think we have to know, understand what we've gotten involved in, who we've gotten involved with."

FRANCE, AD 1198

Once Carissa had lost consciousness, Gabriel moved swiftly to dispose of the body. First, though, he stopped to steal a few sips of blood, cursing himself for doing so. It was not good to drink human blood. Every species of animal had a distinctive taste and some types were far more addictive than others. He had spent too many years drinking only human blood of late to fool himself into thinking it was going to be easy to stop.

Still, he had to keep his strength up. He picked up the body and slung it over his shoulder. He then slipped quietly out onto the deck. The master of the boat was busy steering a straight course between the shores of the river. There had been no letup in the current during the afternoon, which would have allowed them to tie up and wait for the horse and his keeper to catch up with them.

Carefully, he moved to the back of the barge and slowly lowered his burden over the side. He finally let the body go and a small splash was all that marked its passing. If the captain of the barge spotted the body, he would think the man had fallen overboard in the night.

He hurried back below to Carissa. He knelt beside her, awkwardly trying to brush the tears from her pale face. Her chest rose slowly, the only sign of life. He moved the lantern back into position beside her bed and then slowly lifted her into his arms.

He lay down on her bed, propping his back up against the side of the barge. He cradled her body in his arms. His sharp senses would give him ample warning of the captain's approach, though it was unlikely he would venture from the deck until morning.

He stared down at her tear-streaked face and marveled. She had found the courage to attack a man twice her size while trying to protect him. Deep down he had always believed that she would betray him at the earliest safe moment. She was, after all, a good woman, a creature of light. He was a creature of the darkness and no matter what uneasy alliance they had formed between them, light and dark could not long dwell together.

At the most he had hoped that she would not betray him, but would just leave him, fleeing during the day when she thought he could not follow. He wouldn't have blamed her if she had. It would be easier on both of them that way.

Now she had gone and done something for him that could never be taken back nor repaid. Even if he tried for a lifetime he couldn't save her from the pain and she had done it for his sake. He remembered the hatred in her eyes as she stared at him. She knew as well as he that her relationship with him had led her to do things she would never have dared dream about before. Sitting there in the darkness, holding her, he prayed for the first time in years. He prayed that she would forgive him.

The night wore on and she did not move. The boat finally entered still waters and it shook Gabriel out of his light doze. He waited, senses alert. At last he heard a splash and the barge rocked for a moment before settling. The captain had found a place to tie up. It might be another day before they moved again, depending on how fast the horse and man traveled.

At last he settled back again. He could hear the sound of distant snoring and knew that the captain had found some place on deck to sleep. Gabriel closed his eyes and let the darkness claim him.

Before dawn he was up though he left Carissa sleeping. He could hear excited arguing. He emerged from the cabin to see the captain trying to calm down his hired man.

"My brother would not fall off the barge!" the boatman shouted.

"There is no other explanation for it," the captain replied heatedly. "The river was rough last night."

"I think this creature that you're carrying did it," the boatman said, turning to Gabriel. "He is no priest, but a monster."

Gabriel saw Carissa emerge from the cabin. It was regrettable that she would have to see, but what he had to do could not be helped. Gabriel reached up and pulled back his hood. Both men facing him gasped and then Gabriel grabbed the boatman and tore out his throat. The man died, blood gurgling. He barely paused to taste the blood on his lips before sending his body to join that of his brother.

He saw Carissa collapse on her knees even as he turned to the captain. The man was pale and shaking. Gabriel grabbed him by the front of the shirt and forced him to meet his eyes.

"The two men you hired were murderers and thieves. They killed your passengers, a woman and a priest, and you had no choice but to kill them before they killed you. You will speak of this to no one. You don't need that much trouble."

The man nodded dumbly and then whispered, "I had to kill them, for the lady."

"Good, now go downstairs and clean up," Gabriel instructed him.

The man turned and went into the cabin, walking right by Carissa who stared at him uncomprehendingly. Gabriel pulled his hood back up over his head. Once the captain was out of sight, Gabriel crossed to Carissa. She shrank back from him and he cursed under his breath. There was no time for niceties, though. He reached down and picked her up, throwing her over his shoulder. His hand was exposed to the sunlight, but there was nothing he could do about that for the moment.

Carissa cried out and tried to struggle against him, but he silenced her with a stern word and a tone dripping with menace. He hated himself for it, but it, too, was necessary.

He measured the distance to the shore and then leaped off the boat, landing lightly upon solid ground. The horse looked up at him for only a moment before returning to its grazing. It was a good animal and it was a shame to leave it behind, but the captain had more need of him than they did. Besides, the animal wouldn't be as easy to return to a barge, which might be moored anywhere within several days' travel, as it had been to return the one to the innkeeper. He was a monster, but even he had limits. He couldn't bear to take a man's horse.

Carissa hung still on his shoulder and for a moment he thought she might have passed out again, but he could hear her breathing and it was far too fast and frightened.

Before the unfortunate arrival of the boatman, the captain had told Gabriel that there was a tiny village about a day's journey down the river from them. Gabriel began to run. With luck, they would be there before the sun could burn his hand.

On his shoulder, Carissa's body bumped and swayed. Her chin slammed against his ribs twice in a dozen strides. It was barely an annoyance to him, but he guessed that it was painful for her. He would have liked to stop and have her climb upon his back as she had before. He suspected, though, that she would not be in quite so tractable a mood, and he had no patience for a fight.

He began to regret that decision fifteen minutes later when he could hear her crying. He pressed on, though, grimly. He could see the village in the distance, though it was still too far for human vision to perceive. Five minutes later he felt her body go completely limp and he smelled blood.

Worried, he slowed and came to a stop. She didn't move and he could only barely feel the rise and fall of her chest against his shoulder. He bent and eased her down to the ground under a large tree.

Her face was covered with blood and he fell to the ground beside her in horror. Gently he tried to wipe the blood off with a hand that shook. Her chin, which had been banging against his back, had split open and the rest of her face was bruised almost beyond recognition. As fast as he wiped the blood away, more seeped back out.

He fought the urge to lick his fingers and instead wiped them upon the grass. Then he raised them toward his lips and spat upon them. He then moved the fingers gently across the open wound. The saliva caused the blood to congeal fast. It was a means of preserving the life of one he meant to feast upon another time. Within moments the blood had stopped flowing.

He stared down at her battered form and felt the greatest swell of pity and remorse that he had ever known. She had lost everything. She had been the very soul of beauty and purity and now she had been reduced to the pitiful creature that lay before him. He gently touched her bruises and wished for the power to make them whole, to make her whole. All he wanted was to restore to her everything that she had lost, and more, something wonderful to repay her for all the suffering. There was nothing, though, that he knew of that could repay it or even assuage it a little.

He thought of leaving her at the village for some kind person to find and care for. He knew, though, that she would as likely be found by some brute who would only inflict more pain upon her. Also, how could he abandon her before he had guaranteed that she would not be captured within the day and returned to the horror of the cell that they had shared? No, he had to help her, make it so that when he did leave her, she was in a position to never have to worry again.

Hardly knowing why, he bent down to kiss her. When he raised his lips, he wiped the blood from them without even tasting it.

CHAPTER TWENTY

And saith unto them, My soul is exceeding sorrowful unto death: tarry ye here, and watch.

—Mark 14:34

Pain exploded around Carissa as she woke and she cried out. She tried to open her eyes but her eyelids would not move. They felt hot and sticky and she wanted to lift her hands to feel them, but she could not move them either. She cried out again as terror filled her. She was in hell, she must be, after all, that was where murderers went. But if she was in hell, then she was dead and Gabriel was with her, for somehow, she could feel his presence.

A moment later, his hand touched her cheek, setting off a new spasm of pain. "It is all right," he said, his voice sounding rough.

"What has happened to me?"

"You were injured."

"I remember you were running, and I was on your back. Did I fall?"

"Not exactly," he said, hesitating slightly.

"Why can't I move my hands?" she asked.

"They have fallen asleep," he answered. "I will rub them to help the blood flow again."

She felt nothing for a minute and then pain swept through her right hand as it came searingly back to life. She gasped and he unceremoniously dropped her hand. She flexed the fingers, trying to make the tingling go away and just as she succeeded, she could suddenly feel her left hand as though it were consumed by fire. She gritted her teeth and hissed and he dropped that one, too.

She shook both hands until they felt normal and then gingerly lifted them to her face. Her eyelids felt sticky to the touch and there was a sharp pain in her temple when she touched her cheeks. Her chin was covered with what felt like crusted blood.

"The swelling is going down in your eyes, you'll be able to open them in a few more hours," he told her.

"Where are we?"

"Safe for a while," he answered.

She heard footsteps and then a woman's voice spoke. "There, there, lamb, we'll have you right as rain in no time."

Carissa stiffened. "Who?" she asked, uncertainty filling her.

"Tess is the local midwife. She knows a great deal about herbs and is helping to heal you."

The woman made a clucking sound. "I do as I can. You just relax and try to forget those villains that attacked you, miss. It's lucky for you a priest found you."

"What happened?"

"You and your escorts were set upon by thieves," Gabriel hastened to say. "I heard screaming and I came, but, alas, too late to save the others. I am sorry," he said, reaching out to squeeze her hand.

She nodded, though the motion sent fire along her skin. "All dead?" she asked, playing along with the charade he had chosen.

"Yes."

The tears came easily and she let them. There was so much to cry about besides the physical pain that it was no effort. The midwife made more clucking sounds and spread some foul-smelling pastes across Carissa's skin.

"It's all right, dovey. Here, I imagine you will be wanting to be alone for a while."

Carissa managed another nod, then as she heard two sets of footsteps retreating she called, "Father?"

"Yes, my child?" Gabriel asked.

"Would you stay and help me say some prayers?" She was sobbing now, wishing that Gabriel was a priest who could pray over her and absolve her of her sins.

"Of course, child," he answered.

"I'll just close the door, so you can have some privacy," the midwife said and Carissa could hear the compassion in her voice.

She felt Gabriel sit down beside her and take her hand again. She didn't know what to say and she gathered from his silence that neither did he. The touch of his hand was both welcome and repulsive to her. It was familiar and she desperately needed that, as well as the recalled moments of shared warmth and triumph that it brought. It also brought to mind, though, the memory of seeing him remove his hood and kill the boatman. That thought led her inescapably to the memory of killing the man's brother. She wept.

After it seemed like an eternity had passed her tears ceased and soon after Gabriel spoke. "What do you want me to say?" he asked.

"I'm not sure there's anything that you can say," she whispered, heartsick.

"Killing never gets easier, no matter how often you do it. That man was your first and you'll never forget how it felt, the loss of innocence, the power, the fear, the helplessness. God willing you'll never have to kill anyone again. Know this, though. What you did was right. The man was a thief and a murderer. After he had killed me he would have killed you, or worse."

He tightened his grip on her hand as though he knew what she was thinking.

"As much as you don't want to believe it, some people need killing."

"But what about grace?" she whispered.

"I figure grace is God's business, living is ours. If you hadn't done what you did, you wouldn't have been tending to our business, man's business, that of living."

"But you weren't even there, he wouldn't have killed you."

"Just because I wasn't in that bed doesn't mean that he wouldn't have killed me. I'm not entirely immortal, I can be killed, and he certainly knew one way to do it. No, I wasn't in that bed, but he might have still turned around and been able to stab me through the heart if we had fought. Because of you, we'll never know, so as far as I'm concerned, you saved my life. That makes twice."

"Twice?" she asked, shakily, wishing she could believe his words.

"Yes. I was starving to death in that cell and it was only a matter of time before they let me starve for good or killed me outright. You saved me by trusting in me, believing in me, by giving me your blood without reservations and then helping me to escape."

"You helped me to escape as well," she reminded him.

"Just because there was mutual benefit it doesn't diminish what you did. You did save me, Carissa, and as God is my witness, I will find a way to save you."

The tears began to flow again and she couldn't strangle back the sob that escaped her. She clung to his hand as though it were the only thing that could save her, the lifeline that would keep her from drowning. There in the dark, with only his voice to guide her, she searched her soul. She had killed a man, but had he not truly been worth killing? Was Gabriel right, that some people did deserve to die? Her husband thought so, she had thought so, until she was one marked to die. It was harder to judge others when she herself had been so cruelly misjudged. And yet, even then, had she not vowed to kill the man who had done so?

Still, in the darkness, she did know one thing. The boatman would have done his best to kill Gabriel. If she had to make the choice again, she would still kill him. It had been him or Gabriel and she knew that he was the one who had believed in her and helped save her. She would choose his life over any other's. She squeezed his hand and sobbed.

Within two days the midwife proclaimed Carissa fit to travel and it was with relief, tinged with a touch of sorrow, that she found herself once again on the move.

Gabriel had managed to procure them horses and they rode across the fields, the village slipping from sight. A few well-chosen words and well-placed coins had ensured the midwife's silence. In fact, the woman seemed not at all suspicious of them as they rode off, but cast only looks of pity upon Carissa. So, they were traveling again, the lady and her priest, or, as Carissa bitterly thought, the murderess and her monster.

She glanced back at the village before it was lost to sight, then shivered. Suddenly fearful she looked at Gabriel.

He had his head cocked to the side as though listening to something that the wind was whispering to him alone. She kept silent, not wanting to interrupt. At last he turned to her, a puzzled expression upon his face.

"What does the wind tell you?" she asked through lips that were still slightly swollen.

He smiled at her question and it warmed her. She hadn't seen him smile in days. The smile slowly faded though and the warmth it brought faded as well.

"We need to find some shelter soon," he said, glancing worriedly at the sky.

"We could have left at night."

"Not without drawing suspicion. We'll find a place to wait out the day and you can rest some more. We'll be traveling fast tonight."

"There's something else, what is it?"

"I'm not sure," he admitted. "But you are right, there is something."

He kicked his horse into a canter and she did the same. A dull ache spread through her ribs and she pressed her hand to her side. Apparently the bruises weren't all external. Fortunately they soon found what they were looking for. A small copse of trees stood, its shade inviting.

They reined in their horses. Gabriel dismounted and tied up his horse before helping her down. Normally she would have scorned a helping hand down from the saddle, but the pain in her ribs made her grateful for it.

After tying up her horse as well he helped her to a seat beneath an ancient-looking tree. "Try to get some rest," he instructed her.

"Only if you do," she countered.

He stood for a moment, features tense, and lips curled away from his fangs. Finally, he gave her a short nod and took a seat beside her. She let herself relax and put her head back against the rough bark of the tree. She didn't fight sleep as it overtook her.

Paris, Present Day

Notre Dame. It never failed to awe Raphael. He didn't know of a vampire who didn't feel that way in the presence of the great cathedral. He stood in the square in front of it, ignoring the beggars and pickpockets that surrounded him, preying on the tourists who had shown up to see sunrise at one of Paris's greatest landmarks. They all steered clear of him and they were wise to do so.

The cathedral reached toward the sky, terrible and beautiful. The sun would be up shortly and he needed to seek shelter. He briefly thought about concealing himself inside the cathedral itself. It would be too risky, though. If Gabriel had been there with his ability to wake while the sun was still up he would have chanced it.

He was a little concerned that his sire hadn't appeared or called. He couldn't help but wonder what was happening in Spain. Had Gabriel found Richelieu? If so, why hadn't he called?

As the sky lightened he realized there was no use conjecturing about it. It was time to sleep and when it was nighttime again he was sure to have word from Gabriel.

He retreated to a small hotel that catered mainly to artists and writers. They were more than happy to give him a room with blackout curtains. He wasn't the first eccentric night owl to stay there. He propped a chair under the doorknob, ensuring that no one could enter his room easily.

Even though the curtains completely blocked the light from outside it still worried him. With the sun pulling at him and moments to go before sleep claimed him he rolled under the bed, hoping that the extra protection was an unnecessary precaution.

FRANCE, AD 1198

Gabriel awoke and it was still light out. He was worried. There was a step on his trail, a shadow that moved just beyond the reach of his vision, and it was drawing nearer. He strained all his senses. At last in the distance he heard something, the pounding of horse's hooves.

He stood slowly, careful not to disturb Carissa. He took a step away from her to the edge of the shade. Her breathing and heartbeat sounded like thunder in his ears as he strained to keep hold of that other, elusive sound.

At last the rider came into view and his sense of foreboding increased. The horseman was coming from the direction of the village at a dead run. He glanced around and cursed their location. They were beneath the only stand of trees in sight. There was no other shade to be had and he had already spent too much time in the sun. He was trapped. As he watched the rider approach he began to breathe.

"What's going on?" Carissa asked, rousing from her sleep.

"Rider."

She sat up, the color draining from her face. "Who?"

"Don't know."

He could tell the moment the rider spotted them. There was a slight shift in his horse's gait. As he drew closer, he began to rein in his animal until he came to a stop twenty feet from them.

He stopped in the sun, Gabriel noted, well out of his reach. The man stepped from his horse in one fluid motion and took three quick strides forward.

"Greetings, stranger," Gabriel called. "My lady is taking a moment to rest herself from the midday sun."

"Perhaps milady is not the only one needing to hide from the sun," the man suggested, stepping even closer. He was now less than ten feet away.

"It is a warm day," Gabriel replied.

"Indeed."

"Can I do anything for you?" Gabriel asked when the other did not move.

"Yes. I am searching for someone."

"And who might that be?"

"Two escaped prisoners. A man and a woman. The man is actually something more, a kind of monster."

Gabriel crossed himself. "Then I shall pray that you find them quickly. Perhaps these are the same devils who beset my lady and her traveling companions."

"Yes, I heard about that unfortunate incident," the man replied thoughtfully, gazing at Carissa. He bowed to her. "My wishes for a speedy recovery."

"Thank you for your kindness," she replied and Gabriel was grateful for her cool head.

"Milady," the man said and then he nodded to Gabriel. He turned and walked back to his horse. He checked the saddle and then began to tighten the straps.

After a moment he turned back. "One other thing," he said.

"Yes?"

The man stepped clear of his horse and Gabriel saw a torch flare to life in his hand. He threw it through the air and it landed squarely in the branches of the largest tree. The branches caught fire and within moments it had spread to the others.

Gabriel cursed and leaped away, pulling the robe about his head and hands as he did so. He watched from under his hood as Carissa untied the frightened horses and led them out of danger. Then he turned his attention to the approaching stranger.

"What do you want?" Gabriel asked, circling him warily.

"Your heads, yours and the woman's."

"We've done nothing to you."

"That is true, but your deaths will mean my freedom."

"How can the deaths of a noblewoman and a simple priest achieve that?"

"If you are a priest, show your face," the man growled, advancing.

He had him trapped, and Gabriel knew it. "You would seem to know me, but I have not had the pleasure of making your acquaintance."

"All you need to know was that until a week ago I was also a prisoner. I sang every evening, I'm sure you remember."

Gabriel had heard the man's voice every night for years. "They called you the Baron."

"Yes."

"You were promised your freedom in exchange for finding us?"

"And killing you."

Gabriel gauged the ever-narrowing distance between them. He couldn't fight without exposing some part of his body to the sun. He could run and the odds were good he would be out of range before the man could throw the second piece of wood he just lit from the firepot his horse was carrying. That would leave Carissa at his mercy, though. There was no way he could carry her without putting them both at risk from the sun or the fire.

He snarled like the cornered animal he was, the sound wild even to his own ears. Then, swift as lightning, he made a decision. "Let her go and you can have me."

He heard Carissa cry out a protest.

The other man shook his head. "Sorry, see it's her that they really want."

"Her?"

"Yes, the marquis was quite insistent about that. He said I must kill her. In fact, he never said the same about you."

Gabriel and the Baron circled each other warily. The Baron held the torch in his right hand. Without warning he lunged forward and only Gabriel's speed saved him. The torch flashed past, just missing his robes. Then, swift as thought, the Baron turned and pulled a knife from his belt with two fingers. He threw it at Carissa.

Gabriel got there first and grunted in pain as the weapon lodged in his shoulder. He dared not risk exposing his hand, though, to reach up and pull it out. They were in trouble, and for the first time in five hundred years he was terrified.

I can't let her die, he realized. If nothing else she needed to escape.

"Get on your horse and ride," Gabriel hissed at her.

No sooner had he said it than Carissa was mounted and urging her horse forward. The Baron threw another knife and Gabriel took it in the chest before throwing himself forward.

PRAGUE, PRESENT DAY

"'Gabriel urged me to escape while he fought off our attacker,'" Wendy read. And Susan couldn't help but think how like Raphael that was. *Like sire, like sireling*, she thought.

Wendy put down the pages. "I've got to take a break," she said.

"Okay. I'm going to go check on Paul," Susan said, hastily standing and heading for the stairs.

In reality she just wanted to be alone with her thoughts. She was relating a little too much to Carissa's story about Gabriel. She wished she could know what Gabriel had been thinking and feeling during all the events that were happening.

Did he care about Carissa or was he just using her?

And next she thought grimly, *Does Raphael care about me or has he just been using me?*

By the time she made it to Paul's room she was in a dark mood. She crossed to the chair and flopped down in it. She fingered her cross necklace. She was going to have to call Pierre's office and see if her package had arrived yet. She was eager to know how her key ring could help her uncover the secret of the cross.

She glanced at Paul and then sat bolt upright. "Wendy!" she shouted.

She heard feet pounding up the stairs and moments later both Wendy and David appeared in the doorway.

"What is it?" David demanded. She realized suddenly that he had a stake in his hand. She blinked at it in surprise and then managed to point at the bed.

Wendy glanced down and gave out a little scream.

The few patches of skin that hadn't been burned had turned color from white to ash gray.

"Is he . . ."

"I don't know," Susan said, staring in horror. She reached out a hand and then pulled it back. She was afraid that if she touched him whatever was holding him together would give way and he would turn to ash in front of her eyes.

Wendy spun and buried her face in David's chest and began to cry. Susan could make out a few scattered words including " . . . helped Carissa."

Her cousin was right. Reading Carissa's account of her meeting with Paul had made her feel that much closer to the monk. She could feel herself shaking and she slid onto her knees next to the bed.

"Please, God, spare him. Bring him back to us," she prayed. "We need him."

A moment later she heard David add his own entreaties and then finally Wendy squeaked out a prayer around sobs.

Susan pulled her phone out of her pocket and dialed Raphael. It went to voicemail.

"It's me, call me please when you get this. Paul is worse. I don't know what to do," she said, her voice breaking. "Please, tell me what to do!"

She realized she was shouting the last. Too many hours trapped and helpless. And now this. It was too much.

She hung up with a sob and then tried Gabriel's phone. It, too, went to voicemail and she left a similar message. The sun would be rising soon so they probably wouldn't get the messages until nightfall.

But by then it could be too late.

"He was fine two hours ago," Wendy said.

"I know."

"We should keep watch," David suggested. "We can take turns. I'll go first."

"I can't sleep," Susan muttered.

"Neither can I." Wendy hiccupped.

"Then we can all stay."

Susan went and got two more chairs and placed them around the bed. She felt like they were keeping a death vigil. Every few moments she said a word of prayer over the still form on the bed.

"We have to try something," Susan said at last, standing.

"What do you have in mind?" David asked.

"When Raphael was injured fresh blood helped heal him faster."

"What?" Wendy asked, voice squeaky with fear.

"There are those blood packets downstairs. I'm going to get one and try feeding it to him," Susan declared.

She left the room and rushed downstairs, eager to act now that the decision had been made. Gabriel hadn't wanted to touch Paul to feed him, but given that Paul seemed to be worse she felt like they really had nothing to lose.

She grabbed one of the packets of blood from the refrigerator and also grabbed scissors and some paper towels. She ran back upstairs. Once there she opened the blood packet with the scissors. Paul's lips were parted slightly.

"I don't know how to pour it in his mouth without having it run everywhere," she admitted.

"Just do what you can," David urged. "And hurry."

She tipped the packet over and a stream of blood spilled down. It splashed on the monk's lips and then she steadied her hand so that it was pouring straight into his mouth. She emptied the entire bag and then wrapped it in one of the paper towels and stared intently.

Nothing.

She didn't know what she had been expecting, but there seemed to be no change. She couldn't even see him swallow. After a minute she took the bag back downstairs and tossed it in the trash. When she returned there was still no difference. Feeling defeated, she sat down in her chair to wait and watch with the others.

After about a half hour Wendy went downstairs. When she returned she had the diary in her hands.

"You don't have to translate," Susan said.

"Yes, I do. I can't just sit here like a vulture. I have to *do* something."

And because Susan completely understood that feeling she nodded and leaned over to squeeze Wendy's hand.

Wendy found her place and began. "'My terror was great as I kicked my horse away from Gabriel and the man who had come for us.'"

FRANCE, AD 1198

Carissa twisted in her saddle. She saw Gabriel lunge at their attacker, as the man drew a weapon concealed in his belt behind him. A moment later, though, she saw the man bury a stake in Gabriel's chest. Time seemed to stop and then Gabriel crumpled to the ground.

"No!"

She started to rein in her horse to go back. *He died because of me*, she thought despairingly. *No, not because of me,* for *me. I can't let his sacrifice be meaningless.*

She turned away and kicked her horse into a dead run. The wind whipped past her face, stinging her eyes and roaring so loudly in her ears that she knew she wouldn't hear the sounds of pursuit until it was too late. *God, let my horse be faster*, she prayed. She glanced back once and saw her pursuer. She urged her mount to even greater speed.

Carissa nearly went flying as her horse stumbled. She managed to hang on though as the animal regained its footing. The mare was reaching the end of her strength. At last she spied some trees in the distance and she urged the weary horse onward.

When she reached the edge of the forest, she turned her horse's head and plunged off the path into the underbrush. She pulled the horse to a slower gait as they wove through the trees. Finally she reined the animal to a stop and listened for sounds of pursuit.

Only the sounds of the forest greeted her ears. After a minute she slid off her horse's back and the weary animal groaned. *This must be what the fox feels as he runs from the hounds*, she thought. She tied the horse to a tree and moved slowly back the way she had come, stopping every few steps to listen.

At last, she turned back to her horse, loosened the girth on the saddle, but did not take it off, and sank wearily to the ground. Her thoughts turned to Gabriel and she began to weep. He had saved her life numerous times and the last time it had been at the cost of his own. It was a debt that could never be repaid. More than that, she realized she had come to depend on him, and that he was one of the only true friends she had ever known. Her husband had taken even that from her.

When her tears had dried she began to think about the future. Continuing on to Avignon was futile. She would find no aid there. She could turn back and ask for Paul's help, but he had been helping Gabriel and not her and there was no reason to believe that with Gabriel dead there was anything he could or would do for her. There was no help to be found at the palace for who would take her word over that of her husband? Lastly she thought of the assassin following her. He might expect her to do any of those things. There was, however, one place he would be unlikely to look for her.

By the time she had made up her mind the sun had faded. She stood and unsaddled the mare and led her to some water. She stroked the horse's nose. "It's you and me now. Together we're going to end this. We're going to Bryas."

CHAPTER TWENTY-ONE

But thou shalt surely kill him; thine hand shall be first upon him to put him to death, and afterwards the hand of all the people.

—Deuteronomy 13:9

On the outskirts of Oviedo Gabriel finally caught up with his prey. He leaped from the top of a building down onto the vampire running through the alleyway below.

The vampire fell with a grunt and Gabriel flipped him over in one swift move and put a stake to his chest. The cloak the other was wearing fell away from him and the first rays of the sun caused him to scream in fear.

After killing the drug dealer Gabriel's body had knit and his mind had cleared. He had realized that someone other than the vampires who had attacked him must have removed the relic from the cathedral before he had gotten there.

He had circled back and picked up the vampire's trail and now he had him.

It wasn't Richelieu. In fact, his teeth were tiny stubs in the sunlight and his eyes flashed with the kind of terror and confusion most common to young vampires.

Worse yet, he didn't have the artifact on him.

"Where is it?" Gabriel demanded, pressing more firmly down on the stake.

"I don't have it!"

"I already know that. What I asked was, where is it?"

"I have no idea. There was nothing there in the church. I couldn't find anything."

The young vampire's skin began to smoke. He hadn't conditioned himself to be in the sun for very long, as Gabriel had.

"Where's Richelieu?" Gabriel demanded, changing tactics.

"I don't know."

He pressed the stake in deeper, drawing blood, which filled the air around them with a pungent, coppery smell.

"I told you, I don't know! Please, I don't want to burn!"

Unfortunately, Gabriel believed him. It just wasn't the answer he wanted. He growled deep in his throat, impatient.

"How many others like you are going after the relics?"

"I don't know."

It was the truth again, he could read it in his mind.

"What else can you tell me?" Gabriel asked.

"Nothing, I know nothing more."

"Too bad for you."

"Mercy," the vampire begged.

If there was one thing Gabriel had learned in all his years, though, it was to kill your enemies. If you let them live they'd come back to haunt you later.

FRANCE, AD 1198

Gabriel lay as though dead. His chest felt like it was on fire where the stake had been driven into it. Still, the Baron had missed his heart and so he was still alive. He could smell the stench of garlic and it was nearly enough to make him gag, but he hadn't yet located the source. He watched the Baron through his eyelashes as the man circled warily, checking for signs of life. Even though he had the proper tools to hunt a vampire Gabriel could tell that he had never killed one.

He strained his ears but could no longer hear the sound of Carissa's horse. His own horse was too far away to be of any immediate help. He waited until the Baron had retrieved his sword from its scabbard on his saddle. Gabriel forced himself to remain motionless as the man took up position and prepared to cut off his head. The sword swung up, the sun glinted off the metal and then began to descend.

Gabriel waited and then at the last moment rolled away. He jumped to his feet and grabbed the Baron's horse. His hands started to blister as he sunk his fangs into the terrified creature's throat. A moment later his hands stopped burning and he spun to face the Baron, allowing his hood to fall back. He pulled the stake free from his chest and hurled it as far away as he could. Then he lunged forward.

The Baron turned to run but hadn't taken more than a step when Gabriel grabbed him. He twisted his head sideways and was about to rip his throat out when his hands began to burn and he felt suddenly sick. He released the Baron and leaped back.

The man straightened. "I took the precaution of sprinkling holy water on myself a few minutes ago. I've also been eating garlic for the last few days almost nonstop. I think between the two you won't be wanting a taste of my blood. Wish I'd thought to do it for the horse," he said with a short laugh.

Gabriel reached for the sword the Baron had dropped, but stopped, his fingers hovering above it. "Oh, yes, anything you could use as a weapon also got the holy water and garlic treatment," the Baron said with a smirk, confirming his suspicions.

"It would seem we are at an impasse," Gabriel said.

The Baron shook his head. "Only for a few minutes. And even if you take all the blood that horse has, do you really think you can make it to sundown?"

Gabriel glared at him. Already the sun was making him intensely uncomfortable. He had already been overexposed to the sun and he could tell he wasn't going to get as much time from the horse's blood as he might otherwise have.

"You know, if I were you, I'd run. You're free, leave this place and never look back," Gabriel suggested.

"Unfortunately, I cannot return to Germany under the current circumstances," the Baron said.

"There are many places in this world you could be other than Germany and France."

"Maybe for some, but not for me."

"In a few weeks' time I may be in a position to help you," Gabriel said.

"Sorry, I don't trust you and nothing will change that.

The way I see it there's going to be a death right here, right now. It might be you, it might be me, but that's a chance I'll have to take."

Gabriel thought of Carissa and realized it wasn't a chance he could take. "There's a third possibility you didn't think about," Gabriel said.

"And what would that be?"

Gabriel move liked lightning and before the Baron could react his horse slumped to the ground, dead. Gabriel wiped the blood from his lips. He gave the Baron a small smile as the man cursed. Then he ran to his own horse, leaped into the saddle and took off after Carissa.

"This isn't over!" he heard the Baron shouting behind him.

He rode with the robe shielding his body from the sun but his blistered hands hadn't yet healed and the pain of it tore at him more with each passing minute. At one point he thought he saw a rider ahead but a moment later there was nothing but empty road again.

He turned and saw a small run-down building a ways off the road. He turned his horse and made for its shelter. They were not far from Avignon and he prayed Carissa could find her way safely to the castle.

PRAGUE, PRESENT DAY

Susan watched as Wendy folded the parchment back up and stuffed it back inside the diary.

"What else does it say?" David asked.

"There's nothing more on the parchment, but it looks like there's a lot more in the diary," Wendy said with a shake of her head. "I'm too tired, though. I can't translate anymore."

Susan felt deep disappointment but she couldn't blame Wendy for stopping. The story alone was emotionally taxing let alone the work of translating it for them. That coupled with the stress of keeping vigil over Paul had to be overwhelming. If she had a splitting headache she could only imagine how Wendy felt.

She picked up her cross and stared at it some more. Bryas. Carissa had decided to head to Bryas.

And Susan had been there, walked its hallways, slept in a bedroom, what might have been *her* bedroom. She'd been in its dungeon. And in that dungeon she'd had the secret of the cross in her hand.

David agreed to stay awake and watch over Paul while they got some sleep. He promised to wake her if there was any change. Working with vampires had their sleep schedules all messed up. Susan lay awake in the master bedroom long after Wendy had begun to snore beside her.

What is it about this cross? she wondered.

And then her thoughts turned to Raphael. Carissa had written about overhearing Gabriel and Paul discuss him. He had actually set himself up as a tribal god? She shook her head. And apparently Paul had set him on fire.

And because of Raphael and his battle with Richelieu, Paul is now burned and hovering on the point of death.

It was a strange world.

When she finally slipped into sleep she dreamed about Carissa and Fleur.

She woke just after noon and checked in on David, relieving him of duty. She placed a call to Pierre's office. His secretary informed her that a package had arrived for her that morning and she could stop by in the early evening to pick it up.

Susan wasn't thrilled with the idea of being out after dark, but beggars couldn't be choosers. She'd been hoping she could just pick up the package and run, but the secretary had said that the attorney wanted to speak with her, and had clients scheduled all day long.

Her last conversation with Pierre had been unnerving to say the least. But if it weren't for him she wouldn't know nearly as much as she did about her grandmother and the legacy she had left her.

Wendy got up a couple of hours later. They ate a late lunch and talked together quietly. Paul's condition seemed unchanged. David woke just before it was time for Susan to leave.

Wendy offered to go with her, but Susan insisted she stay with David and Paul. After a moment's thought, she also left the cross necklace with Wendy who dutifully put it on. She left while the sun was still up. She walked a couple of blocks and then called for a cab.

"You're early," the secretary noted disapprovingly when she arrived. He escorted her into a waiting room where there were already two other people.

"Sorry, just didn't want to be late," Susan said, unwilling to explain her real reason for being there when she was.

After about half an hour the other two people were called away. She checked her phone every two minutes just to make sure she hadn't missed a call from Raphael or Gabriel.

Just calm down, she told herself. But she was digging her nails into the palm of her hand and her other hand ached because she was clutching the phone too tightly. Susan waited another twenty minutes and then the secretary came to get her. The man escorted her into the same old-fashioned office that she had been in before.

A man was standing with his back to the door. He turned slowly. He had long, blond hair that brushed his shoulders and he wore an expensive tailored suit.

"I will see you later," Pierre said, effectively dismissing him.

The stranger inclined his head and swept by Susan, giving her the faintest of smiles. There was something unnervingly familiar about him but she couldn't place his face.

The door closed behind him and Pierre rose with a smile and came around the desk to shake her hand. "It is an honor to see you again," he said.

"Thank you, it's good to see you as well. Who was that gentleman?" she asked, unable to stop herself.

"A colleague. We were just discussing a business venture."

He waved her to a seat and she sat after only a moment's hesitation. "Are you still enjoying your time in Prague?" he asked.

Susan glanced up at the portrait of her grandmother that was on the wall then forced her eyes back to Pierre. "Yes, although, I did take a short trip to France."

"Ah, did you go to see your holdings in Bryas?" he asked.

"Yes."

"And how did you find the property there?" he asked.

"In serious need of repair," she said. "If it was restored, though, I think it would be a magnificent castle."

"I am sure it would be," he said with a smile. "If there's any way in which my firm can assist you with that, please do not hesitate to let us know."

"I will certainly keep that in mind."

"And now I think you are here to pick up a package," he said with a smile.

"Yes, thank you."

"It's no problem," he said, moving over to the safe in the corner of the room.

"You put it in the safe?" she asked, somewhat surprised.

He glanced at her. "You had a package sent to an attorney's office from your home country. I assumed it was important."

She bit her lip. "Thank you. I appreciate your thoughtfulness."

He spun the dials and then opened the door and pulled out a padded envelope. She stood up and went to take it from him.

The envelope was scuffed in a few places from having come halfway around the world. She turned it over and froze for a moment. It was sealed, but there was no extra tape on it. Her aunt always put a piece of tape on these kinds of envelopes, just like her grandmother had done.

"Anything wrong?" Pierre asked.

Was she imagining it or was there a slight edge to his voice? She remembered the last time she'd been in his office, how disappointed he'd been that she wasn't wearing her cross necklace. She'd lied to him and told him she had left it back home in California. *And not long after that someone broke into my apartment and ransacked it. Were they looking for the necklace?*

"No, it's fine," she lied again.

"If I may be so bold, what is it that you had sent here?" he asked.

"My house keys," Susan said.

"Excuse me?" he asked, looking puzzled.

"My apartment was broken into while I've been gone and they had to change the lock. My aunt sent me my new keys so that when I go home I don't have to have someone let me in."

"Oh. I am, of course, deeply sorry to hear that you've had trouble. Nothing was taken, I hope."

Susan forced herself to smile at him. "The police are still trying to figure that out."

"Of course. Well, if there's any way I can be of assistance, please let me know."

"I will, and thank you for this," Susan said, eager to get out now that she had what she'd come for.

"Why don't you just check and make sure that she sent you the keys you need," he said.

He doesn't believe me, he thinks it's the necklace, she thought. She didn't know how she knew but that inner voice that had prompted her before in times of crisis now urged her to be very, very careful.

She ripped open the envelope, praying he couldn't see the way her hands were shaking. She reached in and pulled out the key ring, relieved that there were actually keys attached to it.

"Just what I needed," she said, faking a smile.

The smile he gave her in return didn't reach his eyes.

Her hand was on the door when he spoke again. "Oh, Miss Lambert?"

She turned, every muscle tense, ready to yank open the door and run if she had to.

"Do let me know if you ever need help getting rid of a vampire. I know people who specialize in such things. Please remember that."

"I'll remember."

Was he threatening Raphael? When she had first met him they had spoken of Raphael and the existence of vampires. Pierre had expressed concern, told her that Raphael was a monster.

Should I have listened to him? she wondered for a moment.

She left the building quickly and once outside she breathed a little easier. She'd had the most uncanny feeling when she was in there. It seemed to her that somehow the fact that her apartment had been robbed wasn't a surprise to him.

Could Pierre have had something to do with it? And if so, why?

He wanted the necklace. It didn't make any sense, but she was glad she'd listened to that inner prodding and left it with Wendy.

Now she was anxious to get back to them both. She just hoped that the key ring would actually shed some light on the whole mystery. She started to drop it in her purse and then, remembering the way her carry-on had been snatched at the airport, she shoved the key ring into the front pocket of her jeans instead.

Somewhere a car backfired and she jumped at the sound. She glanced uneasily around. *I'm not out of the woods yet.* She may have gotten out of Pierre's office but she had walked into the night and the street was dark enough and the shadows thick enough to hide all manner of evil that might be waiting for her.

Anxiety washed over her as she headed to the corner, hoping to hail a cab. She had been foolish not to pay the driver who had dropped her off to wait for her. She twisted around every few feet, convinced that someone, some*thing*, was following her.

She should never have let Raphael go with Gabriel and leave them all unprotected. She walked faster. Her breath came in short gasps.

When a man stepped out into her path she veered and let out a stifled cry.

The guy said something to her she couldn't understand and kept walking. She leaned against the building next to her and tried to catch her breath. A hand descended on her shoulder and she screamed in earnest, spinning on her heel. She took a step back and tripped over something. She landed hard on her back. A figure leaned over her. She brought her hands up, wishing she had brought a stake with her.

"Are you all right?"

A man's face came into focus and she recognized him as the one who had been meeting with Pierre.

"F-fine," she stammered.

He was reaching down a hand to her. Warily she took it and he helped her to her feet.

Standing upright once more she felt foolish and embarrassed. "Thank you," she said stiffly.

"Not at all. Can I walk you to your car?"

"I just need a taxi," she said.

"I would be happy to drive you home."

"No!" she said, instantly regretting the fervor with which she said it.

He smiled. "As you wish. I will help you get a taxi."

Five minutes later they parted ways as Susan settled into the back of a taxi. She waited until the door was closed and they had pulled away from the curb before giving her driver the address. She had no reason to distrust the blond stranger other than that he had been meeting with Pierre. But she stared out at the darkness as they drove, searching it for anything that might want to find her, hurt her. Because there were creatures out there hunting her still.

Is it being paranoid when people really are out to get you?

CHAPTER TWENTY-TWO

And he shall dwell in that city, until he stand before the congregation for judgment, [and] until the death of the high priest that shall be in those days: then shall the slayer return, and come unto his own city, and unto his own house, unto the city from whence he fled.

—Joshua 20:6

As soon as Susan left Wendy had gone downstairs. David was praying over Paul. She had run out of things to say, repeating herself over and over in her prayers for him. She was still feeling like she needed to *do* something, but she didn't want to pick up in the diary without Susan being there. She fingered the cross necklace, frustrated that she didn't know its secrets. She wished she was with Raphael and Gabriel, hunting down the relics.

It would be dangerous and I would be so terrified, but anything has to be better than this. Waiting for Paul to die. Waiting for Richelieu to find us and kill us.

She sighed and sat down at the computer. A web page was still up with some of Susan's search results for relics. She clicked a few links. It was fascinating reading.

She hit Google and started a new search and began to scroll through the pages of information, quickly becoming absorbed in what she was reading.

And then she found something she had never expected to find.

Wendy stared at the computer screen in disbelief. Half a dozen emotions flashed through her one after another.

The front door opened and she jerked her head around and then relaxed slightly when she saw Susan. Moments later David was walking downstairs.

"You're back," he said, sounding as relieved as she felt.

"Yes," Susan said, sounding somewhat breathless.

"Hey guys," Wendy said. "Anyone ever hear of the Sudarium of Oviedo?"

Susan and David exchanged blank glances and then he shook his head. "No, what is it?"

"It's like a sister to the Shroud of Turin. It's the separate cloth that was wrapped around Jesus' head when they were taking Him down from the cross."

"Are you serious?" Susan asked.

"Deadly serious," Wendy confirmed. "It has blood-stains that match up with those on the shroud."

"Wait, are you saying this could be one of the relics Richelieu is going after?" David asked.

Wendy spun around in her chair and faced them. "No, I'm saying this is *the* relic he's going after." She was gratified when they both looked stunned. "It normally resides in the cathedral in Oviedo, Spain, but it's currently on tour to raise awareness and support."

"Where is it now?" David asked.

Wendy felt a grin spreading across her face. "That's the best part. It's here in Prague. It goes on display tonight."

Susan sat down on the couch. "You're sure?" she asked, voice barely a whisper.

"Positive." Wendy glanced from one to the other. She

could see them thinking hard, but neither was saying anything. She had expected a little more than silence. "So, what do we do about it?"

"We get to it before Richelieu or his minions can," David said, face pale but voice ringing with conviction.

"What if he's been here all along, waiting for this relic to come to him?" Susan asked. "What if he sent Raphael and Gabriel away on a wild-goose chase?"

David shook his head. "I don't know if that was his plan but we have to assume he knew about this." He turned to look at Wendy and his eyes seemed to practically glow with intensity. "You're sure there's blood on it?"

"Yes."

"But how can we know if the relic is real, that it's *His* blood?" Susan argued.

Wendy took a deep breath. "I don't think the question is whether or not it's real. The important question is whether or not Richelieu believes it could be real."

"We can't afford to assume he won't," David said. "We have to go, tonight."

"And do what?" Susan asked. "Steal it before he can? That's a bit out of our league."

David took a deep breath. "We're not going to steal it but we can be there in case he tries to."

"Why, so he can kill us? Two birds with one stone?" Susan demanded.

Wendy reached out and put her hand on Susan's arm. Her cousin was shaking.

"What's wrong? I would have thought you would have been on our side in this."

"And I would have thought you'd already be a continent away," Susan snapped.

Wendy jerked back, feeling the color rise in her cheeks.

"I'm sorry," Susan said quickly, reaching out to grab her hand. Tears sparkled in her eyes. "It's just, I know what these monsters are capable of. That day in the palace…"

Wendy squeezed her hand. Susan had only told her a little of what had happened but clearly the images that the Raider had put in her head had scarred her deeply. "Some things are worth fighting for, no matter what the cost. You taught me that." Wendy reached out with her free hand and took David's hand. "You both did," she said, glancing meaningfully at him.

"If there's even the slightest chance that this cloth is real we can't risk Richelieu getting his hands on it," David said.

"You're both right," Susan admitted. "What's the plan?"

Wendy glanced at the time on the computer. "I think we'll have to come up with one in the car. We need to get there soon."

"Give me a minute," Susan said, standing swiftly and heading to the stairs.

"Sure," Wendy said, looking up at David. "I think we could all use a minute," she whispered.

Upstairs Susan splashed some cold water on her face before depositing her purse in the room she was sharing with Wendy. She fished her keys out of her pocket and put them in the purse with regret. She wanted to see how the key ring could reveal the secret of her cross necklace, but that was clearly going to have to wait.

She pulled her cell out of her purse and hastily called Raphael.

"Hello?"

The sound of his voice took her breath away. She squeezed her eyes shut. "It's me," she whispered, knowing he'd have no problem hearing her.

"Are you all right?" he asked, his voice swiftly taking on a hard edge.

"No," she croaked around the lump in her throat.

"What's happened? Is Paul dead?"

"No." She took a steadying breath. He had got her message then. She felt a surge of anger. Why hadn't he called her back?

"We found something. A relic, the Sudarium of Oviedo. It's a cloth that's supposed to have the blood of Christ on it. It's on a touring exhibit and it's in Prague tonight."

"No."

"Yes. David, Wendy, and I are going to see it, to see if...if Richelieu..." She trailed off.

"Susan, don't go, it's too dangerous."

"It's too dangerous to let him get his hands on it."

"Where's it going to be?"

"St. Vitus Cathedral." The place where they had first met. The place where the shadow of darkness had first fallen across her life. The place where she had prayed and reflected on the power of the blood of Christ as she knelt in a pool of red light that had been pouring through one of the stained-glass windows. She wasn't sure if the irony made her want to laugh or cry.

"Susan, I'm on my way. I'll be there as soon as I can, I promise," he said.

He hung up and she stared at the phone. "Hurry, please."

* * *

Raphael was standing inside Notre Dame, staring at the alcove where people lit candles to pray for their dead loved ones. He'd been pondering whether or not it would be appropriate to light one for Paul. He hung up and turned around to see Gabriel standing behind him. He jerked in surprise. He could tell from the look on his sire's face that he had heard every word.

"Where have you been?" he snapped.

"He never had to go to the relics, he just had to wait for the one to come to him," Gabriel said. "He played us for fools. We're over five hundred miles away."

"We'll have to fly," Raphael said grimly. "And we'll have to hurry."

Susan hung up and forced herself to walk back downstairs.

The other two were standing by the door, faces drawn but determined.

"I've loaded David up with weapons," Wendy said. "But I saved some for you."

She held out a stake, a vial of holy water, and a handful of crosses. Susan took them and concealed them in her pockets. Wendy reached up and started to remove the cross necklace. Susan held up a hand to stop her. Wendy hadn't fought a vampire before. Of all of them she was the most vulnerable and she would never forgive herself if something happened to her.

"Keep it, please. Just for tonight. It would make me feel better."

"Are you sure?" Wendy asked.

"Yes."

"Okay. Thank you."

Susan nodded, not trusting her voice at that moment. She just prayed they all survived the night.

They walked outside. They went a few blocks, this time in a different direction than she'd taken earlier, before calling a taxi. It dropped them a block away from the entrance to the cathedral. Thinking of her earlier regret, Susan thought about paying him to wait, but had no idea how long that would be. Plus, there were a number of cabs waiting in the area. It looked like the unveiling of the relic was going to be the hot ticket in town that night.

She wished she could believe that a bigger crowd meant safety. But it would be too easy for a vampire to kill them and be gone before their bodies even hit the floor with that many people around.

The cathedral had mercifully been nowhere near the part of Prague Castle that had been burned. Still she couldn't help but remember that other night.

As though sensing her unease David reached out and squeezed her shoulder. She gave him a fleeting smile. He was walking hand-in-hand with Wendy. At least if they died tonight they would be together.

Raphael, where are you?

She forced herself to take a deep breath as they joined the stream of people heading into the cathedral. Most of them were there as an act of faith, of worship. Many clutched Bibles and crosses. The sight of so many crosses helped her relax a little. Wouldn't it be easier, and less dangerous, for Richelieu to wait until the cathedral had closed for the night before trying to steal the cloth?

But with the next breath she tensed up again as she reminded herself that she wasn't there with the other worshippers. She was there to stop Richelieu from stealing the relic. Which meant she had to find a way to stay even after the cathedral closed if he hadn't shown himself yet.

Surely Raphael will make it back here before then. He will, he must, find a way.

Inside the cathedral the relic was on display behind the altar. Susan, Wendy, and David joined the line of people waiting their turn to see it. As they inched forward she tried to look at everyone around her. She wished she'd made Raphael give her a better physical description of Richelieu so she'd know him on sight.

"It's going to be okay," David whispered.

She wanted to ask him in what reality things would be okay, but she didn't.

The line moved so slowly she wanted to scream. Around her there were people praying, talking in hushed tones. She wanted to warn them that their lives were in danger just by being there.

But would it even matter? Some people could have been waiting their whole lives to see something like this. She glanced at Wendy. Her cousin only had eyes for David.

He's here. That's what's making her strong.

They were finally nearing the front of the line. The closer she got the more terrified she was.

And then suddenly she was the front of the line. She stepped forward and saw the cloth that everyone was there to stare at. And she felt power coming from it.

It washed over her and her memories of that first time in the cathedral combined with it. Peace swept through her blood and bones. It was as though God Himself were whispering in her ear that everything was going to be okay.

And she wanted to believe that more than anything.

After a moment David nudged her. She opened her eyes and turned to look at him. He raised an eyebrow and she nodded slightly. She'd forgotten not everyone could feel the things she did.

Yet another legacy from her grandmother that she didn't fully understand.

They shuffled to the side and sat in some extra chairs that had been set up for the occasion. Some people were lingering after seeing the cloth close up while others were leaving. From where she was sitting Susan could see them all.

What she wouldn't be able to see was someone moving with vampiric speed. But there was nothing she could do about that.

She sat, silent, watching and waiting for what seemed forever. When she glanced at her watch she realized that only a half hour had passed. The cathedral would be open for just over another hour. Then it would reopen in the morning.

Her eyes wandered over the line and she did a double take when she actually recognized someone. She watched as Pierre slowly shuffled forward with everyone else, hands clasped behind his back. When he finally stood in front of the sudarium, he leaned forward, entire body tense. He seemed to be committing it to memory. When he finally turned away a single tear was rolling down his cheek.

It startled her. She couldn't have said why but she hadn't thought of him as a particularly religious man. He looked lost in thought as he walked her way. She debated whether she should say anything and then she remembered that Wendy was wearing the cross, the one she didn't want him to know was here in Prague.

She ducked her head, watching his shoes. They drew opposite her and then suddenly paused. She winced.

"Susan?"

She looked up slowly, feigning surprise. Maybe he'd think she'd been praying instead of avoiding him. "Hello, Pierre."

Out of the corner of her eye she saw David and Wendy exchange significant looks.

"It's good to see you," he said, the ghost of a smile on his face. His eyes were still glassy, as though he were somewhere far away. He turned his head slightly and his eyes slid from her to Wendy and something changed suddenly in his face. His body jerked violently.

"Carissa?" he asked, voice wondering.

Wendy looked at her, eyes wide in panic.

"This is my cousin, Wendy," Susan hastened to say. She stood, putting herself between the two of them, hoping he hadn't realized what necklace Wendy was wearing.

"And our friend, David."

"Pleased to meet you," David said, also standing and blocking Pierre's view of Wendy.

Pierre shook his hand but didn't even seem to notice him otherwise.

"Is everything—" Pierre stopped and shook his head sharply. "My apologies. I didn't mean to interrupt your meditations."

"It's all right," Susan said. "It was good to see you. Have a nice evening."

"You, too."

He turned and headed toward the back of the cathedral.

After he was out of sight Susan sunk back down in her chair. Her stomach was clenched in knots.

"Why would he call me Carissa?" Wendy whispered.

"I don't know," Susan admitted. "From his reaction he's clearly seen a portrait of her. Maybe the same one I have."

"Maybe he thought I was her, changed into a vampire," Wendy said, trying to joke.

Her heart was still racing and Susan couldn't bring herself to smile. After another minute David sat down again as well.

The next hour crawled by and Susan found her mind drifting. Every time she'd force herself to focus back on the task at hand. She was tired. The days of terror and uncertainty had taken their toll. She checked her phone but there were no messages. She prayed that the nightmare would soon be over.

And where will that leave you and Raphael? Over as well?

She gritted her teeth. A couple of days away from him had not made anything clearer in that respect.

Ten minutes until the cathedral was scheduled to close and the crowd had thinned out considerably. There were only a few people still waiting in line. The cloth would be on display at St. Vitus Cathedral for another two weeks according to the sign she had seen out front. There was plenty of time for the faithful to see it.

Plenty of time for Richelieu to steal it.

The final minutes passed, each second slower than the one before. At last it was time to go. A priest stepped forward.

"The cathedral is closed now. You can come back tomorrow to see. We will open at eight in the morning."

"Thank you," Susan said, standing slowly.

He nodded and walked toward the back of the cathedral.

"What are we going to do?" David whispered.

"I don't know. I don't think there's any way we can hide ourselves in here."

"So, what, keep vigil outside?"

She turned, ready to leave. "I don't—"

A man had just entered the back of the cathedral and was walking forward with slow, measured steps.

She shouldn't have worried about recognizing Richelieu because even from sixty feet away she could feel the evil coming off him.

She reached out and grabbed David's arm. He turned and saw the direction of her stare. He reached a hand to the back of his waistband where she knew he had stakes concealed beneath the jacket he was wearing.

All the priests were at the back of the cathedral, escorting people out. The three of them were all that stood between Richelieu and the Sudarium of Oviedo.

"What now?" David whispered.

They were out of time and as much as she wished Raphael was there, he wasn't. She put her hand inside her pocket, wrapping her hand around the stake inside it.

"Follow my lead," she whispered back.

She began to walk up the center aisle, on a collision course with the vampire. It was like some insane game of chicken.

Forty feet.

Thirty.

The distance between them closed dizzyingly fast.

Twenty.

She could hear David and Wendy walking a few steps behind her.

Ten.

She forced herself to make eye contact with the monster.

Five feet.

She smiled even though his presence was making her stomach roil.

Three.

The soul of darkness smiled back at her.

Two.

One.

His shoulder brushed hers as she passed him.

She paused, then spun, raising the stake in her hand.

He turned around and plucked it from her hand before she knew what was happening.

"Sloppy," he said. "Did you think I wouldn't recognize you?"

And without looking he knocked the stake out of David's hand as he rushed him from behind.

"Any of you?" Richelieu said, swiveling his head to include them all in his stare.

Wendy grabbed a fistful of crosses and swung them at him. But he wasn't standing where he had been a moment before. Instead he was behind Wendy, an arm wrapped around her waist and the stake he had taken from Susan in his hand.

"You, Susan, are valued by Raphael. That means that you will be the instrument of his destruction. But your little cousin here—"

He stopped suddenly and his eyes narrowed to slits. "What have we here?"

And she realized that he was staring at the cross neck-lace.

"Interesting," he said, as if to himself.

With a shout David lunged forward and shoved a cross in Richelieu's face. The vampire had been so intent on the necklace that it caught him by surprise. He roared, and tossed Wendy into a row of chairs like she was a rag doll.

Susan ran forward and hurled her vial of holy water at Richelieu. It struck his shoulder and shattered. A moment later she could see smoke rising from his clothes where the holy water was burning through them.

He ripped off his jacket and hurled it at David's face.

David batted it away and pursued, stake in hand. Susan grabbed another stake from David's waistband and they both approached the vampire.

He recovered before they could close on him, though, and with a laugh snapped his fingers in the air.

A man dressed as a priest appeared from the wings of the cathedral. He was wearing gloves and quickly rolled the cloth into a small tube.

"No!" Susan shrieked and ran forward to stop him.

As she passed Richelieu he backhanded her and she went flying several feet through the air. She crashed to the ground, landing on her left knee with a cry of pain. She forced herself to a sitting position just in time to see David jab Richelieu with a stake. The weapon made contact but it was too high up and Richelieu pulled it easily out of his shoulder.

It had gotten his attention, though, and he was now fo-cused on David. Which left Susan free to go after the relic. She tried to stand and quickly realized the knee wouldn't take weight. She crawled across the floor, dragging her one leg behind her.

She reached the altar and the priest turned to look down at her. His eyes were wide, vacant. He had been mesmerized. He was holding the tube containing the Sudarium of Oviedo. She knew she wasn't strong enough to wrestle it away from him.

Behind her she could hear David grunting in pain.

She didn't have much time. She reached into her pocket and grabbed a small metal cross with pointed tips. She pulled it out and then slammed it with as much force as she could into the priest's hand.

He yowled in pain and dropped the tube. She grabbed it and tucked it under one arm, then used the altar to pull herself to a standing position. She couldn't put any real weight on the injured leg, but she was able to hop toward Wendy who was finally sitting up.

Her cousin saw her and rushed to her side. Susan shoved the tube into her hands. "Go, run!"

Wendy headed for the side aisle far away from Richelieu and David and then raced up it and out the door.

Susan turned her attention back to the fight.

Miraculously David was holding his own but he was fast running out of weapons.

She heard shouts and she looked up to see a group of priests bearing down on them, brandishing crosses.

With a hiss, Richelieu retreated from them, eyes darting back and forth.

In five steps David reached her.

He supported her weight as he half carried her toward the back of the cathedral. She could still hear shouting behind her and she said a prayer for the priests as she and David made it outside. A few yards away Wendy was standing next to a taxi, waving frantically at them.

They headed for her as fast as they could.

We're going to make it, Susan thought.

But then she recognized the blond-haired man standing behind Wendy, the same man she had seen in Pierre's office and on the street earlier that evening. Before she could blink, he grabbed Wendy.

The tube with the cloth fell from Wendy's hand, and bounced on the pavement.

With a shout David dropped Susan and charged forward. But the man threw Wendy into the backseat of a car and followed her inside. The driver hit the gas and the car sped past them. Susan screamed and struggled to leap after them, but David held her tight and ran with her in the other direction.

"Vampires!" he screamed.

She looked and he was right. They were exiting a trio of limos a few feet away, fangs bared, eyes gleaming.

We are going to die.

They passed the spot where Wendy had been abducted and David scooped up the tube with the relic in his free hand. The two remaining taxi drivers were driving off in a hurry.

There was no escape.

And then she heard the squeal of tires.

"Get in!" a voice roared.

David dove with her into the backseat of a car, not even bothering to close the door as it peeled out. She righted herself and glanced at the driver. It was Gabriel.

"We have to go back!" she shouted. "He kidnapped Wendy," she sobbed.

"Who?" Gabriel demanded as he negotiated a series of sharp turns.

"I don't know. He was in Pierre's office earlier today. He has long blond hair."

"Pierre?" Gabriel growled, his voice dropping so low she could barely make out the word.

"He didn't take her, the blond man did."

"Did Pierre see Wendy?" Gabriel asked, voice tense.

"What?"

"Did he see her!"

"Yes, in the cathedral. He thought she looked like Carissa. But he wasn't the one who kidnapped her. It was—"

"Didn't you read the journal?" Gabriel demanded.

"Yes! We—"

"Don't you see?" he asked. "Don't you get it?"

"What?" She couldn't see, she couldn't think. They had to go back.

"*Carissa*. He called her Carissa. What was the name of Carissa's husband?"

"I—she never said. She never wrote his name." There was a pause. She looked at David and his face had turned ashen.

"Pierre," Gabriel hissed. "It was Pierre de Chauvere."

"No!" Susan screamed and pounded her fists into the back of the seat in front of her.

Pierre whose family had been watching out for her family for years.

Pierre who had been obsessed with her cross.

Pierre who had not seemed surprised that her apartment had been broken into.

Pierre de Chauvere, attorney, vampire, magistrate,

monster. The man who had betrayed Carissa eight hundred years before had just had Wendy kidnapped.

David grabbed her shoulders and turned her to face him. His eyes were burning with an intensity that frightened her. "Listen to me, Susan. On my life, we will get her back. I swear it."

The world was coming to an end but all she could think about was her cousin.

God, what do I do now?

Susan didn't remember getting back to the house but suddenly she was standing in the middle of the living room. Gabriel was upstairs checking on Paul. David was sitting at the kitchen table, one hand wrapped around the tube and the other cradling his head.

It just seemed so unthinkable. They had kept Richelieu from getting his hands on the one artifact he really wanted and they had escaped with their lives. They had won.

But it felt as though she had instead lost everything. She sunk down slowly onto the couch. Her eyes fell on the diary and she burst into tears.

Wendy and the necklace were now in the hands of Pierre.

At least you know where to find him, a voice whispered inside her head.

The front door opened and she looked up. Raphael walked in and her heart soared then plunged again when he closed the door behind him. She had thought for sure he was bringing Wendy back with him.

He crossed to her, his face grim. He sat down on the couch next to her and took her hands in his.

"By the time I got inside the cathedral, Richelieu was gone. And I looked for Wendy but couldn't find her."

"I know where Pierre works."

"I checked his home and his office. No one knows where he is. And trust me, I didn't ask nicely."

She leaned her head against his shoulder and felt a shudder pass through her. "What do we do now?" she asked.

"Rest. We've stopped Richelieu from getting his hands on the blood of Christ, but this is just one battle. The war is far from over."

He wrapped his arms around her and she clung to him. Something about him seemed slightly different. He didn't pull away from her, but just held her.

The war might not be over but she wouldn't let Wendy be a casualty. There, in Raphael's arms, she made a pledge.

I'm coming for you, Wendy. And I will find you no matter the cost.

EPILOGUE

The prison warden walked the floor one last time, peering into every cell as he passed it. Doors were flung wide and the emptiness was overwhelming. When he came to the last door he stopped. That one was still locked. What manner of monster was inside he didn't know, he only knew that it had been there since long before his time. Now that the prison was no longer to serve that function everyone had been moved. Everyone but the creature.

The warden was curious. He had long wondered what he would find if he opened the door. Even now he wasn't sure what to do. There had been orders not to move the prisoner. Did that mean he was just supposed to leave him there? From inside the cell he heard insane laughter.

He turned to leave and shouted in surprise to discover

a man standing behind him. He was tall, handsome, and self-assured. "Why are you here?" the warden asked.

The man glanced at the locked door. "My name is Raphael, and I've come for him."

"Are you sure?" the warden asked.

"Yes. Two hundred years is a long time. Long enough to give a man pause."

"What will you do with him?" the warden asked.

"Teach him how to live."

With a shaking hand the warden handed him the key and then fled, suddenly sure that he didn't want to see the creature. Behind him he heard the tall man say, "Pierre, I've come to take you home."

Turn this page for a preview of

KISS OF REVENGE

by Debbie Viguié

Available from FaithWords in October 2013

And look for the eBook exclusive short story
Kiss of Life.

G abriel, Count of Avignon, stood in the shadows of
the mosque, watching carefully the carnage that was
unfolding before him. The young knight had entered the
mosque a few minutes before and had been battling his
way toward the front ever since.

Gabriel had been shadowing the knight, Jean, for days
as he tracked down the rumors of a holy treasure. It served
his purpose to let the knight be the one to find it and dispose of him later.

Gabriel reached out with his mind, touched the mind of
the knight. Jean truly believed himself on a holy quest, the
fire of his faith burned bright in his heart and soul in a way
that it did for few others.

As he slaughtered a foe in front of him another was

sneaking up behind him, ready to behead him. Gabriel couldn't allow that to happen just yet.

Turn! Gabriel commanded silently, implanting the thought so intently in Jean's mind that he knew the crusader would probably swear that he'd heard someone speak out loud. Perhaps later he would attribute the word that saved his life to God. If he lived to think on it at all.

Jean moved just in time to plunge his sword through the abdomen of his would-be killer. As the last man died, Jean dropped the body to the floor. He then turned back, approached the altar, and fell to his knees in reverence.

Beneath Jean's knees rivulets of blood coursed and pooled over the stones. Behind him lay the bodies of half a dozen who had stood between him and what he had long sought. Tears streaked down his face and he wiped at them with a bloody hand. He laid down his sword and grasped a silver cross that hung around his neck.

Gabriel studied the cross. It looked like one that would belong to a woman, a token from the woman he loved, no doubt.

Upon the altar there was a small box made of wood, ornately carved and decorated with a few small, glittering jewels. It was beautiful, the creation of some skilled craftsman for a wealthy patron. It was enough to turn any man's head, but Gabriel knew that Jean didn't care about the box, only about what he prayed was inside it.

Gabriel could feel the hunger growing in him as the smell of blood filled the air. He would feed soon, but for now he watched the knight curiously. Centuries of practice had allowed him to control his instincts and urges in a way no mortal man could ever dream of. Jean had killed the men whose bodies littered the mosque's cold stone floor without hesitation. He was not the most skilled warrior, but he had an intensity of purpose, a driving focus, that sustained him in battle. Yet, the same hands that had taken life with such determination trembled when he lifted the box from the altar. The box covered the palm of Jean's left hand and as he opened the lid with his right he closed his eyes.

Gabriel risked moving closer then. He wanted to see if the rumors that had led them both there were true. What he saw inside the box surprised even him. He could feel Jean's fear, his hesitation. He knew that the young knight was desperately hoping that he was right and that his long journey had been worth it.

Open your eyes, Gabriel urged, and watched as Jean did. The surprise on his face mirrored what Gabriel felt. Was still feeling. After a few moments Jean recovered sufficiently to shut the lid and rise to his feet. He tucked the box inside his tunic and picked up his sword. Gabriel moved forward, and Jean spun around, eyes probing the shadows. Gabriel stepped farther into them and even though Jean stared right at him he did not see him.

"I am for God, and I will protect with my life that which He has led me here to find," the knight said, challenging the darkness with a statement that was half threat, half prayer. Gabriel allowed it to go unanswered and watched as Jean left the mosque. Gabriel stepped carefully around the bodies, not wishing to leave any evidence of his presence by so much as a boot print. He moved to the altar where the box had stood and touched it hesitantly.

He closed his eyes and could swear he could feel some sort of warmth emanating from the place where it had been. Whatever doubts he had harbored vanished in a moment.

"So many have searched for so long and it was found by a simple knight," Gabriel mused out loud. It was God's sense of humor, that was what Paul would say. What even Paul could not have anticipated, though, was that there were two relics instead of one.

He turned and glided through the entrance of the church. Night cloaked him as he followed Jean, who left the city far behind before making camp for the night. When the young man finally fell asleep Gabriel considered taking the relics from him. It would have been a simple thing to retrieve the box without waking him, simpler still to retrieve after killing him. Instead he decided to wait. Paul would have said it was mercy that motivated him. There was something else, though. Something about the knight gave him pause. At any rate he knew where the relics were. He could afford to wait.

For the preaching of the cross is to them that perish foolishness; but unto us which are saved it is the power of God.

I Corinthians 1:18

PRAGUE, PRESENT DAY

The cross. It's all about the cross, David Trent thought as he sat numbly at the kitchen table in a house on the outskirts of Prague. He watched the two vampires in the living room pace back and forth like caged animals. There had to be somewhere they hadn't searched yet, but none of them had thought of where yet. Susan Lambert sat silently on the couch, her arms wrapped around herself. If it hadn't been for the tears still streaking down her face she might have looked like she was asleep.

David was not crying. He was sitting, staring into

space, reliving the whole thing over and over. There was nothing he could have done to stop it, he realized. He couldn't have reached Wendy's side any faster when the vampire had grabbed her outside the cathedral hours before.

I should have protected her. Her and the cross necklace she was wearing. There had to be a reason that the other vampires wanted it so badly. Was it just because it seemed to be even more effective against vampires than average crosses? All David knew about the cross was that it had belonged to an ancestor of Wendy and Susan named Jean who had fought during the second crusade. Their grandmother, who had died recently and insisted her funeral be here in Prague, had left it to Susan. She had also left a letter hinting that the cross contained a great secret, but gave no clue as to what the secret was. If Susan had been wearing the cross instead of Wendy, would the vampire have taken her instead?

David wondered if this was what going insane felt like. Just days ago he'd arrived in Prague for work. If he hadn't met Wendy and Susan he'd be sitting at a desk, tapping on a keyboard right now. He'd be blissfully unaware that vampires even existed, let alone that they were at war and one of them, Richelieu, was building a formidable army of them. But he didn't regret meeting Wendy. His only regret was that he couldn't do anything now to help her.

They knew the vampire with long, blond hair who had taken Wendy worked for Pierre, her grandmother's lawyer. Susan had had several dealings with him regarding aspects of their grandmother's estate, but they'd had no idea until a few hours ago he was a vampire. Not only that, it seemed his connection to their family went all the way back to when he was human. Eight hundred years before Pierre was a magistrate in the Inquisition in France and had condemned his young wife Carissa to a fate worse than death. They had read about him in Carissa's journal, never expecting he was still alive, let alone so close. They had also read about how it was Gabriel who had saved Carissa's life. Susan had seen a portrait of Carissa, and swore that Wendy looked just like her.

Is that why he kidnapped her? David thought. *Or did he want the cross?*

"At least Richelieu didn't get his hands on the Sudarium," Susan said, suddenly enough to make them all jump.

David glanced at the document tube clutched in his right hand. Inside it was a relic, the Sudarium of Oviedo, a burial cloth which was purported to be stained with the blood of Christ. Yes they had fought Richelieu and saved the cloth, but they had lost Wendy in the process.

He felt a lump form in his throat. He had come to care for Wendy deeply in the short amount of time they'd known each other. "There has to be some way we can find her," he ground out.

"There's nothing more we can do tonight. The sun will be rising soon," Gabriel said, his voice eerily calm.

David glared over at the two vampires. "You should have told us, warned us that Carissa's husband was a vampire and here in Prague. How were we supposed to know who Pierre was?"

Gabriel gave no sign of the earlier distress he'd expressed over hearing Pierre's name. "We did not know he was in Prague," he said simply.

"I feel like there are secrets you're both keeping from me," Susan said, anger flashing across her face.

Neither vampire responded to that. Instead there was silence for several minutes before Gabriel turned back to her. "We can do nothing now. We must wait for night. The sun is rising."

Raphael, the other vampire, was heading for the staircase, swaying slightly on his feet. David glanced out the kitchen window and could just see past the one curtain that it was, indeed, getting light outside.

"I suggest we all get some sleep," Gabriel said, moving to follow Raphael upstairs.

Susan had reverted to staring vacantly, and he doubted she'd be getting any sleep for a while. She was in shock and he wished there was something he could do for her, but he didn't even know what he could do to help himself.

"We'll find her, you know," he said, his voice sounding hoarse as he choked back his own emotion.

Susan nodded and he was grateful that she didn't ask the question that wouldn't leave him alone. *When we find her will it be too late?*

David forced himself to pry his fingers loose from the tube as he stood up. His body was battered. His fractured ribs were still incredibly painful and the fight with Richelieu had done more damage. He was exhausted and he needed to sleep, but how could he shut his eyes even for a second when Wendy was somewhere out there in the clutches of a monster?

Wendy woke slowly, her mind muddled. She couldn't remember where she was, and when she was finally able to open her eyes and sit up, she realized that was because she truly had no idea where she was. Overhead fluorescent lights gleamed down, illuminating the room.

She looked slowly around her. She was lying on top of a bed that was in a corner of what appeared to be an unbelievably large studio apartment. Across the room was a massive, antique rolltop desk and some other worktables. In the center of the room was a kind of sitting area with a couch, a table, and some chairs. A silver platter with a dome on top of it on the table caught her eye.

She stood slowly, continuing to look around. There were no windows anywhere. What appeared to be a short passageway past the office area led to a staircase. At the top there was a medieval-looking door with iron fittings. She ran up the stairs and tried the door, but it was locked. Moreover, it was so massive and solid that there was no way that she could batter it down. There was a small rectangle about eye height that looked like it could be opened, but not from her side.

She ground her teeth in frustration and turned to survey the rest of the room. There was art on the walls, some of it rare and valuable looking. There were curio cabinets displaying all sorts of knickknacks. She had missed seeing a small kitchenette earlier and after walking back downstairs she headed over to it. There was a refrigerator, a microwave, and a sink. She opened the refrigerator and stared at row after row of bags of blood like you'd find in a blood bank.

She slammed the refrigerator shut and spun around. What was this place? A luxurious dungeon? A panic room for vampires?

The possibilities were frightening. Her stomach growled and she realized she had no way of even telling what time of day it was, let alone what day.

How long had she been here?

She remembered running outside the church, holding on to the tube with the cloth in it when a man had grabbed her and thrown her into a car. After that she didn't remember much. Had she been drugged?

But by whom, and why would they bring her here?

She thought of Susan and David and prayed that they were okay. They would have to be sick with worry over her. She wondered what had happened to them. Had they escaped Richelieu's men and retrieved the Sudarium?

She knew that Gabriel and Raphael were worried that Richelieu had been trying to find a holy relic that had the blood of Christ on it so that he might ingest it. Blood was life, and power, and spirit and when a vampire took the blood of another, he made that other person part of himself. They were afraid what would happen if a vampire tried to make the blood of Christ part of himself.

She pressed shaking hands to her temples. It was all too much to take in.

Can't panic, just have to breathe and think.

Her stomach rumbled again.

And eat.

Her eyes turned back to the table and the silver platter on it. She walked over hesitantly and put a hand on the lid. It was warm. She couldn't help but think that when she lifted it she'd find something terrible like a severed head or a human heart.

She took a deep breath and yanked the lid off.

Steak, mashed potatoes, and roasted vegetables. They were hot, too, with steam coming off them. It all smelled delicious.

She sat down on the chair. The food was for her. There was no other explanation. The question was, why? It didn't make sense for it to be poisoned. It would have been simple enough to kill her if that was her abductor's plan.

She picked up a fork that was sitting beside the plate and pushed it into the mashed potatoes. She gave it an experimental nibble and then wrinkled her nose when she realized that it was laced with garlic.

And now she was even more confused. Was it a test to see if she was a vampire? There were better ways to go about that. Or was it meant to reassure her that she wasn't about to get eaten by a vampire since garlic repelled them painfully?

Either way she was too hungry to question. She prayed over the food, hoping God would protect her from whatever ill might come of it. Then she dug in and ate.

She was hungrier than she had thought and a few minutes later she had cleaned the plate, including the steamed carrots which she normally despised and which had also been laced with some sort of garlic powder.

When she was done she grabbed herself some water from the sink and then got back to exploring her prison. The more she saw, the more she was convinced it was more of a shelter of some sort than a dungeon. There were too many items of a personal nature and the artwork alone was clearly too valuable to use to decorate anything other than a private residence.

So, a vampire must live there or use it as a sort of backup place. The question was, which one? She hardly thought it was Richelieu. It didn't seem his style. Plus he'd been ready to kill her inside that cathedral. The only thing that had stopped him was—

Her hand flew up to her throat and she was relieved to feel that Susan's cross was still there. She searched the apartment for anything that she could use to try and batter down the door but had no luck. Next she sat down at the desk and began looking at the collection of papers she found there, searching for a clue to the identity of her captor.

Finally she found a letter addressed to Pierre de Chauvere. She believed that was the attorney in Prague that Susan had been in contact with. He had been at the cathedral to see the Sudarium and he had remarked that she looked just like Carissa.

"Pierre, what is it you want with me?" she said softly as she looked through the rest of the desk.

There were literally dozens of cubbyholes in the desk and it took time to go through them all. There were a lot of boring-looking legal documents, some of them seemingly quite old.

And then she started yanking out drawers, dumping their contents. She hoped one of them had a false bottom. The third drawer granted her wish when she saw a piece of paper wedged into a crack toward the back of it. She retrieved a paper clip from the middle drawer, inserted it between the back of the drawer and the bottom, and yanked.

The wood came up and inside she found several very old parchment papers with fine, tiny handwriting on them. She felt excitement mounting within her.

It was the same kind of parchment that they had found stuck into Carissa's diary. Gabriel had given the diary to Susan to read and they had eagerly devoured the story of their many-times-great aunt and all the tragedy that had befallen her.

She picked up the pages and moved back over so she

could sit on the bed and lean her back against the wall. She studied the writing more closely and realized that, like Carissa's diary, these pages were in French.

Wendy had studied the language in college and now she scanned the ancient papers eagerly, hoping for a sign of what they could be. Finally she saw the name Jean, Marquis de Bryas, and her heart nearly stopped. That was Carissa's father, the one that had given her the cross that had been handed down for generations that Wendy herself was now wearing.

She put the pages down on the bed and examined the room again. There truly was no way she could see to escape this place. Frustration filled her. There was nothing to do now but wait for her captor to make himself known or for the cavalry to come riding in to her rescue.

She said another quick prayer for all of them, that they were all safe and might be swiftly reunited.

Beside her the pages called to her and she could feel curiosity burning brightly inside her. Maybe they would reveal to her what the secret of the cross was.

When had their lives gotten so fantastical? There were hints, whispers in the back of her mind that they had always been so. Susan and Wendy's grandmother had always been gifted, called upon by God to leave her home at all times of day and night to go and pray for friends and strangers alike. It had always fascinated and frightened Wendy, that amount of faith.

There had also been the recent revelation that her grandmother knew of the existence of vampires and had even known Raphael. Wendy was still dying to know how all of that had come about. But like so many other people in their family, her grandmother seemed to have taken her secrets with her to the grave. It was incredibly frustrating, but it also made sense. Who would have believed her? Wendy herself had only listened halfheartedly when her grandmother would talk about the magic and mystery of her hometown. She'd always put it up to a mixture of nostalgia and overactive imagination.

Right there and then Wendy vowed that if she ever survived this and someday she had kids she'd tell them all the important stuff before it was too late. *God forgives everything. I'll always love you. Vampires are real, watch out for them.*

She was going to have to make a list at this rate to make sure she didn't forget anything. She got up and circled one last time. This time she focused on looking for anything she could use as a weapon. There wasn't so much as a flashlight. Unless she threatened to bash someone over the head with a priceless work of art she didn't see an escape plan that was remotely viable.

Which meant there was nothing to do now but wait. Resolutely she picked up the pages and began to read.

There are days when I hardly believe myself what has transpired in the last two years. How I dearly long to tell Marie about all of it, but I dare not. This secret is too great, too burdensome, and I would not risk her life with it. Still, if I should die the secret will be lost. So, however loath I am to do so, I must make a record of what transpired in the Holy Land and upon my return home from there as well. For I fear that strange things are happening and I worry about the meaning of it all.

The Templars are pressing me sharply to join

their ranks and I fear their wrath if I continue to refuse. I do not know why they are so keenly interested in me in this manner. I fear it is because they guess at the truth, but how could they? From what lips would they have learned of it? For all that knew what I carried away from that mosque should have been silenced.

And then there is him. I saw him again at the party that the king held. He spared my life, saved it, but he still terrifies me like no other could. Is it only a matter of time before he comes for me in the night? And if he spares Marie, what then shall she think?

No, I must leave an account and I will seal it away so that none should find it unless I am dead.

This then is how I, Jean, found a great and terrible treasure...